USA TODAY bestselling and RITA® Award–nominated author **Caitlin Crews** loves writing romance. She teaches her favourite romance novels in creative writing classes at places like UCLA Extension's prestigious Writers' Program, where she finally gets to utilise the MA and PhD in English Literature that she received from the University of York in England. She currently lives in the Pacific Northwest, with her very own hero and too many pets. Visit her at caitlincrews.com.

Riley Pine is the combined forces of two contemporary romance writers as you've never seen them before. Expect delicious, dirty and scandalous swoons. To stay up to date with all things Riley Pine head on over to rileypine.com, for newsletters, book details and more!

D0237681

UNDONE

CAITLIN CREWS

MY ROYAL SURRENDER

RILEY PINE

MILLS & BOON

First Published in Great Britain 2018
by Mills & Boon, an imprint of HarperCollins*Publishers*
1 London Bridge Street, London, SE1 9GF

Undone © 2018 Caitlin Crews

My Royal Surrender © 2018 Riley Pine

ISBN: 978-0-263-26657-3

MIX
Paper from
responsible sources
FSC™ C007454

Printed and bound in Spain
by CPI, Barcelona

UNDONE

CAITLIN CREWS

MILLS & BOON

CHAPTER ONE

EVERYONE WARNED HER not to go to Italy.

They said it was a bad gut reaction that she would regret, bitterly.

"It will be like a funeral march," Maya Martin's older sister, Melinda, had asserted, her familiar body vibrating with the force of her outrage that *her sister* had been treated so shabbily. Maya could relate. She had been in a constant state of outrage—or maybe it was fury, possibly covering up something like grief—ever since Ethan had made his ugly little announcement and ruined all of the plans Maya had made. For her wedding *and* her life. "You can't possibly take your own honeymoon trip alone. It will make you crazy."

"More crazy than being left at the altar? Almost literally?" Maya had retorted, standing there with her hair and makeup exquisite and ready for the ceremony her father had canceled after it became clear Ethan couldn't be reasoned with. "Because that's hard to imagine."

Melinda had made a face. But the facts were simple and incontrovertible.

Ethan, who Maya had been set to marry that very day, was not in love.

Not with Maya, anyway.

"We've always been best friends before we were anything else," he had said, in his usual warm way, his hazel eyes bright and clear, not tormented. That part had seemed significant later. "Haven't we?"

Maya had been sitting in the pretty silk bathrobe she'd bought for precisely that purpose: getting ready the morning of her wedding. Her hair was finally done. Her makeup was pristine and perfect for photos. She'd been about to step into her lovely white dress when Ethan had talked himself past her mother and sister, even though everyone knew it was bad luck for the groom to see the bride before the ceremony and the Martins were nothing if not sticklers for convention.

Everyone was correct. It was very bad luck.

"Of course we're best friends," Maya had said, feeling warm and happy, shot straight through with sweetness.

It made her feel sick now.

She hadn't seen it coming. She'd been thinking

about how she and Ethan had started together at the same Seven Sisters firm in Toronto after their articling placements. They'd worked on cases together. They'd grown closer and closer. Eventually, all those late nights and weekends had led to more. A year after that, they'd moved into a condo in chic, trendy Yorkville together. When Ethan had proposed six months later, it had seemed like the next, perfect, logical step.

Maya's life had always gone according to plan. As a Martin, Maya had been expected to excel from her earliest days in Toronto's tony Lawrence Park neighborhood, through her prelaw studies at McGill in Montreal, straight on to law school at the University of Toronto, a plum articleship with one of her father's impressive friends and into her current place as a senior associate at one of Canada's best law firms.

Ethan fit right in. He was successful, ambitious and attractive. Their life together was filled with shared interests, from work to working out, the odd minibreak when schedules allowed and a very clear focus on how to build the perfect future together.

Maya and Ethan made sense. It was that simple.

"I know I can tell you this, though the timing is off," Ethan had said that morning. He'd come to sit next to her on the sofa in her suite at the Four Seasons in Yorkville with its view out over the city. He'd taken her hands in his, his thumb brushing the cushion-cut halo diamond from Birks he'd placed there himself when he'd proposed at one of their favorite restaurants. "I've fallen in love, Maya."

She still hadn't gotten it. She'd been focused on the plan. The future they'd carefully plotted out together over dinners and on long runs. First they would both make partner at their top-tier law firm. Only when that was nailed down would they move to a tony suburb, like Rosedale or Lawrence Park, to start their own family and continue the cycle of Martin excellence. Martins were lawyers, doctors like Melinda, professors like their cousins or CEOs like their father. Their lives were duly glittering because they worked hard and excelled at everything they did.

So Maya had only sat there, smiling softly at the man she'd expected to marry, practice law with, make babies with and *glitter* with, because Martins didn't suffer hideous public humiliations. Martins didn't make mistakes.

"Neither one of us meant it to happen," Ethan was saying in that engaging way of his that helped him win cases. "Both Lorraine and I feel sick at how this will hurt you, but we were powerless. People fall in love sometimes, even if it's inconvenient."

Maya had finally stopped smiling then, when he'd said her oldest friend's name. "What? *Lorraine?*"

"In time," Ethan had said in that plummy, confident voice that was half the reason Maya had been so enamored of him in the first place, "we think you'll agree that this is actually for the best."

What happened after that was a bit of a merciful blur.

There were guests waiting—family and friends from all over Canada and abroad—but Maya's father had dealt with that in his severe way that brooked no argument or follow-up questions.

There was the dress that Maya and her mother and sister had picked out together, exactly the kind of fairy-tale gown Martin girls deserved to wear. Maya had tried on the winner while her mother had looked proud for once and Melinda had smiled, no doubt remembering her own triumphant wedding. Maya was carrying on the Martin family tradition of marrying well and living better, and the dress was a beautiful indulgence to mark the occasion.

She had secretly loved that dress and not because it "set the right tone," according to her chilly mother. She had imagined herself wearing it, sweeping down the aisle and then dancing the night away at the reception, with all that white surrounding her like a gift.

Now she wanted to burn it.

The details were fuzzy, once it was clear that Ethan was deadly serious, that he couldn't be talked out of it, that he was really, truly calling off his own wedding a few hours before the ceremony.

But what Maya really remembered were the things Ethan had said when he had stopped pretending to worry about Maya's feelings. When he made it clear, at last, that he hadn't worried about Maya's feelings in a long while—or, possibly, ever.

"Come on, Maya," he had thrown at her, his lip curling into a sneer that made him look like a complete stranger. The kind of stranger who might sleep with his fiancée's best friend and call off his own wedding. "You like your sex boring and vanilla, and that's fine. That's your right. But ultimately, I'm not willing to shackle myself to someone who can't satisfy my needs."

"Your needs?" Maya had been on her feet by then. They'd been going around and around for hours, though the damage had already been done. She'd thrown his ring at his head like the cliché she'd never dreamed she'd become. Papa had made the announcement in the chapel, filled already with their friends, their families and, most embarrassingly, their business associates. "What does that mean, Ethan? Lorraine pretends to like anal? She indulges your heretofore-unknown foot fetish? Or, let me guess, she dresses up like a little girl and calls you daddy. Is that what you like? Because you told me you liked a grown woman, not an overgrown child whose life is and always will be a disaster of her own making."

"I understand your childish need to swipe at me," Ethan had said with great dignity, as if he had the moral high ground. "I deserve it, I suppose. But I won't allow you to talk about Lorraine like that."

That hadn't helped.

But it wasn't until Ethan had slunk out, under direct physical threat from Maya's normally icy-cold mother, that the Lorraine part really sank in.

Lorraine had been Maya's roommate at McGill. Maya had tended to her through all the emotional upheavals Lorraine had suffered over the years, from the jobs she'd lost to the relationships she'd sabotaged. Maya had given Lorraine a place to sleep when she'd been evicted, had given her money when she was short and had gotten in more fights with Ethan than she could count over what he'd called her "obsession with that albatross around your neck." Maya had even made Lorraine her maid of honor over her sister, because she'd thought her fragile, thin-skinned friend would have had a breakdown otherwise.

"I don't want her to feel left out," Maya had told Melinda, who was older than Maya by four years and had witnessed many Lorraine fits and breakdowns over the years. "You know how destructive she can be."

The truth was, even Maya hadn't known Lorraine was *this* destructive.

What made it worse was that Melinda had understood, even though Maya had been her maid of honor when Melinda had married Edward years ago. And now Maya was left to feel as horrified about that decision as every other one she had ever made concerning Lorraine.

She honestly didn't know which part of the equation made her feel more ill. Ethan. Lorraine. Or her own unforgivable blindness.

"I think the worst thing you can do right now is run off by yourself somewhere," her mother had said much later that terrible day, when Maya seized on the Italy thing like the lifeline it was. Mother had reverted to her usual crisp, icy demeanor, as if nothing untoward had happened—or nothing she couldn't arrange to her satisfaction, eventually. "What you need to do is come home. You can stay with your father and me until we figure out how best to handle this."

Maya had still been wearing her wedding hair, because nothing short of a tornado could make the elaborate coiffure move. She'd changed into jeans and a T-shirt long before so she could wear something other than her fancy wedding lingerie while she canceled everything. And do things like talk to the guests who had come so far to see a wedding that would never happen.

She had been humiliated. Furious. So much of both that she couldn't see a path through it. She couldn't imagine how she ever *wouldn't* tremble with all that rage and horror.

But what she hadn't been, she'd realized with a sick sort of lurch deep inside as the day edged into evening on that late November day she already wanted to forget, was as heartbroken as she surely should have been.

Maybe that was why it was a little too easy for her to slip into her usual mode as one of her firm's rising stars.

As an attorney she was decisive. Correct. And never ever emotional.

Exactly the Martin daughter her parents expected her to be.

"I'm not going to move out of my condo or slink off back home to my parents," she said, the decision coming to her in a flash. A flash that she knew would irritate Ethan, which made it even better. She was standing in the corner of the hotel suite—the honeymoon suite, of course, just to salt the wound—staring out at Toronto there at her feet. Like it was mocking her. "If Ethan wants to run off with Lorraine, he's welcome to do so. That will involve him moving out, not me. And I would rather he do that when I'm not around."

"If that's what you want," her mother said in an overly patient way, as if Maya was acting irrationally. It set Maya's teeth on edge, but she'd already done more yelling today than she had in years. Maybe ever. She wasn't going to give in to the urge for more when all it did was make her throat hurt. "But I don't see what good it will do you to run off to a foreign country—"

"We booked a month's holiday on the Amalfi coast," Maya said, with the bedrock certainty deep inside her that she thought might be entirely made of fury and rage. "It will be the first vacation I've taken since law school. Yes, it was supposed to be our honeymoon. But I'm not giving it up just because Ethan turned out to be an asshole."

No one had supported this decision. Melinda

had argued against it. She'd recruited her engineer husband to do the same. Her parents had been deeply opposed, nearly frigid in their distaste for Maya's plan. Everyone had argued at her, yet had shied away from addressing the elephant in the room—which was that clearly her decision-making was faulty.

Maya had stuck to her guns, faulty or not. She needed to go away. She needed to put as much distance between this debacle and whatever was on the other side of it. She needed to figure out a new path, a new plan, and she couldn't do that here in the wreckage of the old.

She had flatly refused to see Lorraine. She had declined the opportunity to speak to Ethan further when he'd reappeared outside the hotel suite. She'd had her father inform him that she would be using both the plane tickets they'd booked and the hotel—a charming boutique hotel in the exclusive St. George portfolio—and he could take the opportunity of her absence to remove himself and all evidence of his existence from their condo.

Papa had reported back that Ethan hadn't taken the news well, just as Maya had hoped.

And Papa had allowed himself a slight smile while he'd shared that with the family, which was as close to violence as Maya's stern, dignified father had ever gotten to her knowledge.

The great thing about her decision to leave Toronto, she reflected the following evening when she was at cruising altitude over the Atlantic Ocean with an empty seat next to her, was that no one was there to stare at her and ask her how she *felt*. About anything. She was just another woman on a plane, blessedly anonymous and with no reason to die of her own embarrassment.

She landed in Frankfurt on Monday morning, then transferred to another flight down into Naples in Italy. By the time her taxi delivered her to the cliffside town on the Amalfi coast where she'd be spending the next month suspended over the glorious Tyrrhenian Sea, she was dead on her feet.

She hardly noticed her surroundings. She had the faintest notion of crisp, white walls and a pink-and-blue sunset beyond the lobby, but it took all her energy to focus on the chic, smiling woman behind the front desk.

"You are booked into the honeymoon suite, signora," the woman said in charmingly accented English. "Yet you appear to be traveling alone…?"

Maya stared back at her. She had been traveling for close to twenty-four hours, all told. She had suffered the greatest humiliation of her life and she wasn't sure she'd even scratched the surface of processing that. She had lost her closest friend and her fiancé in one fell swoop, and the real tragedy was that they hadn't died in a freak accident. She couldn't mourn them when they'd betrayed her.

They were both quite alive, apparently perfectly happy, and had each other to lean on.

It was Maya who had to deal with the mess they'd made, alone.

All that and the Venetian mirrors behind the front desk reminded her that she had left her hair in its wedding style, tamed into an elegant chignon that twenty-four hours of airplanes and airports hadn't so much as dented.

She moved her glare from that hair—a walking monument to her humiliation that she was going to have to deal with as soon as possible—to the poor woman standing at the desk, waiting patiently for her answer.

"It will just be me," she said.

And offered no further explanation.

After a beat, the woman nodded. "Of course, signora."

Maya followed the porter up several sets of stairs that felt like an assault on her already over-exhausted system, then down a graceful, sooth-ing hallway. He threw open the doors at the far end, then ushered her into a set of airy, sweeping rooms, bright white with blue accents, and sunset views at every turn.

She saw the sea before her and the darkening sky above. It was beyond pretty, but she couldn't really take it in. When the doors finally closed behind her, she threw herself across the four-poster king bed in the bedroom, fully clothed, and slept like the dead.

And when she woke up the next morning, she was in Italy, a world away from Toronto.

That was the good news.

The bad news was that she hadn't imagined the debacle of her wedding day. There was no ring on her finger any longer, and she frowned down at the place it had been and the dent that was still in her skin. She took herself off to the washroom, scowled at herself in the mirror and applied herself to a long, restorative shower and then returning her hair to its natural state. When it was finally the cloud of black curls around her face that she preferred, springy and free and big, she padded back out to the main room. Then, at last, she pushed her way through the French doors onto the balcony that ran the length of her suite.

And only then, overlooking the stunning, impossible stretch of blue before her that was the Gulf of Salerno rolling into the Tyrrhenian Sea and on to forever on this crisp late November morning, did she take a real, deep breath.

Then another. And another, until she started to feel, if not herself, something other than the prickly ball of horror and humiliation she'd been since Saturday.

Ethan had always been obsessed with itineraries, so the first thing Maya did after a restorative espresso or three was wander out into the ancient village clinging vertically to the side of the steep cliff. With no clear idea of where she was heading or what she ought to do. She wandered down old, uneven stone staircases hewn into the side of the mountains until she found the rocky shore. Then she wandered up again, moving from shop to shop. Some were closed in deference to the off-season, but she had no trouble finding a place to sit and have another espresso with a pastry she couldn't name but tasted like heaven. She spent the morning basking in the Italian sunshine, worrying not at all about the top-ten-sights-to-see lists that Ethan would have brandished before them, forcing them to march quickly from one to the next for fear that they might miss out.

And it was while she was having a peaceful lunch, on a terrace overlooking the village and the sea and more cliffside villages in the distance with clouds rolling in, that she took a good hard look at what remained of her life.

Her father had given Ethan a week to move out. When she returned to Toronto, Maya planned to live in the condo they'd found and chosen, with all the locks changed and no trace of him around to remind her what an idiot she'd been. *A better person would want to talk to him at some point*, she thought as she stared out at the rolling blue waves. A good, decent person would try to find a little empathy in her somewhere, surely, for two people she had loved for years.

Maybe not today. But someday.

Maya didn't think she had it in her. She had yet to cry more than a few appalling tears of rage when she'd been fighting with Ethan. When she'd still imagined she could argue him to the altar.

But she hadn't *really* cried, and that felt a lot like proof that he had been right to leave her. Wouldn't a normal person cry in a situation like this? Shouldn't she have been lying in the crucifixion position in a dark room somewhere? For weeks?

Had she brought all of this on herself?

But she couldn't really grapple with that, it turned out. Because the one thing that kept tumbling around and around in her head was the fact he'd called her boring in bed. Repeatedly. There had been a comment about preferring her vibrator to a flesh-and-blood man. And he'd followed that up by calling her "boring and vanilla," *again*, when he'd been the one who'd had all those *rules*. The showers they had to take before sex and after, the scheduling, the places she could and couldn't touch—

She suspected that the emotional wallop of what had happened, and so spectacularly, would land sooner or later.

But Maya had always been a woman of action, not feelings. She couldn't do anything about the embarrassment she'd suffered or what waited for her when she got back to Toronto after New Year's. She couldn't fix what Ethan and Lorraine had broken.

What she could do, however, was address the boring-sex allegation to her own satisfaction. She'd always thought the sex they'd had together was fun, if not as frequent as they both claimed to want—yet did nothing to change. Before Ethan, she'd always liked sex, like anyone else. It was never as ruin-your-life, scream-for-mercy crazy as movies and books and Lorraine always claimed it ought to have been, but that was life, wasn't it? Always a bit duller in practice than in imagination.

But she had no intention of Miss Havishaming herself. That was letting Ethan win, and she refused to allow that to happen. She was going to prove to herself that if there had been someone boring in their bed, it hadn't been her.

Maya decided then and there that she was going to go out and have all kinds of sex that the fastidious Ethan she'd thought she'd known would have found revolting.

Her life was already ruined, but who knew? Maybe she'd learn that screaming for mercy was a lot more fun than it sounded.

It certainly wouldn't be boring.

There was an extra little swing in her step when she headed back up the cliffside, following one long, medieval staircase after another. She was out of breath when she got to the top again but exhilarated as she made her way back onto the grounds of her hotel. It loomed up before her, a deep magenta color, graceful and pretty. She admired the tiered gardens, bursting with bougainvillea and other flowers she couldn't identify at a glance.

Just as she admired the man working on a fence on the tier closest to her.

He wasn't the kind of man Maya usually found

attractive—but then, it was possible she'd spent a lot of time liking things because she thought she should, not because she truly, deeply liked them. The worker before her was beautiful in the way the rocky shore here was beautiful, hard and rough and more than a little disreputable. He was stripped to the waist, though the day wasn't overly warm, showing off a hard, muscled torso that could have been sculpted from marble. Maya's mouth went dry as her gaze traced over the tattoos that wrapped around one bicep, trailed over one shoulder and made his wide, tough back into a work of art.

His jeans hung low on his hips, and she spent a little longer than necessary admiring the taut curve of his ass, his powerful thighs and even the scuffed boots on his feet.

Heat flashed through her, the first thing that had penetrated the shield of ice and temper she'd wrapped around her since Ethan had told her he was in love with Lorraine.

Maya grabbed on to it. Hard.

The man was sweating in the hot Italian sun, which only seemed to make his shaggy, close-cropped blond hair gleam like gold. He wore a tawny sort of beard and a pair of battered work gloves, and when he swung around to look at her as if he'd felt her standing there, she felt herself shiver into goose bumps.

Because his eyes were as blue as the Italian sky and the sea all around them.

But far more dangerous.

Maya had always maintained certain standards. Her family's expectations had always been clear and she had always aimed to exceed them. Martins were the best, attracted the best and did the best. Even Ethan had been a part of her same pursuit of excellence. He had been as driven as she was, as successful. He was everything Maya had wanted in a man, from his career to his trim, smooth runner's body.

The man before her did not look like he was a runner. He looked like the words *rough and tumble* had been created specifically for him.

"Take a picture, babe," the man said in the kind of American accent that did things to Maya's insides.

She felt...syrupy. Melting hot, like butter. She couldn't think of anything she liked less than being called babe, especially by a stranger, but this man somehow made it feel delicious, not derogatory.

That was the old Maya, she reminded herself. The Maya who had been left so publicly was gone.

She'd died right around the time she'd had to cancel her own wedding.

This new Maya didn't have to worry about what was good for her. She didn't have to concern herself with her reputation or what her parents would think. She didn't have to care if anyone would judge her or what they might say or what her choice of man showed about her to the people who were always watching, always commenting, always looking for chinks in Maya's armor or ways to sandbag her success.

She had no armor here. And better still, she was the only person in Italy who knew who she was, what she'd left behind or even that she was supposed to be sad and broken in the first place.

Fuck that.

And fuck Ethan and Lorraine, too.

"All right," she heard herself say, like a random person with no baggage. She fished her mobile out of her pocket and held it up before her, smiled at him and snapped his picture. "There. Picture taken. Now what?"

She had never sounded like that before in her life. Flirty. Suggestive.

Slutty, a voice whispered inside her that could as easily have been Ethan as her mother.

Another thing Maya had never been was a slut.

Staring into the bright blue gaze of the gorgeously inappropriate man in front of her who didn't know that or anything else about her, she thought that was a crying shame.

Not that she planned to cry. About anything.

"That depends," the man said, and his voice was almost too much to handle. He sounded like the American South, mixed through with what she could only call bad boy, and his amused drawl made her shiver in all kinds of impossible places. "What do you want?"

And Maya had never done an impetuous thing in her life. It was high time she started, she thought. Right here and now, with the kind of reckless behavior she would have shuddered at a few days ago.

Because the man before her, looking at her with all those muscles and a kind of too-hot awareness in his blue eyes, might not be a corporate lawyer. But she had absolutely no doubt that he had reckless down pat.

And Maya wanted to taste it.

Now.

CHAPTER TWO

CHARLIE TELLER WAS no stranger to beautiful women.

He liked to consider himself something of an expert, in fact.

And the one standing before him hit pretty much every single one of his buttons. Hot? Check. A killer body, all generous curves packed onto a lean frame? Check. Soft, dark brown skin he itched to get his hands on? Check.

And better still, a wicked, inviting smile he could feel in his cock?

Hell yeah.

Charlie wasn't a complicated man. His life had gotten a little complicated over the past year, true—but he was doing his best to combat that.

He was here in Italy, a million miles away from everything he'd ever known. Not back in Texas, answering questions that were designed to incriminate him. One way or another.

A year ago he had learned that the unidentified

man his mother had slept with all those years ago, resulting in the pregnancy that had forced her— her words, usually screamed at Charlie while she was wasted—to marry his stepfather, introducing Charlie to a life of outlaw bikers and other rough, often desperate men, wasn't some random drunk in a bar as Charlie had always assumed.

Or if he was, he'd been a very, very rich one.

Daniel St. George had been one of the world's wealthiest men when he'd died. He'd collected beautiful women, fancy hotels and fast cars, and houses in places Charlie had never heard of before. He'd also collected bastard children wherever he went, like some kind of rich man's we-are-the-world power trip. Charlie had found out he had half brothers in Iceland and the Pacific Islands. A half sister living in New York. All as wary of their sudden family connection as he was.

And better by far—or less complicated, anyway— his father had left him a fancy-ass hotel in Italy and a chunk of money to go with it so he could run it.

Given the way things were headed back home in Texas, with federal agents infiltrating his step-father's biker club and a lot of Charlie's own biker-club-adjacent activities under a little too much surveillance, he'd jumped at the chance to get the hell away from a sinking ship.

And who knew? Maybe this was his opportunity to go straight.

It was high time for a little change in his life, he could admit that. He'd lasted a long time hurtling down a dead-end road, but he was a realist. His stepfather had been in and out of jail for most of Charlie's life before he'd met an ugly end in a bar fight gone bad. His mother was too drunk and bitter these days to do much more than exist the same way she always had, moving from man to man in the same small, grim pool of outlaws and grifters. Last he'd heard she was in yet another biker town in the Louisiana swamp.

Charlie had known he'd needed to get out since he was a kid. He'd been plotting out the best way to do that when Daniel St. George's lawyers had found him. And the rich father he'd never known—and couldn't really believe his mother had ever known, if he was honest—turned out to be an excellent exit strategy.

Now he was a boutique hotel owner in a high-class, undeniably beautiful part of the world he never would have seen if he'd stayed in Texas. He had a new life, the new start he'd always wanted and an aversion bordering on phobia for any further complications to his newly simple and easy life.

But he was still him.

And the gorgeous woman smiling at him with all that appreciation in her smile and the November sun playing over her face wasn't complicated at all.

She made him feel simple all the way through.

"What did you have in mind?" he asked her, letting his drawl get lazy. He stripped off his work gloves and tossed them down near the base of the fence post, then rested his hands on his hips.

"What's on offer?" she asked, more of that wickedness in her voice.

And in the way she shifted so he couldn't help but look at that swing in her hips. His mouth went dry.

"The hotel is full-service," he assured her. "Whatever you want, you get."

"I'm delighted to hear that. I have a lot of... wants."

She laughed when she said that, which somehow transformed it from a silly little line anyone might say into something...extraordinary.

Charlie had the distinct impression that if he didn't get a taste of her, it might kill him.

"Tell me what you want," he said, grinning when she did, like they were both caught up in the bright grip of her laughter. "I'll make sure you get it."

She moved closer, and he had to lecture himself not to reach out and sink his hands into the massive cloud of curls around her head. He had to order himself not to wrap his hands around her curvy hips or pull them flush to his, right here, out in the open.

The steep incline of the village fell away behind her, and the ocean was spread out everywhere like a deep blue witness, but all he could see was the flirty skirt she wore that showed off her lean, muscled legs and her long-sleeved shirt with a neckline that drew attention to her delicate collarbones, her firm upper arms and her plump, mouthwatering breasts.

He took his time dragging his gaze back up to her full, lush mouth. She swept her sunglasses off her face, and then he was lost for a moment in the dark brown of her eyes, hot and direct.

He felt it like hands all over him. He wished hers were, and who cared if they were in public.

"I would say I want you," she said, and there was a certain awkwardness in her words, or maybe it was in the way she stood, as if this was out of character for her. But Charlie didn't care. "But I wouldn't want to get you in trouble on the job."

She didn't know who he was. No one had pointed him out to her yet, calling him the American boss or whatever more colorful terms they used in Italian. Capo americano, whatever.

It had taken him and the hotel's longtime manager, Benicio, a solid three months to figure each other out. These days, Charlie left the running of the hotel to Benicio and amused himself with the kinds of things he was good at. He'd always worked with his hands. And there was a deep, unexpected satisfaction in working on something that was his. Something no one could take from him. It felt like an indulgence to spend an afternoon thinking about nothing more than repairing a fence.

Instead of federal wiretaps on the people he'd always considered his family, for example. Or which friends might turn state's evidence and throw him into the middle of it because of things his stepfather had done or boasts his drunken mother had made to the wrong people. It was a relief to be able to simply do a thing without running it through the proper channels so as not to offend anyone, making sure to use a shitty burner phone instead of the technology everyone else enjoyed these days or any of the other things he'd done over the years while he'd danced up and down that gray moral and legal line that all the lawyers he'd known had called, at best, arguable.

There was nothing gray or arguable about a fence. Either it was fixed or it wasn't.

And this woman didn't know he was the owner of this hotel. Charlie could tell from the way she held herself and the clothes she wore that she was high-class. Much higher class than a dirtbag from the Texas dust. She had diamonds in her ears, another one on a delicate chain around her neck, and everything on her curvy body was sleek and quietly expensive. She wasn't dripping with over-the-top, conspicuous wealth the way so many people were around these world-renowned cliffside beach towns—film stars and European royalty and all the rest who flocked to the Amalfi coast because some Kennedy had done the same way back when.

This woman was fancy.

And she thought he was a handyman.

That delighted Charlie all the way through.

"What the owner doesn't know won't hurt him," he drawled. Then he held out his hand, daring her. "Want me to give you a tour?"

He watched her swallow, hard. He watched the way her smile froze, and then the way she forced it wide again.

But what he really cared about was the way she held out her hand after a moment, sliding it into his and holding his gaze while she did.

"I would love a tour," she said, low and a little rough.

Charlie laced his fingers with hers, enjoying the kick of heat that hummed through him at the contact. The way she sucked in a breath. Then he tugged her along behind him, skirting the bottom of the tiered gardens and terraces to duck into the little shed tucked away at the corner of the property.

"This is the best part of the hotel," he told her as he pulled her inside. There was no light, but the ancient windows let the afternoon in through the brightly painted shutters, and it took only a moment or two for his eyes to adjust. And he liked the way the sunshine poured over her pretty face, tipped up to his. "It's nice and private, for one thing."

"Private is my favorite."

And again, there was that hesitation. But it was like she heard it, too, and didn't like it. Because she threw herself forward.

She braced herself on his chest, exhaling in a rush when her palms met his pectoral muscles. Her gaze met his, bright and intense. Then she surged up on her toes and pressed her mouth to his.

Charlie liked that.

And he liked it a lot more when he angled his mouth and took it deeper.

Hotter. Wetter.

And maybe a little bit insane.

One thing he'd learned in Italy was never to deny himself a treat, and this was no different. He found her face with his palms and then guided her head where he wanted. He took the kiss harder. Wilder.

She tasted almost too good. Sweet like honey, with a kick of something that went straight to his head like too much Jack on a long, rough night.

He growled a little bit at that. She made a humming noise in response, and then she was pushing even closer to him, pressing those lush breasts of hers into his chest.

Charlie swung her around, getting her back up against the old stone wall and levering himself against her. He ate at her mouth, demanding and dirty, loving the way she shuddered against him as she met every stroke.

But it wasn't enough.

He picked her up, liking that she was a good, tight handful when he wrapped his arms around her ass and pulled her thighs wide. He pinned her to the wall. She wrapped her legs around his waist like they'd done this dance a thousand times, and he wedged himself there where she was softest and hottest.

And the way he kissed her went savage.

Then she made it worse, because she started

to move. She rocked those hips of hers in a sweet circle, dragging her soft heat all over him, and he thought that he might actually lose it.

He reached back and pulled a condom from his back pocket, and broke the kiss.

She was panting, her mouth faintly swollen and her eyes wild, and he wasn't sure he'd ever seen anything hotter. He fumbled between them to un-button his jeans, pulling himself free. He dealt with the condom, then shoved her skirt out of his way, reaching between them to get a few fingers in all that melting heat.

"Oh my God," she whispered, and he laughed at that, because it was hot. And she was hot. "You just…walk around prepared?"

He thought he might lose it at any second, that was how slick her pussy was, splayed open be-tween him and the wall. Charlie shoved her pant-ies to one side, then put his cock where his fingers had been, moving the tip through her folds, just to play with her.

"I'm always prepared," he told her. "You're wel-come."

Sure enough, she rocked her head back and arched against him, like that could make him do what she wanted.

"I should have mentioned this," he said in a low

voice, gazing down at the picture she made for him, her legs wide-open and wrapped around him. And his cock rubbing this way and that over her proud little clit. "But I like to be in charge. Does that work for you?"

She was panting. Her eyes were unfocused, but still, she laughed at that.

"Go right ahead," she told him. "I can handle it."

"If you say so."

Charlie slammed himself into her, deep.

And felt her come, hot and wet and greedy, like a dream.

Maya couldn't believe any of this was happening.

She couldn't believe the things that had come out of her mouth. She couldn't believe that she'd let a total stranger lead her off into a dark little shack.

But that paled in comparison to the fact that he was inside her.

Thick, huge and impossibly hard.

And more, that an orgasm clenched her tight and hard in its greedy fist, instantly.

She didn't believe in things like this. It wasn't real. It couldn't be real.

Men this beautiful didn't exist, and if they did, they certainly didn't dole out instant orgasms like candy—

But still, she shook around him, one wave crashing into another like they might go on forever. She heard the strangest, most insane noises... that it took her much too long to realize were coming from her.

A lot like a scream, but that was impossible.

This was all impossible.

She choked herself off from any further crazy noises and forced her eyes open. Then she looked down at this beautiful, dangerous stranger who was lodged so deep inside her that she thought she could feel him down into her toes.

His grin was slow and cocky.

And it made her shiver all over again.

She wrapped her arms around his shockingly hard shoulders and held on.

His rough edges were evident everywhere, and it amazed her how much she wanted to lick each and every one of them. His tattoos. His calloused hands. That physical power—when she'd only ever known financial power. She wanted to revel in it.

But she assumed that he would just go for it now, as fast as he could, because she was already taken care of. And it was only fair.

He pulled out, slow and easy, then thrust back in the same way. Like he had all the time in the world.

He did it again, slow and deep. Then that drag out again that made her head spin.

He slid a hand down to her ass, lifting her against him, which made the angle...*more*. More of everything. Intense and deep and too much, all...*more*.

He didn't change his pace.

Maya could feel the remnants of that wallop of an orgasm dancing all along her skin, sinking into her bones, making her feel bright and wild. Time seemed to flatten out on either side of them, and the world narrowed down until there was nothing but that deep, dirty rhythm.

She was aware of everything. How strong he was, that he could hold her so easily and never break that slow, drugging rhythm of his. He smelled like salt and man, something like the sea, and she wanted nothing more than to dip her head and taste him.

But she didn't, because that felt like intimacy, and whatever strange magic this was, it wasn't that.

On some level, she thought that was ridiculous because he was *inside her*—but she couldn't seem to hold on to the things that danced into her head and then out.

There was only that long, smooth thrust. Then the retreat. Over and over and over again.

He braced his other hand on the wall beside her face. She found herself entranced by the corded beauty of his forearm and the particular glory of all those lean muscles.

She could feel the ache in her thighs, but she didn't care. She could feel his chest against hers as she arched into him, then away. Each brush made her nipples ache, and she wanted more. Harder. Deeper. *More.*

Everything—but she didn't say that, either.

This is sex, she told herself. *This is pure fucking.*

And it was more than that, she knew with each thick, deep, thrilling surge inside her.

It was an exorcism.

With every thrust, she was made new.

It was her baptism, and every sacrament thereafter, as he slowly, deliberately, pounded her into madness.

But what a sweet madness it was.

"You going to come again?" It took her a moment to realize that was him, talking to her in that growly, dangerous voice that seemed to scour her body the same way he did. Rough and right. "Are you just going to hang out?"

And Maya didn't know who she was. She never did things like this. She'd never kissed a stranger, much less fucked one up against the wall not even five minutes after laying eyes on him for the first time.

She wasn't this person.

But maybe that was why it was easy to become as much a stranger to herself as the stranger inside her and smile at him. Wicked and flirtatious and nothing like her at all.

"You can either make me come or you can't," she told him, astonished at the words that came out of her own mouth. But she ran with them anyway. "How is that on me?"

"Good point," he replied, and then everything changed.

He gripped her ass harder and lifted her away from the wall. She flowed against him, then bit her own bottom lip as he took that hand of his from the wall and brought it between them.

"Try this," he said, his mouth against her neck, and then he did something to her clit with those big, rough fingers of his—

Maya felt like she'd been electrocuted. It was a jolt, a wild burst of light, and then everything exploded.

She was lost in the white light of it, the wild, impossible commotion, but she held on tight until he finally broke that rhythm of his and went a little wild himself.

And when he groaned out his release into the crook of her shoulder, he tipped her right back over that edge for the third time.

He staggered slightly, then caught himself against the wall again, holding her there between his hard body and the stone.

She held on for longer than she should have, maybe. Until she remembered herself.

Or if not *herself*, exactly, then the facts of the situation.

Total stranger. Random fuck.

Her exorcism was her own business.

She unhooked her legs from around his waist and lowered herself to the ground, shuddering a little at the low noise he made when he pulled out of her as she went.

Her skirt flowed back down over her thighs. He tucked himself away and buttoned himself up again.

And then they were just…staring at each other the way they had outside.

"Hi," he said, with another flash of that grin of his, and a knowing kind of heat in his too-blue eyes. "I'm Charlie."

"Maya," she replied, and then stuck out her hand. The way she always did.

They both stared.

Slowly, with a gleam in his blue eyes that she

could only call unholy, Charlie reached down and wrapped his big hand around hers. And how could that be so hot after everything they'd just done? But it was.

Charlie shook her hand. Very deliberately. Up, then down, in a slow movement that reminded her entirely too much of exactly what had happened here.

She felt too warm. Everywhere.

"Nice to meet you," he said, his voice a low rumble and that crooked grin lodged inside her, somehow. "You want the rest of the tour?"

CHAPTER THREE

"How's Italy?" Melinda asked in her concerned voice, which was exactly like her usual bossy voice, only with a nominal attempt at softness. "More to the point, how are you?"

Maya deeply regretted answering her mobile.

It was another lazy afternoon on the Amalfi coast. She sat out on her terrace in the uncertain, moody weather, wrapped in a whisper-soft throw to ward off the bite of the sea air from below. There was espresso and a selection of freshly baked biscotti and *anginetti* before her. She had been engaged in a rousing debate with herself— should she slip into her infinity pool, always kept comfortably warm to encourage its use even in a changeable, chilly December? Or stay where she was, tucked up cozily with a deliciously fat paper-back at the ready and nothing at all to do?

She really shouldn't have answered the phone.

"I'm fine," she said, trying to drag herself out of the sweet daydream she'd been riding for days now, where this was her life and there was nothing for her to do but gaze at the sea, smell the flowers, watch the rain and pay no mind as one hour rolled into the next. "Good, even."

"You don't need to put on an act for me, Maya."

"I'm sitting on a balcony gazing out at the Amalfi coast, which is even more beautiful than it looks in pictures. There's no acting involved."

Melinda heaved a sigh, and all the ugly things Maya had been doing such a good job barring from her mind since she'd left Toronto squirmed back out and crouched there in the light, disturbing and uncomfortable.

She should hang up, she thought. Right now.

But she didn't.

Maya had spent far too many years being responsible. Available. The sort of person who suffered through whatever conversation someone wanted to start with her, regardless of whether or not she wanted to have it. She'd always assumed that was part and parcel of being a responsible adult.

Today she couldn't recall why she'd ever thought such a thing.

"I didn't want to bother you with this, but I

thought you should know." Her sister's voice took on a familiar, faintly officious tone, because Melinda always functioned best when she was in charge of something. And clearly she felt she was in charge of Maya. Or what life Maya had left behind in Toronto, anyway. "Ethan is resisting moving out of the condo. He says you and he found it together, it's as much his as yours, and you're a single person now anyway, so why do you need all that space? I'm quoting, obviously."

Maya didn't want to think about Ethan. Or the condo she'd called home for the past few years despite the fact she'd seen so little of it, because she was always at work. She didn't particularly want to think about any of the things she'd left behind in Canada. It seemed too far away. Like a bad dream she couldn't quite shake off when morning came, but nothing real.

She'd been in Italy for five whole days now and it felt like a lifetime. As if she'd never truly existed before but had sprung into life the moment her feet hit the endless stairs that made up this village of hers high on its cliff, cascading down to the sea. What concerned her was whether or not it rained. The steepness of her chosen staircase. How many stairs she needed to walk a day to counterbalance all the marvelous food she indulged in with the

same appetite and greed she'd applied to Charlie
the handyman.

Every time she thought about *him*—and she
thought about him a lot—she shivered the same
way she had when he'd been inside her.

But she didn't think her prim, proper sister
would appreciate that anecdote, even if she'd felt
like sharing it. Maya sat up straighter on her comfortable chaise and frowned until she remembered
herself.

She'd wanted to hold on to the condo because
it would irritate Ethan. Because it was the only
revenge she'd been able to come up with a week
ago, however small and silly. But now she was in
Italy and there had been Charlie and the idea of
fighting with Ethan about a condo, of all things,
made her feel…tired.

She was a woman of action, she reminded herself. Not asinine little games of spite.

"You can tell Ethan he has two choices," she
said briskly, sounding like the highly trained lawyer she was. Even if that persona—*her* persona—
didn't seem to fit her anymore. Or not here. "He
can move out and find his own little love nest for
him and Lorraine. Or he can stay in the condo, but
if he does, he needs to find me a different one—

and not in any building where I could conceivably run into him and Lorraine. Ever."

"Why would you let him choose a place for you to live?" Melinda sounded baffled.

"I barely live in the condo we have now. I'm always at the office." There was something about the way she said that, so flat and matter-of-fact, that made something in Maya shake a little. She tried to shrug it off. "Either way, when I come home, it needs to be to an Ethan-and-Lorraine-free space. Feel free to quote me in return."

There was a faint silence, and Maya could hear the far-off sounds of her former life. She could imagine Toronto in December all too well. Dark, cold and snowy.

At the moment, she couldn't think of a single reason to return.

"Are you really going to stay there the whole month?" Melinda made a faint clucking sound. "I know you're stubborn, but this is pushing it."

"There's a reason people talk about Italy the way they do, Melinda. It's magical."

"I'm sure it is, but it's a fantasy world." Her voice turned kind, and that was much harder to take. "Back here in the real world, your broken heart is waiting for you. You're going to have to deal with it. Why would you put that off?"

Maya rubbed her free hand over her face, trying to rub away the creases in her forehead, and did her best not to sound as irritated as she felt when she spoke again. "My heart is right here in my body, thank you. It goes where I go and it prefers a lovely seaside holiday to freezing cold, horribly dark and depressing Toronto."

And her heart didn't feel broken. Bruised, sure. But not broken.

But she was afraid to admit it. She was afraid to say it out loud. Because didn't that say terrible things about her?

"Maya..."

"An Ethan-free, safe space," Maya repeated, with more calm than she felt. "If you want to help, that's what I want."

She sounded smooth on the phone—the way she should, she'd practiced it so much in all her years as a lawyer—but when she poked the button to end the call, she couldn't deny that she was agitated.

Maya tossed her mobile aside. She contemplated tossing it over the balcony's railing so she could be done with it, but restrained herself. Barely. She stood up, suddenly restless and noisy inside instead of happily lost in that same sweet Italian daydream of the past few days.

She wanted to blame her sister for that, but it was her fault for answering the phone, wasn't it?

Maya moved over to the railing, settled her elbows against the metal scrollwork and looked down. It was a long, long way from her balcony jutting out from the highest level of the hotel to the slumbering sea far below. The village was a jumble of brightly colored buildings, houses and shops and ancient structures dating back centuries, as if someone had tossed them there against the steep cliff walls to see what stuck. It had rained yesterday and in the night, and the wind whispered of the kinds of winters she'd left behind on the other side of the world and all the things she'd left there that she didn't want to think about. Not here. She concentrated on the scent of flowers on that same wind instead. The bursts of sunshine. The salt in the air that reminded her of Charlie.

She had seen him only once since that insane first day. And only from a distance.

He had been doing something deliciously physical down by the hotel's big communal pool while she'd been eating in the sunny breakfast room on the main level. He hadn't looked up, and she'd enjoyed that a little too much—because she'd been able to determine that he was not, in fact, an Italian daydream she'd had after running up all those village stairs for the first time. He wasn't something she'd made up out of oxygen deprivation and too much cardio.

He was all too real. Mouthwateringly real, with the tattoos and those old jeans and that *body*.

At the table next to her, a trio of older British women had tittered among themselves, and a glance had confirmed that they were all sharing the same view. Charlie in nothing but those jeans of his, hammering away at something with a sledgehammer. She couldn't remember what.

No one had cared.

She hadn't seen him since. Or really, it was more precise to say she'd gone out of her way not to look for him.

Instead, she'd glutted herself on the sun when it shined, the rain when it fell so much softer and warmer than in Canada, and the sea in all its hues from blue to gray and back again. She'd read books that she found in the library off the hotel lobby. A murder mystery that had kept her up late into the night, her heart pounding. A sweet, tender romance that had made her chest feel heavy and her eyes damp, though she'd refused to give in to all that emotion. And just this morning she'd finished a detective novel, all intellectual shenanigans and arch, clever conversations.

She'd drunk enough espresso to swim her way back to Toronto. She'd eaten— Oh God, had she eaten. Fresh fruit and produce by the armful. Pasta so fresh it redefined her idea of what pasta ought to be, bearing as it did so little resemblance to the stuff she boiled in her own pot back home. Fish, cured meats of every description, olives piled high… She was in food heaven.

She was glutted and besotted, and she didn't let herself think about the mess back home at all. When her mind strayed in that direction, she forced it back to right here, right now. This stunning stretch of coastline in the off-season that felt more and more like hers every day.

And still, when Maya's gaze dropped down to the man standing at the very edge of the hotel property, right there next to the shed where she'd betrayed herself in every possible way and still didn't feel the slightest shred of guilt about it, everything in her…hummed.

She had convinced herself, as one day rolled into the next and she'd had only that one sighting of him, that she'd exaggerated that rough, masculine beauty of his. That she was making it over into some kind of fantasy daydream inside her own head when he was just a man. A pretty one, but nothing more astonishing than that.

To make herself feel better, maybe. Not that she felt bad—now. But it was always possible she might feel guilty or ashamed later. It was possible she was doing what she could to minimize it before she was tempted to care too much.

But when she gazed down at him, she understood that, if anything, she kept undermining how truly—astonishingly—beautiful the man really was.

He was so *physical*. She wasn't used to it. All the men in her life, from her austere father to Ethan, were…attractive enough, she had always thought, but not like this. Not so *raw*. Not all that leashed power and strength, which was as much the kind of energy that burned in him as it was those muscles. Or those tattoos that peeked out from the sleeves of the white T-shirt he wore. None of Charlie's tattoos were trendy. None of them were tribal or vaguely Hawaiian. His looked particular. Specific to him, not something a tourist could pick up on a vacation somewhere. More *Sons of Anarchy* than generic bro.

That made them hotter.

Or maybe that was just the marvel of his biceps. His forearms. *Him.*

He shifted where he stood down there by the shed, then looked up. And even though a great distance and towering height separated them, Maya felt his gaze slam into her as if he was still as close as he'd been in that shed. She made a startled little noise that she knew he couldn't hear.

And still, she was entirely too aware of the way he grinned, crooked and knowing. As if he'd heard it all the same.

She felt…giddy. Silly, almost.

Charlie looked at her for a long while. Then he tilted his head. That was all.

But it might as well have been an engraved invitation.

Maya barely remembered what it was like to date, because she never really had. She had always been too busy, too driven, too focused, which was why meeting Ethan at work had seemed so perfect. And she knew this wasn't dating. Still, she figured the same rules probably applied. Don't act too eager. Don't let him see you care. The person who acts the most disinterested has all the power—

But she didn't care about any of that. Not now, when she'd already proved exactly how overeager she was and had gotten all those orgasms as a reward.

Maya smiled, big and bright to make sure he could see it from all the way down there. And if there was a part of her that knew she was doing a

face dive into this crazy thing that was as far removed from her real life as it was possible to get—

Well. Charlie the handyman was a lot sexier
than a pint or five of ice cream and her own tears.

He inclined his head again, then moved out of
sight, and she knew he was coming for her.

She knew it.

She pushed back from the rail, surprised to find
her whole body felt weak. Shaky.

Ready, something in her whispered.

Maya headed back into her suite, draping the
throw over the nearest chair and smoothing her
hands over the soft denim of the jeans she wore.
She didn't look in the mirror. She didn't want to
second-guess herself.

It felt like free-falling. Like throwing herself
over the side of her own balcony and letting the
Italian wind pick her up and carry her wherever
it wanted.

Maya wasn't this kind of person. She plotted
and planned. She thought about her future and
made sure every step she took in the present led
straight where she wanted to go.

She had never done anything like this in her life.

Certainly not *twice*.

A kind of heat washed over her then, and she
knew what it was. Shame, thick and ugly. *Lorraine*

and I fell in love, she could hear Ethan saying. *All you're doing is whoring around.*

You were always so judgmental, Lorraine added, there inside Maya's head where she lived and breathed and commented no matter how Maya pretended otherwise. *Now look at you.*

And when the knock came on her door, faster than should have been possible, Maya jumped.

Then stared, as if she could make the man on the other side go away with the force of her will.

But you don't want him to go away, something in her whispered.

Maya was the one who had gone away. She had withstood the humiliation of her wedding day. She had ignored the advice thrown at her from all sides and come here. She had ignored every single instinct she'd ever had about her own behavior and she'd had sex with a stranger in a shed, of all places.

She'd already gone off the rails. Completely.

What was the point of stopping now?

She didn't let herself think about it any further. She didn't want the shame in her to win—because it didn't matter what she did here. She would never do what Ethan or Lorraine had done. She would never ever have broken her promises or compromised her loyalty like that. Never.

It didn't matter that she didn't know what she was doing. Hell, it was a good thing she didn't. What had knowing what she was doing, every step along the way, gotten her so far?

She crossed the floor, let out a breath that felt too hot and too shaky and maybe a little bit ugly, too, then swung open the door to let him in.

Charlie had never missed a woman in his life.

Especially not one he'd already had.

He never found himself awake at weird hours, reliving the encounter. Wondering where she was, what she was doing. Wishing they could do it all over again.

Charlie didn't know what the hell it was about Maya that got to him.

He'd seen her these past few days, wandering around the small, vertical village. Aimlessly, to his mind. He'd seen her in the piazza, charming the locals with that smile of hers that rivaled the summers here, a comparison he hated himself for making. He'd seen her race up one staircase, then the next, her attention focused on keeping her feet on the old, uneven steps.

She'd never seen him.

She'd also never looked for him.

When she smiled at him today, he felt like some

kid. The kind of kid he'd never been, awkward and excitable.

He'd told himself there was no way in hell he was running to her like a dog on a leash—

But here he was, five stories up at her door, as surely as if he was wearing a shock collar.

Maya was as pretty as he remembered. Prettier, if he was honest. Her dark eyes were that soft, ridiculously sweet brown, lit up today with something he couldn't quite read. But he could feel it all the same. Her hair was that tempting cloud of black curls he hadn't touched near enough. She wore another long-sleeved T-shirt in an obviously expensive, sleek fabric that only suggested her curves. Her jeans cupped her ass in a way that made his mouth dry, and there was no reason that the fact her narrow, elegant feet were bare should make his chest ache.

She didn't say anything. She stood in her open door, studying him, and he had the strangest sensation that all the odd things he was feeling were plastered across his face. When he had made a dirty career—and lived as long as he had—by keeping his face like stone.

He didn't want to think about that. He didn't want to let it settle into him, like acknowledging the possibility might make it true.

Instead, Charlie reached over and got his hands in her hair, then dragged her mouth to his, making a noise he might have called desperate if he'd heard it from someone else.

This wasn't him. He didn't do desperate.

And still, he was the one moving into the room, kicking the door shut behind him and hauling Maya up hard against his chest.

He was the one getting his mouth on her like he might die if he didn't drown himself in her taste.

He didn't do desperate. He didn't feel those things. Hell, he didn't feel anything.

But he felt her.

He was already on fire, and she threw gas on it.

She met the scrape of his mouth on hers, that dirty, slick tangle of tongue and teeth. Her hands were like lightning, smoothing down his sides and sneaking back up under the hem of his T-shirt.

And it wasn't enough. It wasn't anything close to enough.

He moved her backward, breaking that wildfire kiss only to haul his T-shirt over his head, then throw it aside. He did the same with hers, hissing in a breath at the lacy thing that held her breasts high, then growling a little when he got rid of that, too.

This time when he dragged her close, he hauled

her up against his chest again so her legs went around his waist, and still he kept moving.

Her breasts rubbed against him with every step, those dark brown nipples like sweet torture, and she was so smooth, sugar and heat, and still not nearly enough.

He carried her into the other room, moving until they hit the bed, and then he toppled her down onto the mattress. Then came right down with her.

And once they were horizontal, it all got a whole hell of a lot better.

They rolled. Maya was on top, straddling him and sitting up so he could get his hands on her. He filled his hands with her breasts, then jackknifed up to get his mouth on one taut nipple. Then, when she was arching into him and making greedy little noises that made his cock ache, the other.

They rolled again and he was on top, one hand down the back of her jeans to cup that ass of hers. He ground himself against her pussy, making them both grunt each time his cock pressed hard against the crotch of her jeans.

It was more torture.

He rolled away from her when he wasn't sure his control was going to hold. He kicked off his boots, grabbed a condom from his pocket and then got rid of his jeans, too, never happier in his life that he preferred to go commando.

Until the next second, when she smiled at him, then crawled over to where he'd rolled. That smile widened as she met his gaze, then reached out to wrap a hand around his cock. She tested him, then took him in both her fists.

That was good. So freaking good he almost lost it.

But he thought he might have found religion when she swayed even closer, then took the thick head of him into her mouth.

Charlie's mind went blank.

There was nothing but sensation. Her hands gripping his cock. That sweet, hot mouth of hers. Her wicked, dirty tongue.

He pulled her away, somehow, and the sound of distress she made was almost too much for him.

"I don't want to come yet," he gritted out. "I have plans."

"Plans are overrated."

She sounded irritated, cranky and horny, and he liked the combination so much he was tempted to make it worse. Tie her up to the bed. Tease her until she cried, then make her scream. Something fun like that, but he didn't think he had it in him. Not today. He would have to pick another day,

when she could suck him off the way she clearly
wanted to and he could take his sweet-ass time
with that lush body of hers, making her come over
and over, until he was ready to go again.

It occurred to him that he was doing another
thing he'd never done before. He never plotted out
sex in advance. He had it, then he had more, the
end.

But everything with Maya was different. New.
Crazy, something in him growled.

Charlie told himself it was fury that had him
reaching for her, stripping those jeans off her and
the lacy panties she wore beneath them. He ran
his hand along the silken length of her legs, feeling it shudder through him, all that softness and
strength.

He wanted to eat her alive.

He moved toward the head of the bed, pulling
her with him. Then he set her on top of him until
she straddled him. First his chest and then, tipping her forward, he held her thighs open so she
straddled his face.

"Hold on to the headboard," he ordered her.

He hooked his hands around her muscular
thighs, pulled her down over him to cover himself in all that sweet, melting heat and ate her like
a ripe peach.

She was slippery, made of sugar and need, and the first time she shook apart, he could hear the headboard creak when she gripped it.

But he wasn't done.

He wanted more, so he took it, his hands moving from her thighs to worship her ass. He ate at her until she was making those wordless little sounds again, the ones that had kept him up at night. He didn't think he'd ever been this hard or this desperate to get inside a woman, but he kept going. Until eventually she was grinding her pussy into his face, rocking herself against him and sobbing her way into another orgasm.

Only then did he crawl out from under her. He flipped her over so she was on her hands and knees, facing the big window and the sea and sky beyond. He knelt behind her, choosing not to notice the way his hands shook as he gripped his own cock and dealt with the condom. Then—finally—guided it to her swollen, scalding-hot pussy.

She moaned. He felt it, everywhere.

He felt too damned much.

Charlie notched himself in her entrance, gripped her lush hips and pounded his way home.

CHAPTER FOUR

HE WAS LIKE A STORM.

Elemental. Uncontrollable.

Maya braced herself on her elbows, arching into every thick, deep surge. He was so hard. Not just his cock, but the granite muscle of his thighs she could feel every time he plunged so deep inside her.

And she was already so soft. Melting and spinning, but the rough, perfect thrust of him inside her gave her a kind of focus. She didn't have to think—maybe she couldn't think—but she could lose herself in the demanding rhythm.

It was like disappearing and yet staying fully present, all at the same time.

She dropped her head, surrendered and let him take them both wherever it was he wanted to go.

Maya expected that he would find his pleasure quickly. What she didn't expect was that the way he pounded into her—such an intense, delicious battering that stirred up too many sensations she couldn't count or name—would stir her up all over again.

She almost didn't believe it. But he was so deep, so sure, hard and intense. And before she knew it, that greedy fist—red-hot and wild—was crushing her all over again.

And this time, as he groaned out his own release deep into her, she shattered into a thousand pieces and cried out his name as she fell.

When she woke up, it was to find herself all alone, sprawled across her bed at a careless angle. Maya pushed herself up to sitting position gingerly, feeling much the way she had the other day after the shed.

Used, everywhere.

In the most wonderful possible way.

Outside her windows, cloud cover had moved in over the water, but she liked it. She didn't miss the sun, not when she felt so bright within.

Maya sat for a moment with all that light inside her, telling herself that it was temporary. It would fade. Nothing this good could stay.

Still, she held on to it as long as she could.

She stretched, long and luxuriously. Then she crawled across the mattress, swung her feet to the ground and didn't bother to cover herself as she padded toward her washroom and that huge tub with its sea views she'd been meaning to try—

But she stopped dead as she passed the doorway that led into the main room and saw Charlie.

Still here.

He was damp from what she assumed was a shower, a towel knotted low at his hips, and he was accepting a rolling room-service cart from one of the hotel staff members.

The room-service man didn't look up. He didn't glance around or notice that Maya was there in the other room. He didn't seem to realize Maya was there at all, but Charlie did.

That impossible blue gaze of his flicked to her, then away. He signed something, exchanged a few words in Italian, then let the man out.

"Did you want to give him a show?" Charlie asked after he'd closed the door and took his time turning back to her. His smile was crooked and echoed deep inside her, instantly getting that fire going when Maya would have sworn it had burned all it could. "We can call him back."

"No, thank you." She sounded prim and repressed, as if she wasn't standing there naked. "I'm not really a performer."

"Are you sure?" That wicked gleam in his eyes made her shiver. "So far, I'm a fan."

"I didn't expect you to still be here."

Maya hadn't meant to blurt that out. Not so… baldly, with such obvious recklessness.

It hung there in the air between them.

And she fully expected him to overreact. But he only studied her as if she was the one who didn't make sense and might blow up at any moment. "Why not?"

Maya didn't want to excavate the different layers of the dark things in her gut. What she'd left behind, but worse than that, what she still carried with her. She didn't want to look at any of it. Not when she could look at him instead.

She cleared her throat. "I didn't realize it was that kind of thing."

And maybe she had the dim notion that he would be abashed at that. Had she wanted him to be? But it didn't matter, because all he did was grin wider.

"It can be any kind of thing you want it to be, babe."

"Can it be a thing where you don't call me babe?"

"Right now it's a thing where I'm hungry," he said, no hint of anything like shame anywhere on his beautiful body, much less that gorgeous face.

Maya was still naked, and that suddenly felt very different from before. When they'd been in the shed, her skirt had dropped down and it was as if nothing had happened. She'd clung to that as she'd walked away, reeling.

This was much more…obvious. Vulnerable, maybe.

And she had the distinct impression that he knew it.

That was why she made no move to cover herself, though she wanted to. She stayed where she was, watching as Charlie rolled the cart over to the table in the corner, then settled himself down, as if he had every intention of sitting there, watching the sea and having a snack.

And very much as if she wasn't there at all.

What surprised her was the kick of temper that wound through her at that. As if this wasn't new. As if this was an old fight between people who knew each other.

Get a grip, Maya, she ordered herself.

She decided temper required clothing, so she swept up the throw she'd left on a chair earlier. And wrapped it around herself as she slipped into a seat at the table.

"What did you order?" she asked, as he removed

the big silver covers from a selection of plates and then slid them into the center of the table.

"Food."

There was laughter in his blue gaze, and Maya still didn't know why her heart was kicking at her as if they were in a fight. She hardly knew this man. And sure, the sex had left her reeling and fragile all over again, but he wasn't *doing* anything. A monosyllable just made him a man.

The kind of man she'd read about in books or seen on television shows, because the men she knew never said one word when they could rattle off fifty instead. The men she knew had never missed an opportunity to pontificate. At length.

Charlie had said less in the time she'd known him than any man she'd ever known before had said in the first five minutes of their acquaintance. But it wasn't as if she thought she was misunderstanding him.

She ordered herself to view this—him—as a revelation.

An opportunity to spend time with a man who was completely outside her usual wheelhouse.

Maya took stock of the food herself. It was more of the same simple-yet-delectable fare she now associated with Italy, and she was surprised to feel her own stomach go hollow and greedy in anticipation.

For a long while, neither one of them spoke. And Maya found herself fascinated—or maybe the word she wanted was *compelled*—by how intimate this was. First, sex like that, so untamed and wild. And now food, shared half-naked, which made it all feel sensual.

As if this was the foreplay they hadn't quite gotten around to before.

Either time.

"Aren't you going to get in trouble?" she thought to ask as she feasted on pasta dressed in a simple olive oil. Tart olives, and light perfectly grilled fish. "Won't that man report back that you're up here? Obviously not doing…whatever it is you do?"

"I'll be fine."

"Does the hotel not have rules about staff mixing with guests?"

Charlie sat back in his chair then, that big sculpted body of his looking more relaxed. But it put Maya on alert.

He even smiled, but still, she suddenly felt like prey.

Not, she was forced to admit a moment later while her heart kicked at her madly, that feeling like prey was necessarily a bad thing.

"I know women like to talk after sex," he said.

She eyed him. "Is that a woman thing? I thought it was a human thing."

"I'm not opposed to it," he drawled, as if he hadn't heard what she'd said. "But is this really the topic you want to cover?"

Her cheeks felt hot and she lifted her chin a little, ignoring the way that same heat seemed to roll over her. It should have been embarrassment or some cousin to that kind of humiliation at her own awkwardness, but everywhere the heat touched her it turned out she didn't feel embarrassed at all.

She felt a whole lot more like greedy. Like she wanted to glut herself on him, one way or another, whether the blunt instrument was his cock...or him.

And somehow she managed to hold on to that feeling while harnessing the part of her that had been known to decimate opposing counsel at depositions.

"Okay. You sound American. How did you come to be a handyman at a St. George property on the Amalfi coast?"

"I'm very handy." He grinned when she frowned at him. "Sometimes jobs fall in your lap."

"Do they? That hasn't been my experience."

"You don't seem like you have a whole lot of experience."

Her frown deepened. "If you're talking about sex, I don't have a lot of experience with random strangers. I've never viewed that as a bad thing. And as far as jobs go, they've never fallen in my lap. I plotted them out, then pursued them to the best of my ability."

With single-minded focus, sacrificing everything she could if it would help her get where she wanted to go. But she didn't say that, because she already sounded like she was in a job interview.

Charlie laughed. At her, in that low charged way that told her too many things about him. Chief among them that he wasn't that worried about finding work. Not the kind of work that had always been the center of Maya's life.

"That doesn't sound like any fun."

"A career isn't supposed to be fun. It's supposed to be a career."

"You have to ask yourself what the point of all that crap is. Why do it at all? Because someone told you that you were supposed to?"

Maya felt strongly that, given the slightest provocation, the strange sensation in the back of her throat could turn into a scream. At him.

And she didn't need to fully understand the inherent danger he wore in that hard and rangy body of his to know he wouldn't like that very much. She knew she certainly didn't want to become the kind of woman who made scenes. Her parents had raised her to be calm and collected in the face of any and all provocations. Maya figured a departure from her usual reserve was allowed on her wedding day. But giving in to it now would mean she'd turned into someone else entirely, surely.

"You don't strike me as one of those follow-your-bliss hippies," she managed to say in a perfectly even voice. Or close enough, anyway. "Are you?"

"Not at all." He shifted and she told herself he was uncomfortable, though she suspected that was nothing but wishful thinking. "I had what you might consider a career. I wouldn't call it fun. It required loyalty. Commitment. But when the chance came to do something else, I took it."

"That doesn't sound a whole lot like loyalty."

She knew she wasn't imagining it then, when his smile went dangerous.

"You might want to be careful questioning a man's loyalty. Where I come from, people take shit like that seriously."

Maya should have been more concerned. Worried that this stranger might react in a way she didn't like. They were in a hotel, yes, but the walls were thick and it was the off-season. There was nobody nearby. If she yelled for help, would anyone hear her?

Yet in the next moment, she realized she wasn't afraid of him. She recognized that she ought to have been, but she wasn't. She still felt that temper inside her. She still felt that odd scrape at the back of her throat.

But she had always been more afraid of setting off Ethan's temper—because he was so sensitive, so easily wounded, so quick to take offense—than she was now. When she didn't need anyone to tell her that Charlie was a far more formidable man than her ex.

"I'm not questioning your loyalty," she said, aware that something had shifted in her. She couldn't put a name to it. She only knew that there was emotion attached to it, and she could feel it at the backs of her eyes. "I'm questioning loyalty itself. Everyone claims they want it. But who actually lives up to that kind of ideal?"

That ended up more raw than she'd intended.

"Some people live their life by their loyalty," Charlie said in a low voice, as if he felt that same shift in him, too. His blue gaze made her ache when it met hers. "I spent most of my life keeping old promises. I expected to keep right on doing that until the day I died."

Something occurred to her. She had to fight to keep her expression blank. "Is that your way of telling me you're married?"

His bark of laughter surprised her, but it also cleared the air. The tightness between them—or maybe it was only in her—eased as he sat back again, looking relaxed again.

"Hell no. I'm not married. I've never been close." He nodded at her left hand. "Divorced?"

Maya lifted her hand, frowning down at the dent that showed all too clearly where her ring had sat.

"Almost married," she said.

She waited for it to hit her. For any of those ugly things that her conversation with her sister had stirred up to come back, and harder.

But instead, she kept her chin high and it didn't hurt the way she'd expected it to.

His eyes gleamed. "It didn't take?"

"He decided he liked my maid of honor better. On the day."

She couldn't read the expression she saw on his face then, there a moment and then gone. But she liked the way his mouth curved in one corner. "Dumbass."

"That was my take," Maya agreed. "But we were talking about you."

"You were talking about me. I don't talk about me. Call it a habit."

"I've already broken all kinds of habits since I came to Italy," Maya said with a cheerfulness that should have felt forced. She was surprised to discover that it didn't. "It's fun. You should try it."

He stretched his legs out in front of him, leaning back farther in his chair. "There's not much to tell. What you see is what you get."

"Oddly, I doubt that."

"I'm a simple man." He grinned. "Feed me, fuck me, and I'm good."

Maya grinned back. "Then this must be a tragedy for you. I'm pretty sure you did the fucking. Then you went ahead and ordered the food, too. Maybe you're not quite so simple after all."

She wasn't sure he'd laugh at that, and he didn't make a noise, but she could see it there in all that blue.

"I think you're looking for complications, babe. This is Italy. Everything is simple here, if you can afford it."

"Simple is what I'm after."

"Good."

And Maya had the strange notion that she'd just agreed to something, though she couldn't have said what.

Charlie stood, then helped her to her feet, though she didn't need the help. She assumed he knew that. She didn't say anything as he tugged her along after him, leading her out to the infinity pool tucked there on the edge of her balcony, promising views of nothing but sky and sea forever.

He stripped off his towel, showing off that impossibly perfect butt of his. Then, while she was still trying not to swallow her own tongue, he waded in, and there was a part of her—the part that was used to men who quizzed her in every possible scenario, the better to negotiate what they both wanted out of anything from a take-out order to a life together—that was astonished that this man simply got naked and assumed that she would follow him.

But maybe he assumed it because that was what a woman did when faced with the perfection of his naked body. She dropped the throw she'd wrapped around her and found her way into the warm, inviting caress of the water.

And for a long while, they floated there, as the weather turned grim all around them. It didn't seem to matter. If there was a better place to wait out the storm than tucked up in warm water with a man so big and so imposing, she couldn't imagine where it would be.

They clung to the edge together, their arms brushing, and it felt a lot like healing.

Maya didn't say that out loud, either.

Until suddenly they weren't brushing up against each other. Charlie turned, pulling her over him. She straddled his lap, her knees on the slick tile bench beneath the surface of the water. And she couldn't help the moan that escaped her lips as he slid inside her. Still stretching her, so thick and hard.

"Shit. I left the condoms inside," he muttered.

"I'm on the pill," she offered.

Another thing she never thought she'd say. Not to a man she hardly knew, who was already so deep inside her that she couldn't seem to keep herself from clenching around him, then releasing, over and over, as if she could create her own rhythm that way.

He muttered something and she thought he was going to get up and go—

But instead, he wrapped his arms around her and surged deep inside her.

His gaze locked to hers, and she didn't know

what was hotter: the fierce, possessive look on his face or the way he filled her.

And as he moved her, taking control and guiding her body instead of letting her rock herself against him, it began to rain.

The rain was cold, little shocks against her too-hot skin, but Maya didn't care.

He moved slowly, almost tenderly, though she knew better than to say something like that out loud. Or any of these things she kept thinking about this man whose last name she didn't know. And hadn't asked.

There was nothing but the sloshing of the water in the pool and their breathing. The patter of the rain against the stone buildings and, far off, bells ringing out the time.

And it was too much to hold his gaze like this, because she didn't know what he could see in her. Maya didn't feel simple at all. She felt split wide-open, naked and vulnerable, but she couldn't seem to stop. She couldn't look away.

She had no idea what it was that gripped her—and him—so that every sensation felt sacred.

No exorcism this time. Only the weight, the glory and the searing perfection of the way he fit inside her. The way their bodies moved together as if they'd been made to interlock just like this.

The way she cried out as he came inside her, scalding her.

Changing her.

And better still, the way he said her name.

CHAPTER FIVE

THE NEXT MORNING when her phone rang, Maya saw that it was her parents' home phone number. And ignored it.

She felt guilty about it the second after she did it, but she couldn't bring herself to answer it. She didn't want to hear what else was happening back in Toronto. She didn't want to explain—again— why she hadn't chosen to stay there to drown in all the pity and embarrassment after her disaster of a wedding day. Not to mention the weather.

And to add to her newfound rebelliousness, she declined to check her email, too. For the first time in…as long as she could remember.

Work would have to get along without her.

That was such a scandalous, insane, brand-new thought that she laughed out loud, startling herself.

Thankfully, she was alone.

Charlie hadn't snuck away in the night as she'd

assumed he would. He'd woken her up, rolled her beneath him and made her scream. Ruinously. That had been when dawn was only just beginning to turn the sky outside pink. He'd flashed that easy grin at her while they both lay there, panting. And then she'd stayed right where she was, wondering if she'd ever fully recover from the things that man could do to her, while he'd sauntered off to her washroom.

She'd heard the shower go on, but she'd been too drowsy and dizzy to do much more than notice the sound of the water. She'd still been lying right where he'd left her, boneless and smiling, when he'd walked back out and pulled his clothes back on.

He'd stamped on his boots, run a careless hand through his hair and then fixed that bright gaze of his on hers. He hadn't flashed his grin. He hadn't drawled something to break the mood.

And Maya had felt her heart thump. Hard.

She knew better than to read anything into a moment. A look. She was being ridiculous and she'd told herself so, then and there. He might have spent a long afternoon and the longer night with her, but all they'd done was have sex and eat.

That wasn't the kind of thing that led to good-bye kisses. Or should.

But she thought a kiss would have been a lot simpler than the moment that had stretched out between them, fraught and hot and shot through with layers of things she was afraid to name.

She'd been wide-awake when he'd left, without saying a word.

Maya had decided that it was unwise to lie about in that bed, reliving the things that had gone on there, all over the wide king-size mattress. Besides, there was no need to relive it when she could feel it in every inch of her body. When she stretched. When she breathed.

Every touch. Every thrust. His mouth and hands on every square inch of her body—

It had been enough to make her dizzy all over again.

She'd taken a shower, sorted out her hair, then had set off into the village.

She'd seen a flyer in the piazza a day or so before, heralding a yoga class at the only larger hotel that was open this time of year. She hurried down through the hotel's stacked levels, then headed outside to make her way down the tiers of the garden and pool areas, letting herself out at the gate near the shed that now felt like *theirs*—another thing she knew better than to let herself think. It was a chilly morning with a faint bite in the air, though the sky was clear. But by the time she made it down all the many staircases it took to get to the piazza that was set roughly halfway down the cliff-side, she was warm.

And proud of herself, too. Every day she got quicker. Less out of breath. As if all these stairs were changing her the more she ran up and down them.

Then again, maybe it wasn't the stairs that were making her feel so different—electric and intense—inside her own skin.

She slipped into the yoga class just as it was starting, situating herself in the middle of the room and giving herself over to an easy, peaceful hour and a half of stretching. Breathing. Clearing her head and settling into her body.

Making it hers again.

When the class was done, she walked out, pleased to find the day a little bit warmer, especially when she moved from the shadows into the sun. She found herself espresso and a pastry from one of the cafés that stayed open year-round, and then she sat on the broad lip of a fountain. It was at the base of the wide stairs that led up to a pretty church with its bell tower, and Maya thought she could spend a lifetime gazing up at the ancient buildings surrounding the square. Pastel colors ac-

cented with iron balconies, all of it faintly weathered, reminding her of the sea in the distance and
the long, hot, crowded summers that made the
Amalfi coast famous.

Her pastry was flaky and sweet and gone too
soon, and still she sat where she was, soaking in
the sounds of feet on old stones. The sounds of
Italian being spoken all around her. There were
Christmas lights strung up that she needed to come
back down and admire when it got dark.

The quiet did something to her. These hours
with no stress, no phone calls, no messages. Day
after day without the stress she'd always prided
herself on managing so well. She'd never stopped
to take the time and wonder who she'd be without
all of those things. Without a to-do list that could
stretch across the width of Canada. Without too
much work to ever truly finish. Without a busy
city heaving all around her, rush rush rushing just
as she did.

But now that she'd stopped running, she
couldn't imagine starting up again.

Every time she had an encounter with Charlie,
it got harder and harder to imagine going back
home to Toronto. Whether to her own condo or
some other one, assuming Ethan actually did as

requested. Maya couldn't imagine slipping back into her life.

Melinda seemed to think there would be some kind of operatic reckoning when she returned, but the more Maya considered it, the more she doubted it. There would only be as much of a reckoning as she allowed. People could discuss what had happened with her only if she let them. The firm would be alive with gossip as long as both she and Ethan continued to work there, sure. But Maya didn't have to indulge in any of it.

She didn't have to talk about her misfire of a wedding at all if she didn't want to.

It was almost frightening how easy it was to imagine. She could lose herself in the work the way she always had, because there was always more. She could quietly request of her managing partner that she not be put on cases with Ethan, but as that hardly ever happened anyway, there was almost no point in asking. No one would want them working together anyway, as their personal issues were neither good for the clients nor billable.

And didn't that say everything there was to say about the life she'd so meticulously and carefully built? That she could have a fiancé, then lose him, and it would make so little difference?

That she could get jilted on her wedding day,

run off on her honeymoon by herself and have yet to truly mourn what she'd left behind?

Maya tried to find it in her to grieve the loss of her life with Ethan, but she didn't seem to have it in her. Maybe that was why, when she couldn't avoid it anymore, she finally allowed herself to think about Lorraine.

Fickle, reckless, messy Lorraine. Maya could come up with all kinds of words to describe her best friend. Or *former* best friend, she supposed, given what had happened. And all the words she'd choose were true.

But she'd be lying to herself if she didn't admit that she loved Lorraine anyway. She always had and that was the part she didn't want to admit to herself. Because that didn't just disappear overnight. She'd caught herself picking up her phone to shoot Lorraine a text or send her a picture more than once since she'd come to Italy. It was second nature after all these years.

Her heart hadn't caught up to reality yet.

Lorraine had been so much *work*. There had never been room for too many other friends and never close ones, not with Lorraine there to take up all of Maya's emotional energy. And maybe there was a part of Maya that had taken a certain pleasure in doing that work. In turning herself inside out for her friend, again and again, with no expectation of return.

Friendship isn't about measuring everything to make sure it's equal, she had told Ethan when he'd complained about the Lorraine situation—because there had always been another Lorraine situation. *Friendship is about love. The end.*

She'd believed that. She really, truly had.

But here in this faraway place that still felt like a fantasy despite the hard, cold stone she sat on, she wondered. Maybe there had been a part of her that had gotten off on loving Lorraine despite everything. Lorraine had been her opportunity to take care of someone else when no one else in her life required it. Her parents took care of themselves with a ruthlessness that was only surprising to people who'd never met them before. Melinda had never needed anyone to take care of her. She took care of everyone else and had made it her calling. It was why she'd become a doctor. Ethan, too, had needed very little in the way of maintenance. Their issues were all in the scheduling, or so Maya had thought. But they hadn't *needed* each other.

The only person who had ever needed her—often desperately—had been Lorraine.

Maya had been raised to take care of herself and trained never to expect anyone else to provide something for her if she could do it herself. Lorraine had been the first person she'd met, at eighteen years of age, that she could care for.

Was it her fault? Had it always been leading here? Maya blew out a breath where she sat, then brushed a few stray crumbs from her pastry from her leg. There had been a part of her that had pitied Lorraine. *So broken,* she had always thought. *So lost and lonely.* Had that been nothing more than the worst sort of condescension all this time?

Had she done this to herself, one patronizing offer of help at a time? She'd never meant to condescend to Lorraine. But that didn't mean she hadn't.

She didn't mean to do it, but one second she was sitting there fiddling with her empty espresso cup, and the next she had her mobile in her hand again.

It wasn't until the line started ringing in her ear that her stomach dropped and the reality of what she was doing kicked in. But then it was too late. Even if she hung up, the phone would record the call.

Maya shut her eyes, tipping her head forward as if that could ward off the foolishness of what she was doing.

She heard Lorraine pick up, though there was nothing but silence. One beat, then another.

"I didn't think you would call me. I didn't think you would ever speak to me again."

Lorraine didn't sound quite like herself. She sounded distant and shaken, maybe. Or maybe that was more wishful thinking on Maya's part.

She lifted her head in the piazza and watched the clouds move in above the bell tower of the ancient church that commanded the far side of the square. "I haven't decided."

"Is that what you're calling to tell me? That you haven't decided whether or not you're ever speaking to me again?"

"Ethan had his chance to explain." Maya was proud of how cool she sounded. How unaffected. Thank God Lorraine couldn't see how she shook where she sat. "Of course, some of that was lost in the unfortunate business of canceling our wedding an hour before the ceremony started. I *think* there was an explanation in there somewhere, but to be honest, it's a blur. And I've known you a whole lot longer."

Another long pause. The Lorraine Maya knew would have been weeping, because she was always weeping. Anything she felt, she cried out in great sobs, tears tracking down her cheeks in rivers.

But maybe all of that had been an act. It was entirely possible she'd never known Lorraine at all.

"We didn't mean to hurt you," Lorraine said, just when Maya was starting to think she wouldn't say anything else.

"But you see, you must have meant to hurt me," Maya said. Softly. Very, very softly, the words were coming out of her, though she had no idea where she was going—which was counter to everything she had ever learned about the art of argument in law school. But she couldn't seem to stop herself. "Because if you didn't want to hurt me, you wouldn't have. It's that simple."

"It wasn't like that. It wasn't…"

Maya waited. But it didn't seem as if Lorraine was going to speak again. Or maybe she was fighting the same wallop of regret and self-recrimination, guilt and fury, that Maya was.

She could feel that stinging at the back of her throat again, like a scream that had nowhere to go. And then something far bigger than a scream rolled into her. Through her. A grief so big and wide and impossible that she wondered it didn't tear her apart where she sat.

The rain started then, little drops that felt like a tickle, but she didn't move.

She remembered their first day at university. When all the hubbub had subsided, they were left alone in the room they were expected to share for a year. Maya could see Lorraine as she'd been back then as if she was standing before her all over again. Lorraine had been almost gangly then, though Maya could see that only when she looked at old pictures. At the time she'd thought Lorraine was beautiful, so enviably skinny where Maya was curvy, with the long, straight black hair and dark olive skin of her Persian father and light green eyes of her French-Canadian mother.

This is going to be great, eighteen-year-old Maya had promised the stranger before her, who had struck her as terrified. Maybe she'd made that up, too. Maybe she'd caused all of this from the start. *We're going to be best friends.*

And they had been, which wasn't to say they'd always gotten along. Some years, Maya had wondered if they only even spoke anymore because she had made that proclamation. Maya had followed the path that had always been laid out so carefully before her. Lorraine had…drifted. Maya had remembered their first day a thousand times since then, sometimes with nostalgia, sometimes with irritation. She'd wondered what would have happened if they'd been placed with other first-year roommates instead of with each other.

But today, on a rainy afternoon in a tiny fishing village in Italy, the memory made her nothing but sad.

"I didn't mean to hurt you," Lorraine said again.

"It doesn't matter what you meant," Maya replied. "Because you did."

And that grief was too much in her voice, so she ended the call. She waited until she was sure her knees wouldn't give out on her, and then she stood. The rain was coming harder now, but there was a part of her that welcomed it. Rain on her head felt…right, somehow. She ran her espresso cup back into the café, then found herself outside again, and she couldn't tell if the rain was in her face or if her eyes were blurred for a different reason.

She half walked, half ran for the little tunnel dug out beneath one of the buildings, this old village like a labyrinth built vertically, twisting and turning and piled high on itself. She plunged herself into the shadows, only to find that escaping the rain didn't make her able to see any better.

Maya let out a sound she didn't want to admit she could make, then picked up her pace. She kept her head down, telling herself that people had cried on these stones since the days of the Roman Empire. Her grief over one or two relationships that had ended terribly—and all at once—was nothing compared to the things others must have cried about here.

Not that it helped.

And when she nearly slammed into a person coming in the opposite direction, she tried to duck around and lunge for the rainy, gray daylight a few feet away—

But he caught her.

And she knew it was Charlie in the same second she came up hard against his chest.

The last thing in the world she wanted to do was let someone *look* at her. Especially this beautiful, lazy, entirely too relaxed, American handyman she never should have met, much less touched.

"You look a little too serious for someone who's supposed to be on vacation," he said, the low rumble of his voice reminding her of a motorcycle or one of the Italian sports cars that took the winding roads through these villages much too fast. She could feel it inside her, like an earthquake.

It made her eyes blur even more, and she didn't know which one of them she hated more just then, her or him. Maya swiped at her eyes and focused on Charlie, scowling at him.

He was too beautiful. He wore a leather jacket against the weather and looked like something out of an old movie with his perfect mouth, that golden beard over his perfectly sculpted chin and the rain making his blond hair both darker than usual and brighter where the gray light caught it.

"This is an accidental vacation," she threw at him, that scream in her throat making her voice harsh. "It was supposed to be my honeymoon. He broke the news that he wanted my best friend instead while there were already guests waiting in the chapel. I decided that was humiliating enough and came here. Where sometimes I can't tell if it's raining on me or if I'm grieving something that obviously wasn't real in the first place."

His grip got tighter. His eyes blazed, the blue almost too bright and fierce. Then his mouth firmed into a hard line.

"Sounds like you had a lucky escape," he said, and then he very carefully released her and took a step back.

And as betrayals went, especially lately, this one hardly made the list.

But something inside Maya snapped. She actually felt it crack and was amazed he didn't comment on the fact she was now ripped wide-open right there in front of him.

"I'm sorry," she said, and there was no modifying her voice. There was no containing this or making it sound calm when it wasn't. "Is that more information than you wanted? Am I too much? Too intense?"

"It's not my business."

"I just made it your business."

Charlie's gaze went glacial. "Maybe if you go lie down or hang out in that pool of yours for a while, you'll feel better."

She laughed at that, a wild, unhinged sort of sound, and it was amazing how little she cared that she was making a spectacle of herself out here where anyone could happen by and see it. "Really? You think *a nap* is going to make me forget my called-off wedding and the fact the two people who were supposed to love me the most in the entire world were betraying me behind my back for who knows how long?"

He held his hands up in a gesture of surrender that, on him, looked like an invitation to further aggression. Maya doubted he'd ever surrendered to anything in his whole life. Something she would have said about herself, too—until now. Because there was something about Charlie that made her question her own strength. There was something about him that made her want to pile all her problems—and herself—on his big, strong shoulders and let him carry it all.

She'd never felt that way about Ethan. They had

called their relationship a partnership and they'd both taken the egalitarian nature of it very, very seriously. She had expected Ethan to take care of himself while she did the same.

The fact she was imagining things she'd never known she wanted about a man who very obviously wanted nothing to do with her unless she was naked just made her…a little insane, maybe. Or more insane.

"Do what you want, Maya" was all he said.

"This is not my problem" was written all over his face.

And Maya, who prided herself on her control under all circumstances and had made that control the foundation of her entire life, lost it.

"Forgive me for ruining all the lazy, easy sex with no conversation. What a buzzkill." Her voice was scathing. "Don't worry, I get it. You're perfectly happy to fuck me silly, but heaven forbid I admit I have a *feeling*. I understand that's terrifying even when it isn't about you."

He was still studying her in that predatory, watchful way of his that should have made her nervous. But if it did, she didn't care. "None of this is about me."

Maya laughed again, and this laugh was even worse than the one before, wild and obviously, inarguably upset. "You're absolutely right, Charlie. It's not. You're nothing but a quick route to oblivion, and really, I'd rather chug a bottle of vodka. It has more emotional intelligence, and guess what? The hangover is a hell of a lot more fun."

And she wheeled around, tears nothing but a memory though her temper was racing through her like wildfire, and tried to put as much distance between her and her latest mistake as quickly as possible.

CHAPTER SIX

HE SHOULD HAVE let her go. Charlie knew it without question as she started away from him, all that mess and fury visible in every sweet line of her body. It was like some kind of blazing neon sign, telling him to stay the hell away from her.

Those were the kind of gut feelings that had kept him alive after his stepfather's death, when he no longer had the old man's protection back there in his very rough part of Texas. He'd learned fast to always, always pay attention to his gut.

In the case of Maya, his gut was clear. He needed to walk away.

So there was absolutely no reason that he should have found himself lunging after Maya as she stormed off, out of the old tunnel beneath the church and up an ancient stairway that rose steeply between two pastel pink buildings.

He caught up to her on the next uneven landing and didn't think it through. Maybe he was beyond thinking, too bound up in all this rage—and this had to be rage, because he wouldn't let it be anything else—that churned in him with no acceptable outlet. This wasn't Texas. He couldn't pick a fight with the wrong fool in a dangerous bar to let off a little steam. He couldn't follow the worst of his impulses, not here in this tiny little tourist town where his reputation had to stay more in line with the hotel than his own bad decisions.

And still he spun her around, backing her up against a wall that had been right here since long before there was anything called Texas.

"Don't you throw your shit at me," he growled. "I didn't leave you at the altar or anywhere else."

But she wasn't smiling back at him the way she always had been before. Not today. Her eyes were stormy and dark, and she tipped up her chin like she thought she could fight him.

It amazed him how much of him wished she would try.

"I think we both know it's only a matter of time."

"We had sex, Maya. I don't know about you, but that's not exactly revolutionary for me."

"Then go have more," she invited him, her voice like acid straight down his back. "You're the one chasing people down and manhandling them because you don't like a little dose of reality in the middle of your nonrevolutionary sex."

"You didn't seem to mind how I handled you before. If that's changed, all you have to do is say so."

"Don't worry, Charlie." And her voice was too bright. Too sharp. "I don't expect anything from you. You're just some guy who works with his hands and thinks that makes him special. What do I even know about you?"

"Not a goddamned thing."

She leaned forward, and she was smiling again. Not nicely. "I know you like to smile because you think that if you do it enough, no one will notice all the other things going on in there. I know you think that sex and emotion aren't connected, and if you fuck enough, you won't feel. I know that you talk about loyalty, but only in the past tense. And that's fine. You don't owe me or anyone else a thing."

Charlie agreed with her. He didn't owe her anything. She still didn't know who he was. He liked it that way. There was no reason whatsoever he should feel like she'd sucker-punched him.

He couldn't explain why he had his hands on her shoulders. Why he was leaning over her, somehow unable to just let go and walk away. The way he knew he should.

"You really think you're going to shame me into doing what you want?" he demanded, his face much too close to hers.

"It wouldn't occur to me that shame was something you were even remotely familiar with."

"I didn't ask you for anything. You were the one who approached me."

"Right, yes. You were a poor innocent handyman, trying only to do your job half-naked in the sun, when the big bad lawyer stormed in from Canada and forced you—"

Charlie didn't think he moved. He didn't mean to move. But one hand left her shoulder and found its way to her jaw, and then he was tipping her head back. He didn't like anything about the situation, but he couldn't seem to stop himself.

And he couldn't seem to make himself let go.

They were all alone on the landing, the staircases above and below them empty this late in the year and the shutters closed tight against the cold. There were echoes in the distance. The sounds of footsteps, the odd muscular car engine and the bells from the church. But all Charlie could really hear was his own breath, the clatter of his heart inside his chest and what felt like a drumbeat in his cock.

Most people had the good sense to keep their distance when he had a temper on.

But Maya held his gaze like she was the one daring him. He could feel that she was trembling, a light fluttering beneath his fingers, but there was nothing but fire when she stared back at him.

He tried to keep it calm, but his own voice sounded rough, there in the narrow space between old, high buildings. "You keep poking at something you don't understand, Maya, and you're not going to like the response you get."

She continued to glare straight at him as she lifted up her hand, slowly extended two fingers and then poked him in the chest.

Hard.

"You're not very smart, are you?" he asked, his voice soft with menace, and he could see the shiver she fought back.

"I always thought I was very smart, actually, but I apparently left my brain on the plane when I landed in Italy."

She angled her head to one side as she stared up at him, as if she didn't care at all that he had his hand right there on her face and her back to the wall.

And then she proved how little she cared when she poked him again. Harder.

"I'm not your bottle of vodka, Maya. You're not going to like this hangover."

"You know what I like most about vodka?" she asked, her eyes glittering. "It doesn't talk."

And Charlie was…undone.

He didn't know what the hell he was doing. He couldn't remember the last time someone had challenged him, not without firepower and half an army at their back, anyway. Certainly not a woman.

And he didn't want to feel a thing, because he didn't do feelings and he certainly didn't do *this*. He didn't want anything she was hurling at him to hit its mark and the fact it might have was a problem he should have been off fixing. With prejudice.

But it was like he didn't have a choice.

He crushed his mouth to hers, right out there in the open. Anyone could run up the stairs or come down from above, but he didn't care the way he knew he should have now that he was all respectable. And known. And the things he did might actually affect the lives of the people who worked for him.

Responsibility pissed him off. And somehow made him harder, too.

He slanted his mouth over Maya's, letting the addictive taste of her flood through him. She was sweet and spicy and intoxicating, and he'd been boned before he started.

Because she threw him off balance. She made him do things he never did. He didn't know why he'd left the hotel today. Only that he'd seen her run off down the stairs, and when she hadn't come back hours later, he'd set out looking for her while pretending that wasn't exactly what he was doing.

And when he'd found her, she hadn't smiled at him the way it turned out he really, really liked her to do. She'd shown him what was beneath that smile instead, and he didn't know whether he wanted to punch the stone behind her head, fly to Canada to punch her ex or, better yet, slam his own head against the nearest wall until he snapped out of whatever spell this was.

But with her mouth beneath his, he understood that this was what he'd wanted all along.

He wanted to eat her alive. He wanted to drown himself in her taste, those wild little sounds she made and the way she launched herself against him, up on her toes to press her body into his.

He took her mouth, kissing her hard and deep and something like punishing, but whatever he was doling out, she was returning it. And then some.

And it wasn't enough.

He used his chest to press her back against the wall, pinning her there, and then he lifted his head to study the expression on her pretty face. Need and passion warred for control. Her lips were parted, she was still trembling faintly and her eyes were slick and bright with blind desire.

The only thing Charlie had ever seen that was prettier than this was the face she made when she came.

And he needed to see it again. Right here, right now.

He slid one hand over her collarbone and pressed the weight of his palm there. Not choking her, but holding her steadily on that knife's edge.

Her pulse kicked at him, rapid and wild. Her breath got short, but she didn't say a word.

He crowded into her, slicking his hand down to find her hip and the deliciously stretchy pants she'd worn that held her ass like an offering. He traced the shape of it, firm and tight and round, then moved to the front. He caught that bright, shining gaze of hers, pressed a little harder against her collarbone and then slid his hand beneath the waistband of her pants to cup her between her legs.

Maya jolted, and her breath went ragged, but all she did was rock her hips toward him as his fingers found their way beneath her panties and into the slick folds of her meltingly hot pussy.

"You like to shoot off your mouth, don't you?"

he growled at her. He found her clit and pinched it, hard enough to make her squeak a little. She rose up on her toes, but he felt the way she flooded him, telling him the truth. "You think you can taunt me into giving you what you want."

"Looks like I was right."

He circled her clit once, then again, then stroked down so he could slide two fingers deep inside her.

"Problem is, now I'm pissed." He thrust into her, deep, making sure his thumb grazed her clit with each stroke. "I could do this all day. Your pussy is tight. Sweet. I like how it feels on my fingers. And I like the way you taste."

He pulled his fingers away from her then, lifting them to his mouth and licking them clean, still holding her gaze.

Her panting was a little more high-pitched now, and he could feel her shudder against him, over and over.

Slowly, taking his time, he retraced his steps. Hip to ass, then back to that delicious pussy of hers. He found her clit again, playing with it until she bucked against him and then stroking his way into her again.

She was wetter now. Hotter. She moved her hips in that insistent, drugging rhythm that he knew could bring him to his knees if he let it. And that only pissed him off more, so he drew it out. He brought her higher and higher—

And then, instead of tossing her over the edge, he held her there.

"No…" Her voice was broken. Rough. Her eyes were glazed over with need.

But Charlie was merciless. And more, he wanted her to suffer. He wanted her out of her head, wild and beside herself.

He was only getting started.

He pulled his hand away again and took his time licking her sweetness from his fingers while she trembled, caught between him and the stone wall at her back.

"Fine," she panted at him. "If you won't do it, I'll take care of myself. It's the fucking anthem of my life."

Charlie laughed at that, hard and maybe a little mean. "Not today, babe."

He caught her hands as she brought them down to her own waistband, then hauled them above her head. He pinned her there, holding her wrists in one hand and pressing them back against the wall so she was splayed out before him in a sweet, curvy arc. All woman. All his.

"You bastard," she threw at him, but she didn't try to pull her hands away. She didn't struggle to do anything, except rock her hips toward his and arch herself against his chest.

He laughed again, even darker this time. "As a matter of fact, yes. I am a bastard. My mama had me after a long night with a stranger she met in a bar. I didn't know his name for most of my life. And I don't really think you give a shit about the life and times of an illegitimate dirtbag from Nowhere You'd Want to Go, Texas."

"You can't—"

"But I can."

He showed her, just to get his point across. This time, he only reached down between them to cup her pussy through the stretchy pants she wore. He held her there, working her back up toward that ragged edge again.

And then, once more, leaving her there at the last second.

Her breath hissed out from between her teeth. He could see that she was sweating, her skin deliciously hot in the cool air.

This time, she didn't call him names. She rocked her hips almost helplessly, and he could feel the tension in her wrists where he held them above her head.

"You don't get what you want by sandbagging me with your crap," he told her, his voice dark.

There were too many things inside him, and he couldn't name them all. But he knew this: he knew the dark side of desire and the sharp edge of control. "I'm not the kind of man you can manipulate with your temper. Piss me off all you want, Maya. But you don't get to come unless I say so."

Her dark eyes sparked with defiance. "I can make myself come. I don't need you."

"I can tell how much you don't need me," he growled as her hips jerked toward him, seemingly of their own accord. "You might think I'm an asshole, babe. And you're not wrong. But your body thinks I'm God."

"An orgasm is an orgasm."

"Keep telling yourself that."

"I don't need—"

Charlie got closer, pressing her farther into the stone at her back. "Did he make you come at all? Or, let me guess, he told you that you had to get there on your own. No wonder this greedy little pussy wants me to tattoo my name all over it."

She shook at that, and he kept his hand where it was, holding her so he could feel her heat and dampness, but refusing to move his palm to give her the pressure she needed to get off.

"You had to come all the way to Italy to find

someone to fuck you right. Now you don't know what to do with yourself, do you?"

"I told you. I can handle myself just fine."

He dropped his head down close to her. "But you don't want to, Maya. Do you?"

She made a ragged sound, equal parts sob and frustration.

"You want to dump all your feelings all over me, that's fine. But this is the price. It's easy enough to get my hands on you, sure. You can depend on it if you shoot your mouth off. But if you want me to make you come? You're going to have to beg."

It was like he jolted her with electricity. He could feel it go through her, a wild, intense current that charred him, too.

Her breath sobbed out of her. "I don't beg."

He leaned closer, then ran his teeth over her neck, grinning when she broke out in goose bumps. "Then don't."

When she turned back toward him, dislodging his mouth and no doubt looking to throw up more walls between them, he claimed her mouth again. This kiss was even dirtier than the ones that had gone before. He knew he tasted like her, so he took the kiss wetter. Harder.

Until she was shaking, everywhere, and making low little sounds in the back of her throat.

"Beg me," he ordered her against her mouth.

He moved his hand from between her legs, but only so he could find his way beneath the waistband of her yoga pants again. He found his way to her pussy, stroking his way into her slick folds. He traced patterns in and around her, skidding around her clit without ever touching it, until her hips were rising to meet him again while she thrashed, arching out from the wall in a bow, making the kind of helpless sounds that went straight to his dick.

"Beg me, Maya." And his voice was harsher now. "I can do this all day. You look like it might kill you."

She fought herself. He could see the struggle in her as her breath heaved hard enough to make her breasts move. But every time she let out one of those glorious, needy pants, her pussy got wetter.

"Please," she said finally, as if the words were torn out of her. "Please, Charlie…"

His smile was merciless. "Please, what? Be specific."

"Please," she moaned again. "Please make me come. Please."

He claimed her mouth. He ate at her as he twisted his wrist and drove his fingers deep inside her, pressing his thumb hard against her greedy little clit. She went stiff in the next second, then wild, rocking herself against his hand as she broke apart.

But he didn't stop. He kept driving into her, throwing her from one shuddering, melting, clenching crisis straight on into another one. Until she was limp, so boneless that he thought that if he took his hand away from the wrists he still held pinned above her head, she might collapse into a ball at his feet.

He did it anyway. Slowly. Carefully, so when she did sag, it was into his chest.

He didn't know what swelled in him as she breathed raggedly against his chest, only that the soft weight of her made him ache. Even as his cock was so hard against the fly of his jeans that he was surprised he hadn't legitimately hurt himself.

This was supposed to teach her a lesson. So Charlie didn't understand why he was the one who felt torn into pieces.

But he didn't do anything but hold her, for what felt like a long, long time.

Eventually he felt her stir against him. She blinked as she opened her eyes, then focused on him.

There was a beat.

Then Maya shoved at his chest and he let her do it for a moment, just in case she thought that she could ever move him if he didn't want to go. Then he stepped back, narrowing his eyes when she shoved at him again, harder.

That time not to move him, because he'd already moved. But just to slap at him, which was new. Most people didn't dare insult him with a slap.

"Congratulations," Maya threw at him, because she obviously wasn't worried about pissing him off. Did he like that about her? Was that what his insatiable cock was trying to tell him? "You know how to use a woman's body against her like a Neanderthal."

He smirked. "Is this where you use big, fancy words to put me in my place? Better hurry up and remind me that you're the fancy lawyer and I'm the lowly handyman. Wouldn't want me to get ideas above my station."

She shook again, but he was pretty sure this time it was temper. "You're the one who told me I wasn't very smart. Why would a dumb person's vocabulary threaten you? And what does your job have to do with it?"

"You don't threaten me at all."

He threw that out there, but he didn't need the echo of his own words bouncing back at him from the old stones to let him know what a liar he was.

He could feel it. He had the threat of her all over him. It was like her taste, intoxicating and maddening. He was still hard and pissed and he didn't know what to do when everything inside him was so messed up. When she'd done it.

And somehow, the fact he was hiding who he was from her seemed to sit on him funny.

"Of course you're not threatened." The curve on her lips was much too smug, and she actually rolled her eyes. At him. "Thank you for this object lesson in how not to behave. I made the mistake of thinking we had a connection. When what we had was sex. I appreciate the clarification."

He glared at her. She smiled.

"But don't worry, I'm not going to inflict my inconvenient emotions on you again. I'm more than happy to run along and find someone else to not threaten. Maybe a lot of someone elses."

He didn't know how to handle that defiant tilt to her chin then. Not when his hands weren't on her. Worse, he thought she knew it.

"First you were going to punish me by making yourself come. Now you're going to what? Roll around the village until you find someone else to do it for you?"

"Why not?" And this time her smile was bright and sweet and made him want to break apart the stone walls all around him with his own hands. "I owe you an apology. I walked straight from my wedding into you and had the bad taste to bring all those yucky feelings with me. Thank you for pointing that out to me. You don't have to worry yourself about any sexual escapades I might feel I need to undertake as a newly single woman. You've already done your part."

That smile of hers took on an edge Charlie could feel slice straight into the center of him, lodging in his gut and his cock and making his jaw ache.

Making all of him ache, if he was honest—and he didn't particularly want to be honest.

About anything.

She leaned forward a little, like she wanted nothing more than to take that knife and shove it in deep.

"Godspeed, Charlie," she said, in a sweet, light voice that very clearly told him to go fuck himself.

Which he was considering.

And this time when she walked away from him, he didn't follow her.

CHAPTER SEVEN

MAYA SET OFF that night with a whole lot more trepidation than she intended to let show.

The ancient stairs littering the village—so charming and picturesque by day—were a lot more difficult to navigate in heels. Still, she forced herself to do it. Very, very carefully. She'd slicked herself into a little black dress, put on her most delicate pair of heels and settled a luxurious cashmere wrap in a deep rose around her like a cape. It was more than enough to combat the cool December night.

It did not, however, do much for her nerves.

She made her way down the stairs to the piazza again—a lot more slowly than she had before, thanks to her heels—heading for the gleaming bar she'd seen in the grand hotel where she'd taken yoga that morning.

The stairs were steep and far more treacherous on a cold night, especially given the shoes she'd chosen to wear, but it was amazing how righteous indignation fueled her. It kept her moving when she might have turned around. It burned right over the snap of the cold air, the uneven stairs and the fact she could be tucked up in her lovely suite with a paperback right this minute instead of out here…"rolling around the village," as Charlie had called it.

She did not want to think about Charlie the handyman, and so, of course, he was all she could think about. He could go straight to hell. She would like to send him there herself, in fact. Every time she thought about the way he'd pinned her there against the wall, then worse, made her beg…

Well.

Her body responded instantly and enthusiastically to even a hint of that memory, but Maya was still furious.

She had stormed away from him again, expecting that at any moment she would feel those beautifully weathered hands of his on her again. But he hadn't followed her. When she'd looked over her shoulder at the top of the next flight of stairs, there was nothing below her but shadows.

And she had told herself that she was grateful for that—not disappointed or, even worse, hurt—all the way back up the hill to the hotel.

Maya had been so grateful, in fact, that she

had stewed on it for hours, while her own flesh seemed to conspire against her. She was too over-heated. Too needy. She wanted all the dirty, de-licious things she knew he could do to her—and she had no idea how to handle wanting like that. She'd always enjoyed sex, vanilla or otherwise. Who wouldn't enjoy sex? Orgasms were always a delight. But she'd never *hungered* for a man's touch, so wildly and deeply and insistently that she thought she might actually make herself sick if she couldn't touch him again.

You need to snap out of this, she'd lectured her-self. Repeatedly. *This is all misplaced emotion. These are feelings you have for Ethan, focused on Charlie because he's here. That's all.*

She was sure that must be true. Even if she'd never thought about sex and Ethan in these terms. She'd never thought something might happen to her if he didn't touch her. She'd never felt as if she was at war with her body—as if it had its own needs and desires, regardless of what she wanted.

Still, it didn't make sense that she should feel this much—or anything—for a stranger she hap-pened to have slept with repeatedly, so she told herself it was the situation. Not him.

And the best way to make certain that was true, the way it should have been, was to do precisely what she'd told him she would. To do what she'd meant to do all along and explore her options, not settle on one man and create whole worlds around him the way it seemed she always did.

She had never allowed herself to enjoy being single. Surely it was high time she took advantage of the fact she was entirely without ties or, here in Italy, responsibilities of any kind.

When she got down to the piazza, she took her time walking across it, breathing in the crisp night air. The Christmas lights gleamed brightly and happily, transforming the square where she'd sat earlier. In the thick, enveloping dark with its suggestion of fog from the water, the lights shined like cheer. Hope.

All that sparkle soothed her as she made her way across the square and ducked into the grand hotel. The hotel was one of the Amalfi coast's most famous and beloved locations, splashed across postcards featuring glamorous people from way back when. It was known for its luxurious summers, but even here at the end of the year it was special.

Maya slowed as she walked into the grand, soaring lobby, featuring a selection of evergreens in its center, roped with lights and gold and silver balls—far more impressive tonight, set against the dark backdrop of the windows over the ocean, than they'd seemed this morning. Pretty music played from on high and everything smelled deep green and faintly like cinnamon.

The fact that she was here in December and that Christmas was coming hit her harder than it had before.

So hard she was tempted to go a bit wobbly.

Everybody feels lonely at the holidays, she told herself crisply as she skirted the massive trees and headed for the bar. She wasn't lonely. She was on her own. They weren't the same thing.

Maya intended to illustrate the difference to herself tonight.

She'd spent most of the day psyching herself up for this. According to every man she'd ever met, any woman could walk into any bar anywhere on the planet and find a man to have sex with her.

Maya planned to put that theory to the test.

Because as the hours after her hot, humiliating episode with Charlie had inched past, Maya had grown more and more disgusted by her own behavior.

Not that she'd had sex with Charlie in the first place, because of course she couldn't regret that. That had been the correct impulse, she'd decided. She'd felt something like victorious that she'd

stepped off the plane and found him so quickly.
No one could claim that she was broken if she was
already tearing up the sheets with someone else.
No one could possibly think that she was mooning around after Ethan if she was having explo-
sive, impossibly good sex with a man who could
eat the likes of Ethan for breakfast.

And, sure, she had some concerns about how
broken her heart wasn't and how easy it was to
imagine a life without the man she was supposed
to have just started a whole new life with…

But today she'd understood, with an uncomfortable level of clarity, that she had thrown herself into the Charlie thing not just because he was
the most beautiful man she'd ever met—and not
simply because she had no idea sex could be a
driving compulsion instead of a pleasant pastime
until him—but because she had been keeping a
mental scorecard.

The trouble with that was, she was the only
one playing.

Her conversation with Lorraine had brought
that home. Had she expected that Lorraine might
fall all over herself to assure Maya that it had all
been a mistake? Had she called so that when Lorraine told her to come back—when Lorraine told
her that she'd ended things with Ethan now that the

horror of the wedding day and life without Maya had shown her the error of her ways—Maya could swan back to her old life? Had she imagined that Charlie could be her tit for tat when she took up her carefully plotted-out life with Ethan again?

Was that why she hadn't really grieved the loss of that life?

She wanted to deny that she had ever thought such a thing, because she didn't want to be the kind of woman who would ever consider taking back a man who had cheated and humiliated her, no matter what, but there was something in her gut that told her otherwise.

Maya walked into the bar, all dimly lit reds and golden wood, and smiled sweetly at the bartender as she ordered herself a vodka martini. The first sip went down crisp and good, hitting her belly and warming her up from the inside out.

Kind of the way Charlie did—but she wasn't going to obsess about him tonight. Charlie was entirely too dangerous for the likes of her, anyway. A fling with a man like Charlie was one thing, but she hadn't taken her own honeymoon in defiance of literally everyone she knew to tangle herself up with some other man. She could already hear the heavy sighs from her sister if she were to admit to such a thing when she got home. She knew perfectly well how Melinda would view a holiday fling with a lethal-eyed American she suspected had a less than perfectly legal background, if those functional tattoos of his were as *Sons of Anarchy* as she imagined.

On the other hand, if Maya were to use the weeks she had left to give herself the kind of Christmas gift all the magazines she pretended not to read—unless she was in a doctor's office— told her she should *want* to give to herself.

No-strings sex. With as many men as took her fancy. Because she was a third-wave feminist and sex positive and whatever else she was supposed to be these days. The truth was, she'd never had time to while away her days worrying too much about her love life.

Maya had always focused on one man at a time, because how could she be expected to juggle all her work and school commitments and date a variety of them? She'd had two boyfriends in college. Another for most of law school. And then Ethan. She felt confident she knew everything there was to know about the particular joys of sex with intimacy, inside the bounds of a committed relationship.

At some point today, it had occurred to her that dumping all her feelings on Charlie was a knee-jerk reaction based on those experiences. Emotion was something people in intimate, committed relationships did—it was the *point*, she'd always thought—but this trip wasn't about that.

This was her time to do things she hadn't done with her newfound independence. And the one thing she'd never done was joyfully and deliberately slept around. By choice and design.

If the debacle with Lorraine and Ethan had taught her anything, it was that she needed to take a step back from intimacy and commitment and focus a little more on honesty, excellent sex and her own damned self.

And that meant she was going to have to learn how to pick up men in bars.

A fancy hotel bar in a faraway Italian hotel in the middle of the off-season, festooned with Christmas lights and featuring a suggested dress code at the door, seemed like the perfect place to practice.

After all, Maya had a certain stature back in Toronto. If she was going to start going out on the prowl—*as Lorraine had always called it*, she thought with a wince—she would have to figure out how best to do that in ways that could never come back to haunt her in the light. She would have to learn how not to embarrass herself or, worse, her firm. Or worst of all, her family. That meant she had to be careful how she went about things and certainly couldn't use one of those dating apps. The very thought made her shudder.

This would have to be her new normal.

She swirled her drink in her hand, letting her gaze move around the dimly lit space. How hard could it be? She'd never propositioned a man before in her life, but she'd done that already this vacation, too. Charlie hadn't been wrong. She was the one who had started things between them. She was the one—

If all you're going to do is sit here thinking about Charlie, you're defeating the purpose, she snapped at herself.

She applied herself to the task the way she would with any other project. She'd overheard her colleagues talking about how, when they went out to bars, apparently all they had to do was set foot inside and they were besieged by all kinds of men. "Beating them off with a stick" was the phrase she'd heard, more than once.

Maya swiveled around on the bar stool, waiting for the siege. Assuming a little encouragement wouldn't go amiss, she smiled anytime she caught a man's eye when he wasn't sitting with a woman or a family. There was that one in the corner who was fiddling with his drink in a way she liked, his eyes hooded and his lips full as he looked back at her, like every Italian fantasy she'd ever had without realizing it. There was the older gentlemen at a nearby table, exuding a distinguished, authoritative air, who kept pausing in his conversation with two other far more portly and even older men to look at Maya appreciatively. And yet one more, entirely too young for her, who was nonetheless offering her a cheeky, suggestive grin from farther down the length of the bar.

Was it that easy? Did she simply…choose one? Because if it was that simple, it suggested to her that she'd simply failed to notice male interest for most of her life. Not, of course, that interest led to sex—but maybe that was the point all the men she'd known had been making. If she wanted it to turn from eye contact into sex, it could. And wasn't that revolutionary?

She ordered herself a second drink and wondered why the drinks and her realizations didn't make her feel more…buoyant inside. Why the thought of doing whatever she had to do to transform one of those smiles or heated glances into more filled her with something too much like sadness.

But she was not going to sit here mooning over Charlie any longer. She was not.

Maya squared her shoulders, lifted her chin and started to turn in her seat again to make a choice and get the ball rolling—no pun intended—when a hard hand came down on the nape of her neck.

Then held her there.

With a certain gentle implacability that should have infuriated her but instead made her melt. Everywhere.

"I wouldn't do it if I were you." Charlie's drawl was low and laced with a fire that swept through her, lighting her up like one of those Christmas trees. "The pouty one in the corner is Alessandro. Known con artist. He prefers rich, bored housewives to play with in the summertime, but he'll take anyone this time of year. On the very off chance he could make you come at all, he'd fleece you on the way out."

Maya tried to turn to glare at him, but he wouldn't let her. His hand kept her in place—unless she wanted to make another scene—and she felt the heat of him in the moment before she felt him behind her, not quite pressing into her. There was no mirror behind the bar, only polished wood, and she gritted her teeth, wondering how a man she'd never seen in anything but battered jeans and maybe a T-shirt had wandered in past the prissy hostess out front.

"The old man is an expat from somewhere cold. Denmark. Norway. One of those. The wife stays behind in Rome collecting pretty young boys to call her own, but he likes it here, where he can relax. Rumor is he's a kinky motherfucker, so maybe you'd like that as part of your downward spiral. Though you don't really strike me as the golden-shower type."

Maya stiffened and then hated herself for it, because of course he could feel it. "I don't remember asking you for consultation," she managed to say.

"And the kid would be energetic, I'll give you that." Charlie sounded amused, though the grip he kept on her neck suggested otherwise. "I doubt he'll last that long, but the upside is he'd be ready to go again pretty quick."

"Lucky for you, then, that you're not planning to sleep with any of them."

Charlie's hand tightened at her neck, and her curse was that she liked it.

"Are you planning to *sleep* with them, Maya? Or are you looking for a cheap, petty revenge fuck because you're pissed at me?"

"I beg your pardon. That sounds like you're talking about feelings, which I was under the distinct impression was forbidden."

"Here's the thing, babe."

He spun her stool around, and it couldn't have taken more than a second or two, but that was ample time for Maya to reflect on the fact that she didn't find that word—*babe*—as offensive as she should have. As she would have if anyone else had called her something like that. Not the way he said it.

But then he was in front of her, and her heart kicked at her. He was dressed in a dark, impossibly well-fitting suit that did uncomfortable things to her body while it made a symphony out of his. It was obviously bespoke, tailored to his every muscle and sinew, making his rough power elegant. A different kind of raw.

His hard, gorgeous face was grave as he stared down at her. Those blue eyes of his, on the other hand, blazed.

And in case that possessive grip on the back of her neck had failed to announce to the entire bar that he was claiming her, he made it worse by stepping too close and wedging himself between her knees.

"Step back," she hissed at him, aware that if she moved too much—or at all—her dress would roll too far up her thighs and expose her to the entire bar.

She could tell that he knew it, too.

"Here's the thing," he said again, that blaze in his eyes like a terrible fire deep inside her. "I don't feel like sharing you."

Her stomach flipped over, then dripped like fire deep into her pussy. But it was more than that. His words rolled through her, changing her and ruining her in one fell swoop.

Because the truth was, she didn't want a random man in a bar. She wanted him. But surely there was something wrong with her for that. Surely she should want to prowl, totting up her numbers and having healthy, no-strings sex with as many men as possible, the way she kept reading women her age were meant to do.

She scowled at him. "You don't get to decide. I'm not a possession."

"Maybe not." Charlie shrugged. "But I'm possessive."

"Really." She didn't believe him. Or maybe she *wanted* to believe him a little too much. "Is that a thing you do? You have sex and then get all possessive? Does that happen a lot?"

He did something that made his eyes glitter even more and sent something like chills shuddering down her back. Except she wasn't the least bit cold.

"I'm not generally a possessive guy when it

comes to women," he said after a moment, his voice gruff. And she had the distinct impression he was as overwhelmed and furious about it as she was. But no—that was a story she was telling herself. That was what she wanted to see, not what was real. "But for you, I'm willing to make an exception."

"Lucky me." She held his gaze and tried to look like the sexually liberated woman she should have been but never had been. "But I think I'll pass."

She wanted to sweep off somewhere—possibly to the washroom to have a cry—but she couldn't move without exposing herself to the whole bar. And he settled into his stance, even widening it a little. Effectively trapping her.

He didn't have to say a word. He just…kept her right there, her pulse a disaster and that blazing fire too hot and wild inside her.

"You can go straight to hell," she threw at him.

"I can guarantee you I will," Charlie said. There was a different note in his voice then, tangled through with what she might have called sorrow or self-disgust, if he'd been someone else. "But we're not debating what's going to happen to me when I'm gone. We're debating what you're going do with that tight little pussy while you're here."

Maya should have been appalled that he was

speaking to her like that. That he was using such vulgar words. And she was horrified, certainly— but at herself.

She made herself look all the way up the acres of his chest, despite the fact he was dressed like a captain of industry instead of a handyman, which should have confused her more than it did. "I have no intention of entering into another relationship, though I'm sure you wouldn't use that word. And if I did, it certainly wouldn't be with you."

"Sure." His crooked grin was much too smug. "That's why, every time you see me, you get so wet."

"That was before you threw me up against a wall in the middle of the village."

His grin got even cockier. "You were soaking wet then. I bet you are now, too. Should we check?"

Her breath shuddered through her. Out of her. He was electrifying—because he wasn't anything like the men she knew, all of them as worried about public perception as she'd been. Charlie wasn't like them. He wasn't like her.

Maya had absolutely no doubt that if he wanted to, he would go right ahead and get his hands on her—right here in this high-class bar—in a way that would get them both arrested.

And the craziest part was she didn't think she'd do a single thing to stop him.

"Charlie..." she managed, breathing out his name like it was a prayer.

His blue eyes were so bright they hurt. She held her breath.

"There you are," came a plummy, rich voice that hailed from the British Isles. "I thought you'd run for the hills after that tedious exercise."

Maya blinked, confused. An expression she couldn't read crossed over Charlie's face. He muttered something she couldn't hear, so there was no reason it should pierce the wall of her chest and make her heart ache.

The same way she ached when he stepped back to a respectable distance.

"So sorry to butt in," the man standing there beside Charlie said in the same merry way. "Your man raced off after yet another disgracefully boring business-owner's dinner and I confess I followed, grateful to get away. I have no idea why they insist on boring us to death, as if the taxes aren't sufficient to that purpose."

Maya gaped up at the man, dressed in another gloriously bespoke suit that whispered of the kind of wealth and consequence that could afford that level of artisanal tailor. Exactly as Charlie's did.

Something kicked in her at that. Something she didn't want to face.

"I beg your pardon," the round-faced British man continued, smiling down at Maya. "I'm Sebastian Fawkes-Morton, owner and proprietor of a far more modest establishment than the glorious hotel our Charlie owns. What I would give for his view!"

Maya stared up at Charlie, pieces she hadn't wanted to put together slamming into place. His presence here, dressed like that. His total unconcern about his job. His nonchalance about ordering food into a guest's room where he'd been lounging about half-naked.

As she gazed at him, he watched her, his expression daring her to get it. To make the logical connection.

"Hold on a moment," she heard herself say from very, very far away. As if she was trapped in another dressing room, hair and makeup exquisitely prepared for another wedding that would never take place. "The hotel. You own it?"

Charlie's eyes had never been so blue. Beside him, the man let out a whoop and surely risked death by pounding Charlie on the back.

"This is one of the long-lost St. George sons, my dear!" he crowed, putting the final nail into the situation. It felt like he was hammering it directly into Maya's head. Because everyone knew about the late Daniel St. George and the hotels—and wealth—he'd left to the sons he'd never met. The kind of wealth that made it deeply, breathtakingly humiliating that she'd ever believed Charlie was any kind of handyman. "That hotel is his birthright!"

CHAPTER EIGHT

CHARLIE HAD SEEN all kinds of bad shit in his time. Things he could never scrub from his head no matter how he tried. Nasty old nightmares that came out in the dark sometimes and kept him awake. Of all the things that he liked about leaving his life in Texas behind him for good, cutting down on scenarios that left that kind of dank residue inside of him ranked pretty high.

But he couldn't remember any of those tonight. Because the look on Maya's face as she stared back at him, his identity no longer a secret, was the thing that was going to haunt him forever.

He had liked Sebastian well enough before this, but as the man kept braying on, Charlie thought he might actually have to kill him.

St. George this, St. George that—Charlie barely heard him because Maya had gone too still. He watched her gaze darken, stormy and shocked and something much worse. Much too close to betrayed. He watched, frozen himself though he would have denied it, as she swallowed. Visibly.

And when she stood from her bar stool, gathering that soft cloud of pink around her, he could see that her hands were shaking.

The last time his heart had beat this hard he'd had a gun in his face.

"If you'll excuse me," she said in a perfectly smooth voice. But it wasn't *her* voice. Not the one he recognized. "I have to get back."

She aimed the same smile at him that she threw Sebastian's way. Blank. Absent.

As if she was already back across the ocean, tucked up in freezing cold Canada. As if nothing had ever happened between them, which was what he should have wanted.

Instead, Charlie felt like he was running for his life when he knew perfectly well he was standing still. Maya was so elegant, so composed, and he hated it. She pivoted around on one of those heels that did things to her legs he wanted to get down on his knees to taste and started for the door.

"Hold that thought," Charlie growled at Sebastian, finally shutting up the other man midway through a long lecture on the life and times of Daniel St. George, who had somehow found himself in a bar in Houston, Texas, long enough to make

Charlie all those years ago. Back when Charlie's mother had been young and hot instead of beaten down and bitter.

Charlie set off after Maya, not really caring if the entire village and half the Amalfi coast saw him chasing after a woman for the first time ever. All he cared about was that he caught up to her— and he didn't want to ask himself why that was.

He already knew he wouldn't like the answer.

He caught up to her out in the hushed hotel lobby, with its piped-in music and designer fragrances. He skirted the over-the-top Christmas trees, the kind of thing that usually put his teeth on edge given how little holiday cheer he'd experienced in his time, but he couldn't bring himself to care about that now.

"Maya."

His voice was a command. He didn't bother to pretend otherwise.

And still, he was surprised when she obeyed.

She turned slowly, as if she wanted to torture him with the perfection of her figure. All those lean, stacked curves, enough to make his mouth water and his hands twitch of their own accord.

But he wasn't dumb enough to pretend he couldn't see the fury in her dark eyes when she fixed them on him.

"I have no one to blame but myself," she said, her voice somehow thick and crisp at once. Not loud enough to disturb the self-conscious fanciness of this lobby but pointed enough to slice him in half. "What handyman lounges around for half an afternoon and a whole long night with a guest? Or answers the door half-naked when he orders room service? Or orders room service in the first place? There were red flags all around that I guess I ignored."

"I didn't lie to you." He sounded much rougher than he should have. But he wasn't planning to think on that, either. "I never told you I was a handyman. You assumed it all on your own."

"You let me assume it," she fired back. But then shook her head, cutting herself off. She even slashed her hand through the air. "It doesn't matter. You and I both know that you could have told me the truth. You didn't want to. And it only makes you more of a liar."

"It's not a secret," he growled, and maybe the reason he was so pissed off by this was because there was a part of him that knew she had a point. He'd liked that she didn't know who he was. Even back in Texas, he hadn't been anonymous. He'd liked the novelty. But he didn't like defending that choice. "Everyone in this village knows I own the hotel. You would have known it, too, if you both-ered to look. My face is in the brochure sitting on your living room table."

She let out a laughing sort of sound that con-tained absolutely no humor. Charlie drew closer to her, his hands at his sides—not in fists, though he was pissed enough, and not on her, either, which was what he really wanted.

"You know what? I've already had this conver-sation," she said, with another one of those laughs that weren't laughs. And this time when she shook her head, it was very clearly at him. Not at herself. "I'm not having it again."

"The fact that you made an assumption about me is not my problem," he heard himself saying, like he was arguing the point.

Maya made a sniffing sound, dismissive and rude. "Okay."

And she didn't wait for him to react to that. She turned around again, setting off at a much faster clip than before.

Charlie's jaw hurt, and he realized he was grit-ting his teeth like he wanted to break them all off. And his hands had stopped pretending to be civilized, curled into fists he knew were useless in this. Unless he wanted to punch himself in the face.

He didn't understand what was happening inside him, because he hadn't lied. Not directly. He'd let her think what she wanted to think—how was that on him?

His heart was kicking at him again, but he ignored it. And he should have let her walk right off into whatever temper tantrum she wanted to have, because that wasn't on him, either.

But no matter how self-righteous he felt about it, there he was following after Maya like he wasn't in control of his own feet. Like he was a puppet on a string and she'd yanked him close so he could fall into line behind her.

His worst nightmare, basically. But he couldn't seem to stop himself.

She made it across the lobby, then pushed out through the doors into the dark December night.

And Charlie was right there, following behind her like he couldn't bear to let her out of his sight.

What the hell was happening to him?

Outside, the village was brightly lit and deserted this time of year. Anyone who wanted to experience the holidays in coastal Italian splendor was tucked up inside somewhere, enjoying the more sedate pace in the area's otherwise well-trafficked tourist areas. It was as if he and Maya were the only people left in the world—not an image that helped him get a hold of himself.

He didn't know how to feel the things that moved around inside him. He would much rather feel her instead.

"Is this what you do every time you're pissed off about something?" He fired the words at her, his voice louder than the sound her heels made against the stones of the ancient square, and all of it echoing back at him in case he'd missed the part where he was being a dick. "At some point you're going to have to stop running away from the things you don't like, Maya. Don't you think?"

She whirled on him then, and he didn't realize until he saw the sheer, undiluted fury on her face that he'd expected her to be crying. Upset, anyway. Not like she wanted to rip him apart with her own two hands.

"I'm not running away from anything. And I told you I don't want to repeat this conversation."

"Babe. I don't know what you think is happening here, but we haven't had this conversation before."

She made that scornful noise that wasn't a laugh again, and Charlie liked it even less out here where there were no witnesses but the manic Christmas lights. And he couldn't pretend she wasn't doing it *at* him.

"You might not have had this conversation, but I have. Let me jump right over the gaslighting and get to the good stuff."

"Gaslighting?"

But she ignored that. "I'm not going to stand here and take responsibility for your deceitful behavior. That's on you. You knew what I thought, you chose to let me keep thinking it and the only thing I can assume is that you took some sick pleasure in imagining I thought you might lose a job you didn't even have."

This time when she laughed it was a hard, brittle sound that seemed to crack through the cold air. Or maybe that was just his rib cage, shattering into pieces. To spite him.

"The difference between you and me, Charlie, is that I haven't lied to you about anything. I'm a wide-open book. Canceled wedding. Cheating fiancé. Best friend who it turns out probably wasn't much of a friend at all. And this trip to Italy that was supposed to be my honeymoon. I'm not hiding anything from you." Maya shook her head, her cloud of curls dancing slightly with the movement. "You can't say the same."

"We've fucked a few times," he gritted out.

"What makes you think you deserve to know my life story?"

And he couldn't have said why the disappointed look she aimed at him then made that shattering sensation in his chest that much worse.

"It's not about what I deserve. It's about what you choose to tell someone in the course of getting to know them, even a little." She lifted a perfectly rounded shoulder, then dropped it again, and Charlie felt it like a punch. "I don't understand how people can have as much sex as we have and share absolutely no intimate details about themselves, so really, I should thank you. You've taught me something."

He felt like he was ripping wide-open, and he panicked. There was no other word for it. If he could have shoved the pieces of himself back into place, he would have. But he didn't have the slightest idea where to start—or any idea how she'd done this to him in the first place—so he scowled at her instead.

And he didn't know how his hands made it to her shoulders. Not to punish her. To touch her, because he had to touch her. He thought he might die if he didn't touch her, and that was one more thing he didn't want or understand or need.

But touching her just made it worse, because he wasn't inside her.

"I don't share the details of my life with anyone." The words sounded like they came from far away. He was only dimly aware he'd said them. "That's not personal, Maya. That's who I am."

"There's a difference between reticence and lying. Guess which side you fall on."

"I never actually told you a lie."

"What's funny is that I understand why that's the hill you want to die on." She shifted then, tipping her face into his. He wanted to grip her harder, drag her closer—but he didn't. There was too much knowledge in her dark gaze. "Keep ranting on about a technicality and you won't have to have the discussion about *why*. Because *why* is the scary part. *Why* might actually force you to be intimate with someone for five seconds of your adult life. And of course we can't have *that*."

"You don't know the first thing about me."

"You're right. I don't. And whose fault is that?"

He didn't understand why all those shattered pieces of him seemed to rattle around inside him, slicing him into shreds. And he definitely didn't understand why he was just…standing here. Letting this happen.

Why he'd chased her out here to keep letting her get under his skin.

She wasn't wrong. He had no interest in that why.

But here he was, opening up his mouth and talking anyway. When he used to pride himself on his ability to say as little as possible.

"I already told you more than most people know," he said, the words torn from a place inside him he hadn't known was there. "My mother met Daniel St. George in a bar in Houston during the brief window of time she wasn't propping up bars out in the dirt, which is where she raised me. One night, that was all it took, and here I am. Not that the rich asshole stuck around to help or, you know, say hello. All these years later, I had fancy lawyers up in my face, offering me a hotel in Italy and the means to run it. Are you satisfied now? You already had most of that information. Are we going to pretend that you're actually upset that I'm not a broke loser moonlighting as a janitor?"

Her lips twisted into something that bore no resemblance at all to her beautiful smile, which landed on him like one more gut punch.

"Right. Now I'm mercenary as well as stupid and overstepping."

He made a sound that could only be described as a growl. "I don't know what you want from me."

Maya didn't growl. But the look on her face made him feel as if she had.

"News flash, Charlie. I don't know what I want from you, either. I don't know what I want at all. I never pretended otherwise. And therein lies the difference between you and me." She leaned in. "*I'm* not pretending."

"Maya…"

But there was a ringing, then. He scowled, looking around for the sudden noise, but it was nowhere to be found. Not until he remembered that he carried his own set of obnoxious alarms around with him now.

It was his phone. Making that irritating sound it made when it was trying to connect with a video call. Something Charlie—who had been using shitty burner phones for most of his adult life as a matter of course, because he'd always preferred to be untraceable—found horrifying.

"Better get that," Maya said quietly. "I'm sure it's much more important than a boring conversation with a woman you fucked a few times and don't plan to bother with."

She stepped back then, and he had a choice. He could either keep a hold of her, grabbing for her in a panic, or he could man up and let her go.

He let his hands drop. His fucking phone kept ringing.

And she looked at him like she had already

disappeared back to wherever she'd come from to ruin his life in the first place.

"Maya," he said again, hardly recognizing his own voice.

"Keep taking comfort in the fact you never actually lied to me directly," Maya suggested in that soft, devastating way of hers. "I'm sure that if you think about it long enough, you'll find a way to make it true. Liars always do."

And he had to take that, like a kick in the face, as she wrapped that ridiculously soft, pink thing around her again and set off.

Like she was the one cutting this thing off, the way he should have done after that afternoon in the shed. The way he *had* done, always, before she turned up at the bottom of his property and turned his supposedly brand-new, much-better life upside down.

His phone stopped ringing. Charlie muttered out a curse, still watching as Maya walked away from him, her hips swaying like they were keeping time with the heart attack he kept having.

But in the next moment, the wailing from his phone started up again.

He yanked the damned thing out of his pocket and scowled at the screen, still not sure how he'd ended up toting one of these things around when he'd been perfectly happy with ancient flip phones whose only purpose was a quick call. And then, because he knew they would be relentless until he answered, he hit the button to accept the call.

The two faces he had never seen before a year ago—and now saw entirely too often—stared back at him from his phone.

"Aloha, bitch," came a loud, booming voice that belonged to his half brother Jason Kaoki, from far off on an island in the Pacific somewhere. "Did someone lock you in a crypt, brother?"

"I'm outside," Charlie bit off, already moving back toward the hotel and stepping into the lobby of the grand hotel.

As he moved toward a more private area, he could see Jason on his screen with no shirt, his too-long dark hair scraped back wet, suggesting he'd been surfing the way he claimed he liked to do every morning. There were palm trees dancing around in the sun behind him and ocean in the distance. The other half of his screen was a whole lot colder. A cavernous stone room, empty and stark, that reminded him of a spacious prison. And his other half brother, who was actually called Thor. Thor Ragnarsson, who ran their late father's luxury sex hotel up in Iceland, which made Charlie feel frostbitten just thinking about it.

This was his first winter after a lifetime in Texas and he found it much too chilly, here on the coast of Italy where everyone assured him the weather was mild. Or maybe he was the chill, frostbitten down into his bones by a woman who hadn't looked back when she'd walked away from him.

"Better now?" Charlie asked, sitting down by a fireplace in a part of the lobby that had been made to look like a comfortable sitting room. Or the kind of library that would normally have made him feel itchy, because he was a man who did things. Sitting around reading made him antsy. But tonight, all Charlie cared about was that no one else was there. "This isn't our usual time for a call. Is there a hotel emergency somewhere? That I need to care about?"

His tone made it clear he couldn't imagine what "a hotel emergency" would have to do with him, unless it was his hotel.

"Are you wearing a suit, brother?" Jason's voice was taunting, his wide grin wicked. "Look at that. Spend long enough in Italy and a man turns into a baller. Can't even help it. And after claiming the funeral was the only time he'd ever put one on."

"I was at a monthly meeting of local businessmen," Charlie bit out. "I guess I am one. Why are you talking about my clothes? You want to come over here and braid my hair? Brother?"

Jason let out one of his booming laughs that had likely served him well during his short career playing pro football. But Charlie kept his eyes on Thor, who was blond and blue-eyed like Charlie, but there was no dirty in Thor's Scandinavian blond. And his Viking blue eyes were glacial.

More glacial by the second, in fact.

"If we can return to matters of business," Thor said in that icy way of his, "it appears that our half sister has fulfilled the terms of the will."

Their heavily tattooed half sister, who Daniel St. George had messed with from beyond the grave. Bold, take-no-prisoners Angelique Masterson from New York City, with her dyed black hair and bright blue eyes. Unmistakably a result of yet another run-of-the-mill affair, and yet the only one required to jump through hoops to get her inheritance.

"You're going to have to remind me what that means," Charlie said now, making his drawl a little heavier than necessary. "And also why I should care."

"It means she hooked herself the big fish," Jason

replied. He lounged back in whatever chair he was sitting in, looking lazy and amused.

"Correct." Thor still sounded icy, Charlie thought, but maybe there was a hint of something like a smile lurking around the older man's mouth. Maybe. "She achieved her objective. The hotel property in the kingdom of Sadat is now officially hers. And so, too, will our dearly departed father's estate present her with her quarter."

"Why does this require an emergency call in the middle of the night?" Charlie asked. "This feels like it could be an email. One I could ignore, because I have shit to do."

Jason laughed at that. Thor only arched an eyebrow.

"I assure you, I have no intention of wasting your precious time, Charlie. Our next call is set for Friday, as usual. Angelique will be on it. That is the purpose of this call. To prepare you."

"I don't need preparation," Jason said, as if it was all a big joke. But then, that was the way he said everything. And given the way he was holding off developers who wanted to turn the island he'd inherited into yet another strip mall—singlehandedly, from all the reports Charlie was required to listen to every week as part of the thousands of things he'd signed at the will reading—he used it to hide behind. Charlie could relate.

But he didn't want to relate to these men who were family by blood, but who he'd met exactly once.

"Meanwhile, I still don't care," he said gruffly. "Two sisters. Twelve sisters. Or just the one. Makes no difference to me."

"Noted." Thor actually rolled his eyes, which Charlie thought was revolutionary. Normally he didn't crack at all. Charlie figured it was that purple-haired professor he refused to talk about. "I, personally, prefer to know what I'm walking into. Call it a personal fetish."

"Says the man with the sex hotel," Jason said, with another laugh.

But all Charlie could think about was Maya, calling him a liar. Calling him out, ripping him to shreds and walking away.

Again.

"Is that it?" he asked, not bothering to pull out his own lazy drawl and pretend nothing got to him tonight. "I'm actually in the middle of something."

He would have hung up already, but they'd all signed those damned papers. He was forced to be a part of what the lawyers had called "the St. George family." Charlie knew better than to get carried away at the sound of that word. The only family he'd ever had was his mother and stepfather. His mother was all smiles when she wanted something and a raging bitch every other minute of the day. She'd never treated him like he was anything but a burden. His stepfather had groomed him to be a weapon and had knocked him on his ass when he didn't act as ordered, when ordered. And while his half brothers and half sister hadn't exactly achieved those levels on anything so far, it wasn't like he trusted them.

Do you trust anyone? a voice inside him asked. *Do you have the slightest idea* how *to trust anyone?*

It sounded far too much like Maya for his taste.

"*Mahalo*, assholes," Jason said cheerily, as always. "I have a wave to catch."

And he disconnected with his middle finger.

Charlie went to hang up, too, but something in the way Thor was studying him stopped him. "What?"

"Are you well?" the glacial Icelander asked.

Coolly, the way he did everything.

Charlie frowned. "Why does that feel like a loaded question?"

"You look different," Thor replied. "Less...aggressively relaxed than usual."

"I'm going to make 'aggressively relaxed' my new band name." Charlie forced a smile, but it didn't feel right. Nor did it appear to impress Thor. "I told you I was in the middle of something."

"If I could offer you some brotherly advice," Thor said, a rueful expression on his face, suggesting he knew exactly how ridiculous that sounded.

"Is that a thing we do now? Because that's a hard pass on my end. I'm fine."

"Yes, of course." Now Thor looked amused. "I have also been as fine as you look. And all I will say is this. A little something I've been considering. It is always possible that our father's manipulation was not to control us with these hotels and these lives he set out for us in his will. It is always possible that the aim was to free us from our other lives instead."

"This sounds like the raving of someone who finally got himself a girlfriend," Charlie bit out. "Getting it on the regular must have fried your brain, Thor. So let me remind you. Our dear, departed father never did a goddamn thing to *free* anybody. He was a piece of shit. Where I come from, the kind of piece of shit he is would end up dead after he betrayed the wrong person. But it's always different for rich assholes, isn't it?"

"In the spirit of all the families I've ever known,

you certainly don't have to take this advice. I'm just sharing it."

"*Family* isn't a word I like all that much."

This time, there was no mistaking the way the other man's mouth curved, just like there was no mistaking the perfect awareness that sprang between them. They were brothers by blood, called family by the world, but that only made the word more meaningless. It had nothing to do with what Charlie had called his family back home. Those ties of obligation like claws, sinking in deep.

He'd never been to Iceland, but if he had to guess, he'd say his newfound older brother had some experience with those same claws and the damage they did.

"I understand," Thor said. "Enjoy your evening."

But when Charlie finally hung up, he felt... shaken. He didn't understand what was going on. When had he turned into this easily shook fool, who cared what a piece of ass said to him? Who let some stranger who happened to share half of his blood get in his head?

He needed to shut this down. All of this.

But when he found himself out in the village again, out in the dark and the cold and running up those stairs like a maniac, all he could see was Maya.

And it occurred to him that despite everything he had no idea who he was if he wasn't pretending… something. Wearing a mask. Smiling when he was murderous. Laughing when he wanted to punch a wall.

Pretending he felt nothing when the truth was, he felt too much.

What would happen if he stopped?

CHAPTER NINE

MAYA CHANGED OUT of her slinky dress, throwing it across her bedroom as if that could spare her another dousing rush of the embarrassment that had chased her all the way from the piazza. Her heels followed, one after the next, clattering against the floor as she tossed them aside. With force. She stripped down completely, as if the outfit was to blame for what had happened in that bar. And all her choices leading up to it.

When she dressed again, it was in soft, flowy, comfortable clothing that was as close to a hug as she was likely to get tonight.

Or ever again, a dour little voice inside her pronounced.

She told it to shut the hell up.

That was when she heard a faint noise from the other room. She stormed out of the unlit bedroom, her bare feet slapping against the floor.

And maybe she had been expecting him. Because when she looked at Charlie standing there on the inside of her door, his blue eyes brilliant and the hint of exertion making his cheeks ruddy, she felt a whole mess of things.

But none of them was *surprised*.

"Now you're just letting yourself into hotel rooms?"

"It's my hotel, Maya. I have the key. I have all the keys."

He sounded even more dangerous than usual. It made something in her tip over, then hum.

But she thought she'd rather die than let him see that. "I shouldn't have to tell you that the owner of a St. George hotel should not be breaking into a guest's room. That's not the sort of thing you're going to want to put in your brochures."

"What is it you think I'm keeping from you?" He threw it at her, and he sounded different than he had down in the village. More dangerous, yes. But also more raw, if that was possible. "This whole song and dance about how I'm lying to you is bullshit."

"I'm somehow unsurprised that's your take."

"You're always running from something, Maya. That's how you got here, isn't it? Well, now it must be time to run from me. But I'm not that douche-bag who left you at the altar. I didn't do anything to you except make you come."

Maya sighed. "I keep forgetting how blameless you are in all of this. Everything is happening around you, but it's never about you. My bad. You're like the eye of the storm."

She did something theatrical with her hands that made his entire rangy body go stiff. As alarms went, that one was loud and clear—but she didn't back down.

"Are you standing in front of my face telling me I don't know how to take responsibility for myself?"

The way he asked that question suggested that she had better not be telling him anything of the kind. A smart woman would have backed down, happily and quickly.

Maya chose to tilt her head to one side like he was some kind of specimen in a zoo. "Why? Is that a trigger for you? I wouldn't know, would I, because I don't know anything about you."

"I don't know what you think this is, but where I come from you don't spill your guts for a fling," Charlie growled out at her. "No matter how hot she is in bed."

Maya was shaking, but she couldn't tell if it was happening inside her—or everywhere. And oddly enough, she didn't have it in her to care any longer if he saw it. If he saw everything.

"Fine," she said, her voice even but not remotely mild. "Then why are you here, Charlie? Why did you chase me all the way back from that bar and let yourself into my room? If this is a fling that's gotten out of hand, why come back for more?"

He moved as if he was going to put his hands on her—and God help her, she wanted that. She thought she would commit crimes to feel those battered, tough hands on her skin again.

But he raked them through his hair instead.

And his voice was as grave as that expression on his beautiful face when he spoke again. "You want things from me that I don't have to give."

That should have wrecked her. Instead, she rolled her eyes.

And for a moment, she didn't know which one of them was more shocked.

She compounded it with another sigh, this one bordering on irritated. "I'm going to go out on a limb here, but I don't think you've ever been intimate with another person in your entire life. I don't think you have the slightest idea what you have to give."

He stared back at her, looking astonished. And darkly furious, all at once.

"Terrific. I guess this is the night for inspirational speeches. I'm a changed fucking man."

Maya shook her head at him, while inside there was something like grief mixed in with the sadness that she knew had everything to do with this man. Charlie, particularly. Not anyone she had left behind.

"Tell me one true thing," she challenged him. "Just one, Charlie."

He looked at her as if she had hit him. As if she'd hauled off and landed one on his face. She imagined he would prefer that.

"You have no idea how I was raised. The kind of man who raised me. What I had to do to earn his approval. And worse, what it was like when I figured out I was good at it."

"One true thing," she said quietly. "Everything you just said is a story."

"You said you were a lawyer, Maya. I don't think you want to know what it was like to be raised by a lot of outlaw bikers. Almost one of them, but not quite. And not because I didn't want to be, because I did. Believe me, I did. But I look the way I do. Clean me up and put a smile on my face and I can convince anyone of anything—and that made me useful. A kind of useful that wearing biker shit and getting myself arrested would ruin." His hard mouth tightened. "My stepfather raised me up right. I ran cons."

"One. True—"

"It wasn't just my stepfather who thought being kind meant an ass kicking that *didn't* take out an eye or a tooth. It was that whole dusty, dirty world. The club. My stepdad and his dirtbag friends, who I considered family. My mother, who's never been anything but a pain in the ass. Some kids play cops and robbers, but they grow out of it. Not the people who raised me. Not me."

He took a step toward her. Maya held his gaze, though he looked as close to tortured as she'd ever seen him. His blue eyes were blazing. Wild, even, with so much emotion and fury she almost couldn't bear to look at him. Almost.

Charlie stopped before he reached her. Jerkily, as if he didn't know what his own body was doing. And Maya had to lecture herself, harshly, not to reach out and touch him herself.

"My stepdad was killed in a bar fight a few years ago by some real nice individuals he met in prison and tried to cross," Charlie told her in that same voice, dark and low. "And then I was really in trouble. Don't get me wrong. Carl wasn't a nice man. There wasn't one shred of decency in him, he was proud of it, and no one missed him when he was gone. But he protected me in his own way. With him gone, I had to figure out how to live in that world on my own." His blue eyes flashed, like his own kind of lightning. "It was brutal, but fine. I survived."

"You survived, sure. But are you really fine?"

"This is what I'm trying to tell you, Maya. There's no part of me that's fine." And the laugh he let out then was dark. Barbed. "And you wouldn't care either way if you didn't like how I look. How I fuck. You think you want this?" He took one hand and slammed it against his own chest, hard enough that the noise made her flinch. "You can't handle what I carry around in here."

She took a moment. She looked at the fury blazing from him, bright blue and powerful. At that set to his jaw. The way he held himself, as if he was seconds away from throwing himself into his own bar fight.

And keeping her hands to herself had never hurt her before. It had never actually *hurt*. "I'm not sure I'm the one who can't handle it."

He made that low sound that made her think of a wild thing growling. "When I say there's blood on my hands, I mean it. Real blood, not some story one of your tight-assed lawyer friends tells in a bar to sound interesting. I'm talking about real life. Real shit. The kind of stuff that people like you need to pretend doesn't exist so you can sleep at night."

That was supposed to wound her, she understood. She only shook her head. "I don't think I'm the one who's pretending, Charlie."

He made another noise that sounded as if it was ripped from deep inside him. It made every hair on her body want to stand on end.

"This isn't a door you want to open, Maya. I don't know how many ways I can tell you that."

"Then don't open it." She was aware of how much she was shaking. Shivering, everywhere. As if she was lit on fire and freezing cold, all at the same time. "You're the one who came after me. You're the one who let yourself into this room. Or was that another accident? Something else that just happened near you while you were pretending not to notice?"

"What the fuck are you doing to me?"

That was torn out of him, too, his expression anguished. His tone worse.

She shouldn't have laughed. But she couldn't seem to help herself. "I'm not doing anything to you. I'm just trying to see you. Call me crazy."

He moved then, a big rangy predator, and she knew she should have been terrified. She should have screamed. Run. Done something—anything—

to save herself from the man who advanced on her with all that barely leashed ferocity.

But instead, she melted.

And when he swept her up against him, plastering her body against that ridiculously well-cut suit he wore, he gripped her shoulders in his big hands and bared his teeth directly in her face.

And that didn't scare her, either.

On the contrary, she felt it like fire, delicious and intoxicating. It swept through her, lighting her up everywhere it touched.

"I don't have any truth to tell you, Maya," he told her, up close and practically bristling with all that power and fury he carried around inside him. "The man I used to be died in Texas, and it's better all-around if you leave him buried there. There's not one part of who he was that matters now. Here in Italy I own a hotel I wouldn't have been able to afford to stay in a year ago. I go to business meetings with men who would never have acknowledged my existence. I'm a goddamned upstanding member of society."

"I don't think you believe that, either."

He let out another one of those noises that rolled through her like a storm.

And then his mouth was on hers.

By now she expected the kick of it, that wild

passion that flattened her and exulted her. She expected the impossible glory of his mouth on hers,
the sheer, shaking madness of it.

This time, as his tongue plundered hers, he set
his hands on either side of her face. To hold her
still, she thought—

But then his mouth gentled. The kiss changed.

She wouldn't call it *soft*. There was nothing
about this man that was soft.

Still, she felt tears well up behind her eyes as he
kissed her, again and again, not as if he wanted to
toss them off an edge of a cliff, but almost as if…

But she didn't dare use words like *cherish*, not
even in her own head.

"I was conning men out of their money when I
was ten years old," Charlie said against her mouth.
"No one trusts a thing I say, not even me."

And it was the agony in his voice that made all
that emotion she was fighting flood her eyes and
start down her cheeks.

"Charlie…"

"Don't trust what I say," he told her, his voice
gritty and things in his gaze she was afraid to
name. "Trust this."

He bent, then swept her up into his arms, carrying her like some kind of fairy-tale princess as he
moved across the room. Out of the light, into the

dark bedroom, where she hadn't bothered to turn on the lamps. He didn't, either. He lay her down on the wide bed as if she was indescribably precious to him, and then he crawled there next to her.

And she thought she knew him. She expected the rough beauty of his hands streaking over her, hard and wild. The kick, the magic, of that mad rush to the finish.

But instead, he stretched there beside her, turned her toward him and touched her as if he had never seen a woman before.

His blue eyes were bright. His expression was something like grave.

He helped her out of her clothes and shrugged out of his. Then he took his time, moving like some kind of prayer in the hushed, dim light, as if he was worshipping every square inch of her.

It was like a dream. The slide of skin against skin. The scrape of his teeth, his beard. The bright fire every time he tasted her with his mouth.

Until finally he settled himself between her legs. He made an approving noise and then slid his hands beneath her, lifting her to him like an offering.

And when he licked his way into her pussy, she lost it. She tumbled end over end, rolling over and over and over again as if she might not stop. Ever.

She didn't know if she was breathing or sobbing, or both. It was possible she was laughing, and she couldn't tell. It was all *too much*. She was already weak and out of her head when he climbed up beside her again, sat up in the center of the mattress and then pulled her over to straddle his lap.

It wasn't the first time she had taken him this way, but this was different.

His gorgeous cock reared up between them, hard and thick and satiny soft, and he let out a shaky breath when she wrapped her hands around it. But this was no time to play, not when he had his gaze fixed on her like that. As if he had been blind all his life until this moment and only now could he see.

As if the only thing he could see was her.

She knelt up, using both hands between them to guide the thick head of his cock to her entrance. Then, relying on the way he gripped her around the waist, she sank down over him. She took him into her in a rush, reveling in that deliciously deep stretching as her body made room for him. Or tried to.

And this, too, felt like an act of worship.

She couldn't tell which one of them moved. She only knew that together they flowed over each other, into each other. She saw something in his face that she couldn't put into words, but she felt it. With every slick, deep thrust of his body into hers, she knew it.

She became it.

Over and over and over again.

And maybe he had lied about a thousand things, but this was the truth.

She knew it the way she knew the span of her hips, the jut of her breasts. She knew it as if it was already a part of her, bone and sinew, need and longing.

She lost track of how many times she tumbled over one cliff only to find a steeper one, a wilder fall.

Until he flipped them both over, coming over her in the dim light that felt like a caress, pounding himself into her at last.

And calling out her name when he fell, like a vow.

Hours could have passed after that. Or mere moments. Maya would never know.

She was off somewhere, then she was back, and Charlie's hard, beautiful arm was her pillow.

She didn't know how she knew he was awake, only that he was. She drew a circle on his skin with her finger, then laughed at her own display of sentimentality.

"I'm sorry," she said, breaking the quiet.

"What did you do now?"

She smiled at that, there against his side where he couldn't see. "Your childhood doesn't sound like a lot of fun."

Another man might have shifted in the discomfort of that. Charlie went still.

"Was yours?"

"No," Maya said, surprising herself, because she'd never said that out loud. She would never have *dared* say that out loud. And she kept going. "Now that you mention it, it really wasn't any fun at all."

Charlie made a low, rumbling sort of sound that she decided to interpret as encouragement.

"My parents are the coldest people I've ever met," Maya told him, the words spilling out of her, as if there was a fissure inside her she could no more contain than she could stop the flow of lava from a volcano. "I don't think I've ever seen them touch each other. I know I've never seen a hint of affection from either one of them toward anything or anyone. As far as I can tell they have a business arrangement. And they raised my sister and me to be perfect little vice presidents of the family firm. Cold. Focused. All achievements, no excuses. That's the Martin way. My wedding was the only time I've ever seen them show anything even resembling emotion."

Charlie didn't say anything, but she knew he wasn't asleep. More than that, she knew he was listening to her.

And it occurred to her that for all the endless conversations she'd had with Ethan, he had never truly sat there and listened to her. He had always been far too busy strengthening his own arguments.

How had she never seen that when it mattered?

"I worked so hard to meet their expectations for me. I spent my entire life trying to succeed enough to get their approval. But the truth is, I don't think they know how to be happy with anything. Certainly not with me."

"That's what kids do," Charlie said at last, and his hand moved to the back of her head, his fingers gripping her curls and making her feel safe, somehow. "You try to live up to what's in front of you. It's the only thing you know."

"Here's something I know you don't want to hear," she said into the dark, because he made her feel safe and the fact that he could told her things about her whole life she would have given anything not to know. "I think the first real thing I've ever felt in my life is you."

"You're right," he growled down at her, shifting then so he could look at her face. "I don't want to hear it."

But he didn't let go of her. He rolled with her instead, coming over on top of her and pinning her to the bed.

"I wanted to fuck a beautiful woman in a shed, because I could," he told her, his gaze fierce and challenging, and she should have been disgusted, surely. But instead, she was thrilled. "Instead, I got you. I don't like real, Maya. It's not who I am. I told you, I was raised to run cons. Not to get real."

She knew she should say something. She should do something about the way her heart was pounding, as if it was telling her to run.

But he was shaking his head at her, and there was something in that blue gaze of his that made her pussy ache, even while it made her feel all those things she shouldn't feel. Cherished. Safe.

He reached down to pull her hands up and over her head.

"I didn't want real, but here we are." His mouth went dangerous. Maya shivered. "Now we'll see how real you want to get."

"Is that…a challenge?" she asked, need stampeding through her, mixed up with something a lot like terror, but not because she was afraid of him.

She was far more worried that, really, she was afraid of herself.

"You're going to hold on to the headboard again," Charlie told her in that voice of his that was nothing but command. "And this time you're not going to come until I tell you to. That's the challenge."

He dropped his head down next to hers, and the look on his face made her heart skip a beat. Then kick in so hard she was surprised he couldn't see it.

"You wanted real, Maya. You wanted the truth." Charlie's blue gaze set her on fire, but she wasn't sure she'd even started to burn. Or if she'd survive it. "Let's see how much you like it."

CHAPTER TEN

MAYA WOKE UP in a panic, as if she'd had a bad dream.

But if she'd been dreaming, she couldn't remember about what.

Her heart careened around in her chest, her skin felt clammy and she could hardly manage a full breath. She squinted at the clock on the bedside table, certain that it would be the dead of night. But it was one of the long, dark mornings this time of year, and somehow the fact that it was a new day and yet still so dark made her…shiver.

Then again, maybe that had more to do with the way Charlie was sprawled next to her in the big bed, taking up more than his share of room on the mattress.

She wanted to curl into him. She wanted to bury her face in his chest, feel his heavy arms around her and let him make her feel safe again—

But she couldn't let herself do that. Because she

knew she would wake him up if she touched him, and he would see that she was losing it, and the very idea of that made her heart beat faster and her throat feel tighter.

A sob, trapped in her chest like some kind of time bomb, threatened to break free.

And Maya couldn't have that, either.

She eased herself over to the edge of the bed, then rolled out of it, expecting her body to react to that much movement after the night she'd had. Expecting to feel twinges, little pulls or scrapes, instead of...the strangest feeling that suffused her from head to foot. As if she was lit up with something too bright to contain.

It didn't make sense.

Charlie had turned her inside out, with an intensity and a deliberateness that made her knees feel weak. He had taught her things about herself that made her shiver all over again, just remembering.

He had taken control of her in so many delicious ways that she was surprised she'd survived it. But maybe the real truth was that she hadn't. She felt like ash. She was charred straight through, waiting for the faintest breeze to blow her away.

Her heart was still kicking at her like it wanted out of her chest. She couldn't breathe. And looking at the impossible, sculpted beauty of the big hard man sprawled across her bed made her…weak.

She made her way across the bedroom in the dark, carefully stepping over the shoes she'd thrown on the floor last night. Once she made it to the washroom suite, she eased her way inside and gently, carefully closed the door behind her. Then she stood there, her back against the door and her heart hammering at her, as if something was chasing her.

Maya stood there for a long time. Until her feet grew so cold against the tiled floor beneath her that she could feel the chill of it climb up her calves. When she pushed away from the door, she felt older, arthritic, as if the force of whatever panic this was had aged her immeasurably.

The funny thing was, she believed it.

She'd thrown her clutch on the washroom counter when she'd stormed into the room last night, and she moved over to it now, unclipping it so she could pull her mobile out and scroll through her notifications.

There were several voice mails from her parents' house phone and individual mobiles, but she didn't need to listen to them. She could feel their cool disapproval of her choices from across the world and knew exactly what they'd say. That they were disappointed that she hadn't risen to the occasion and shown her mettle as a Martin should.

They would have shown her the same frozen disappointment if she'd ever, say, gotten a bad grade in school or made a scene in public. Not that she'd ever dared do either one of those things.

Her sister had moved on to text messages:

Ethan is not cooperating. He insists he needs to talk to you, personally. Please advise.

Maya waited for that familiar rage to sweep through her again. That deep, comprehensive fury at the man she was supposed to be married to right now that had been keeping her aloft all this time. But it was gone. And the room it had taken up inside her was filled with that brightness…and its matching panic.

She knew why. The *why* was out there in her bed, fast asleep, beautiful and golden and capable of making her body sing like some kind of celestial instrument only he knew how to play. He'd proved it again and again.

But she had spent these weeks secure in her anger and she hadn't spared a thought for what might wait there on the other side of it. A different kind of grief, maybe. For the life she had thought she would be living by now. The life she and Ethan had built, one conversation and goal at a time, year after year…

A life she not only didn't want any longer but couldn't imagine how she'd ever wanted.

That thought felt slippery and treacherous. She slid a hand over her own chest as if that could soothe her poor heart.

Maya hadn't understood how black-and-white her world was—and always had been—until she'd come to Italy. Or how gray her emotions were, or the sex she'd had was, until she met Charlie and he'd turned her inside out.

Now the colors were too bright.

And there was no pretending that she could go back. Not to the life she'd left behind in all those embarrassing wedding-day pieces. She wasn't the same person whose wedding had been canceled in such a humiliating fashion.

Maybe you were never that person, a voice inside her suggested.

But that kind of heresy made her entire life some kind of sick joke, didn't it? And the notion that might very well be true only made it harder to breathe.

Maya moved farther into the rambling washroom suite that was larger than the dormitory room she'd lived in with Lorraine a lifetime ago. She made her way to the huge, dramatic bathtub that was perched in the big arched window, offering a view—by day—of the patchwork, pastel quilt of ancient buildings stuck to the side of the steep hills and the beautiful stretch of the sea beyond.

She climbed into the tub and sank down into it, not minding at all that it was dry and it was too dark outside to see much more than the lights and the suggestion of the water, far below. She felt as if she was in some kind of cocoon, tucked up and safe from the world.

Or maybe the truth was, simply, that she felt safe here. That was what Italy—and Charlie, if she was honest, and maybe *mostly* Charlie—had done for her. And it wasn't until she had started to feel that remarkable sense of safety that she'd truly understood how deeply unsafe she'd felt for most of her life, in a variety of ways. And with just about everyone she knew.

But that was a breakdown for another time.

Right now, she needed to clean up her own mess.

She swiped her phone open, found Ethan's number and hit the button.

The phone rang and rang. It only occurred to her that it was after midnight in Toronto—long past Ethan's preferred bedtime, since he liked to rise at

4:30 to get his run in every morning before work—when she heard the fumbling noise that suggested he was picking up his phone from the nightstand.

"Do you know what time it is?" Ethan demanded, his voice thick and annoyed, and Maya could picture him perfectly. He would be scowling, his eyes even more bleary than usual without his glasses on. His dark hair would be standing straight up and his jaw would be rough.

She waited for a wave of regret to crash over her. Longing, maybe. Yearning, despite the likelihood that he wasn't alone in that bed they'd picked out together.

But all she felt was a kind of soft sadness.

"I beg your pardon, Ethan," she said crisply, the way she might in a fractious deposition. "Is it inconvenient for you to talk to me now? It's obviously very important to me that your convenience take center stage here."

"That's not what I meant." Now he sounded aggrieved. "For fuck's sake, Maya. You really are making this harder than it has to be."

"Out of curiosity, how hard do you imagine something like this ought to be? Is there a certain level of reaction you would find acceptable, under the circumstances? Am I allowed to react at all? I'm guessing not. Because—and correct me if

I'm off base—I suspect it's possible that you don't like being so clearly and inarguably in the wrong."

She heard a sound like a sigh—even more aggrieved than before, which she would have said wasn't possible—and a faint clattering noise that she knew was Ethan fiddling around on the table beside the bed for his glasses.

And maybe because she could picture it all so clearly, as if she was standing in the corner of the bedroom herself, Maya knew she didn't want to go back to that condo. Not even if Ethan removed himself. She didn't want to live there, surrounded by so many ghosts of a life that would never happen. Not to mention, though she couldn't hear another person, she was sure he was sharing that bed—and the couch and the soft rug in the den and God knows which other surfaces—with Lorraine. She had to assume they had been sneaking around in her home for some time.

Which meant Maya could never touch anything in it again.

That notion might have hurt her before. And then made her angry, because who didn't prefer a little spurt of righteous anger to the pain that lay beneath it? But today she could hardly muster more than a shrug.

"You want to hurt me. You want to punish me. I

get it." Ethan actually sounded *self-righteous*, she realized. As if he saw himself as the victim here— and more, *wanted* to be the victim.

It should have made her furious. Instead, she wanted to laugh.

And instead of gulping that strange urge down because it was unseemly, she…let herself laugh.

At him. And better yet, unapologetically.

"I don't want to hurt you, Ethan." She wasn't sure that was true. She didn't want to *actively* cause him pain, maybe, but she doubted she would work too hard to keep from smiling should karma catch up with him. "And I think we both know that the life you've chosen is punishment enough."

"If that's meant to be another nasty little dig at Lorraine, you should know straight off I won't allow it."

"Good to know." She was sure he could hear the way she rolled her eyes, and she was fine with that, too. "I'm not being unkind when I point out that the smooth, easy life you always claimed you wanted? That's not going to happen. Whether you stay together or don't, you've chosen a roller coaster."

"I don't expect you to understand." Ethan was using that fussy, offended voice that, once upon a time, had made her wish that she could do anything at all to solve whatever the problem was. And she usually had.

But that was the old Maya. The black-and-white, rule-following Maya, locked away in all that gray.

"The funny thing is, I do understand," she told him, in the spirit of some generosity that she couldn't have named if her life depended on it. "I wish the two of you could have handled this better. Not left me at the altar, for example. But I understand."

It was the greatest gift she was capable of giving, here in the run-up to a Christmas she'd imagined would be very different. But it was a time for forgiveness and grace, if she was capable of it. She was surprised to find she was.

And she knew it would have been impossible even twenty-four hours before.

But Charlie had shown her what true power was and where it waited deep inside her, if she dared surrender to it.

She had dared. And Maya felt like a different person in the aftermath.

One who might be a little shaky, sure, but one who was capable of giving gifts to those who least deserved it.

So, naturally, Ethan ruined it.

"Of course you don't understand," he retorted,

in that superior voice of his that she'd used to think was cute. Because it reminded her how smart he was, how accomplished, how successful. Today she just thought he sounded like a dick. "You don't know what it's like to truly love someone like this. I don't expect you to. But the problem is, you hiding out in Italy is making things awkward for us."

She ran her tongue over her teeth. "What a nightmare. Heaven forbid you feel *awkward*."

If he heard her sarcasm, he ignored it. "There's friction at work. You know what it's like in the firm when there's any hint of scandal. And your sister is hounding me day and night about selling the condo." He let out a baffled sort of laugh. "It doesn't make any sense. Why would you want to live here?"

"I hardly know where to begin with any of that."

"You need to come home, Maya. Sulking in Italy isn't solving anything. We need to put on a good front for the partners, as soon as possible, before they start jumping to unfortunate conclusions about our dependability."

Maya was shaking her head at the darkness on the other side of the window before her.

"That sounds like a you problem, if I'm honest."

"Don't be childish, please. It demeans us both. I'm talking about our careers."

"And somehow, I don't think I'm the one demeaning anything. What good front do *I* need to put on? I'm the one who was left at the altar." She made her voice as bland as possible. "All I have to do is put on a brave face and I'm the heroine of this story. Your road is a little rougher, I'm afraid."

"I'm aware of the optics," he snapped at her. "That's why we need to do this together."

"The last thing we did together was plan a wedding. You'll understand if I'm less interested in joint projects from here on out."

"This is what I'm talking about. This childishness. Who is that helping?"

"You're going to have to rehabilitate your image on your own," Maya said coolly. "But if it makes you feel any better, I'm sure you'll quickly discover that no one really cares that much about your personal life. I can assure you that I certainly don't. In fact, I would prefer to never hear about your personal life or your deep and abiding love, ever again."

"I knew you wouldn't understand." He sounded lofty then. Like some kind of *martyr* to love.

It was maddening.

Maya's temples were pounding, and she pressed the fingers of her free hand against her forehead, urging herself not to give in to the wave of temper.

"Here's the thing, Ethan. You and I both know that the only thing you will ever love is yourself. Luckily, Lorraine is more or less the same. And I'm sure you'll do wonderfully together."

"I already told you I won't tolerate your nasty asides."

"I think we both know that you don't care about me, my feelings or anything else, or none of this would have happened."

A funny thing happened when she said it that way. Out loud. Stark and matter-of-fact. And *to* him. Especially when he didn't argue. It put the years they'd spent together into order. It highlighted all the things she'd told herself were just a part of a long-term relationship—one that greatly resembled her parents' businesslike arrangement.

I don't want to be my parents, she admitted to herself. They were as cold as a Canadian winter, frozen straight through, and she'd tasted fire now. She'd burned alive—and she liked it.

She felt free and sad at the same time. Unmoored. "Let's be clear about why you're really stonewalling my sister. It would be *inconvenient* for you to relocate. That's why you don't want to leave the condo. Not because it has any sentimental value to you and not even because you're trying to hurt me, somehow. Because you would have to care to do that."

Ethan sighed. "If I'm such a sociopath, why did you want to marry me?"

"A question I'm sure I'll spend the rest of my life grappling with," she shot right back. "But today, happily, that's one more thing that's not my problem. If you want the condo, you need to buy me out. And if I were you, I would think long and hard about lowballing me, as I know you're going to try to do."

"This is ridiculous. I'm not going to play these adolescent games with you in the middle of the night. We'll talk when you get back from Italy."

And impossibly, laughably, he hung up.

He hung up on *her*.

For a long moment, Maya didn't move. She sat where she was, her mobile in her hand, staring at the screen in disbelief.

But then something shifted inside her.

It had something to do with the glorious way Charlie had taught her how to surrender. To move into the things she feared or wanted, or both at the same time—and discover who she really was on the other side of it.

Her heart kicked at her at that, but she couldn't think about him yet. Not quite yet.

She thought about what she knew instead. All those grays, the black-and-whites and Ethan in the middle of it, so certain that she would do as he wanted.

Because she always had.

She had been more dedicated to the idea of their perfect life together than she had been to him, personally. They had rarely fought, because there was nothing to fight about. Maya had always done that math and come up with the same conclusion. Keeping their busy, glossy life running smoothly had been her priority. Always. If she hadn't been sure about something, Ethan would argue her into it. He would sit her down, lay out his argument and treat her like a recalcitrant jury.

And she had accepted that. She had enjoyed it, even. If asked, she would have said that it was one of the things she loved about their relationship. They were so logical. So rational. Even when things got emotional, they managed to talk their way to an equitable solution.

Things she hadn't done with Ethan, for example, included yelling at him in the street. Engaging in sexual acts in public when anyone might happen upon them at any time. She had never begged Ethan for anything.

Ethan had never made her come over and over,

ignoring her when she said she couldn't and making her body do things she'd never imagined it could.

Again and again.

It was as if Ethan was a cold, gray rain. And Charlie was sunlight.

And there was no pretending, now, that she didn't know the difference between the two.

Ethan wanted her to come back to Canada so he could argue her into compliance with whatever rational, self-serving plan he had in his head. About how Maya would slip into the role of ambassador for Ethan's relationship with Lorraine, smoothing over all the rough edges socially and professionally, and making it all okay. Ushering him into the future he wanted, just with someone other than Maya at his side.

Would she have done it? If she hadn't met Charlie, would she simply have tucked her tail between her legs and run back home to do Ethan's bidding now?

But she already knew the answer, nauseated as it might make her.

She was a Martin. And Martins did not behave irrationally. They were not motivated by emotion. They did what was expected of them and, whenever possible, exceeded those expectations.

She swiped through to her parents' most recent message and lifted the phone to her ear again.

"Everyone is sympathetic, of course," came her mother's frosty tones. "But surely it's time to handle the fallout and put your spin on it. It would be a shame if Ethan and that Lorraine were left in the position to have the final word on this mess. You must see that. Hiding away with your head in the sand never solved anything."

Maya wanted to laugh at that the way she'd laughed at everything else today, but couldn't quite get there.

Her heart was kicking at her again, because her immediate instinct was to leave her mobile tucked away, out of sight, again. And to run back out to that bed, crawl into it and lose herself in the sweet, shattering oblivion that Charlie offered.

But she was kidding herself.

Her life in Toronto wasn't going away, no matter how little she wanted to think about it here. She would have to go home soon enough, and when she did, there would be no big brawny American with all that danger stamped in his bones, just waiting to make her feel new. And alive.

Maya had claimed she wanted the truth. And he'd given it to her.

She could do no less than give herself the same courtesy.

And the truth was that Charlie terrified her.

He made her feel safe, sure, in a way that no one else ever had. Certainly not her frostbitten parents, who were forever disappointed in her. Or her sister, who always wanted to fix her. Or Ethan, who had seen her only in terms of a valuable merger. Things that were so obvious to her now she didn't understand how she'd failed to see them before.

But she knew color now. All the rowdy, boisterous color of the Amalfi coast. The shock of the flowers, the serene self-possession of the pastel houses.

And all that Italian sun, even in the dark of December.

She knew better now, and that was a gift.

Maya could never go back to the life she had before, and she knew that however painful this had all been, that was a gift, too.

Outside the window, the sky was beginning to lighten. Pinks were creeping in, hinting at the blue day to come.

Christmas was coming. The year was ending.

And Maya wasn't in any way the person she'd believed she was when she'd come here. The person she'd imagined she was all these years—the person she'd worked so hard to become.

Charlie had forced her to see herself.

And this was what she knew now. She couldn't be with a man like Ethan, so self-absorbed, so consumed with making the best argument no matter what, so convinced that he could monologue her into submission. She didn't want a life that was all compromise in such a cynical, deliberate way. She didn't want all those external markers. The right address. The right law firm. The impeccable pedigree.

None of the things she thought mattered had saved her from the humiliation of her wedding day. None of her successes had made her parents proud of her. Nothing she'd achieved had made Ethan love her or made Lorraine loyal.

But here on the Amalfi coast she'd abandoned everything she'd thought was true about herself. She'd had sex with a stranger. She'd gotten loud and dirty, publicly. Her attempt to prowl for more casual sex in a bar hadn't ended the way she'd thought it would, but she'd tried. She'd acted like someone else's daughter, for once. Someone who didn't care about appearances. Someone who would throw herself at a man she'd thought was a caretaker. A handyman.

She had let her libido lead her. And this was where it had led her.

To sex so raw and shattering that she'd forgotten her own name.

Intimacy so ferocious and all-consuming that she was still reeling, halfway into a panic attack.

Charlie was the antidote to Ethan. That was clear.

But she'd convinced herself that she was in love with him, and that was insanity.

It had been one thing when she'd believed that he was a shiftless laborer who'd ended up in Italy by accident. It had been easy then to sink into all the things he made her feel without worrying about what they meant or what repercussions those feelings could have.

It had been easy to imagine herself in love with a man she had known with a bedrock certainty she would leave behind forever when she left this place.

But Charlie wasn't a lackadaisical drifter, blown from here to there and back again as the whim took him—a kind of life Maya couldn't imagine or understand. He was one of the St. George heirs. He was a profoundly wealthy man. And he was powerful in ways that had nothing to do with that danger stamped all over him, but everything to do with the world Maya knew best.

There had been no possibility that she could really, truly get serious about the man she'd thought he was—and she knew exactly what that said about her.

But now…he'd come after her. She had dared him to be real and he'd more than met that challenge.

And the truth was, she thought as she stared out the window as dawn snuck its tendrils over the ocean, she hadn't been with Ethan by accident.

Maya didn't know what to do with *real*. With *raw*.

With emotional and physical intimacy—not just the shared life two people could build out of habit and goals.

It had been so much easier to feel persecuted. To be the victim, yet again. To wrap herself in her own self-righteousness, her own martyrdom, and console herself yet again that she was the one who loved and was lied to, even here in Italy where she'd gone to heal from the last betrayal.

She'd gotten a lot of mileage out of that, hadn't she?

But then Charlie had made her grab that headboard. And he'd taught her a very deep lesson about the reality of surrender. About what *real* meant in practical terms. About her own power and her own need.

Over and over.

Maya put her hands over her mouth to stifle the

huge sob that had been lurking in her chest since she'd woken up in such a panic.

She was in love with him. God help her, she'd fallen hard, and she didn't have the slightest idea how to crawl back out of that pit.

But none of that mattered, because the only love she knew how to give was shallow. If she'd loved Ethan deeply, or at all, she would have been broken now. Not…imagining herself in love with someone else. Not capable of arguing with Ethan on the phone as if they were debating where to get takeout. Not able to think about forgiveness for him or Lorraine ever, and certainly not so soon. How many times did she need to prove this to herself before she believed it?

Maybe the truth was that she was nothing but a sad, gray puddle reflecting bright colors she could see but not touch. But Charlie…

Charlie was like an ocean.

And Maya needed to get the hell out of here before she drowned.

CHAPTER ELEVEN

TORONTO WELCOMED MAYA back with a bitch of a
snowstorm, just in case she might have forgotten
where she lived.

It was like a very cold kick in the gut. But then,
leaving Italy had been a lot like peeling off her
soul with her fingernails and then leaving the best
parts of it behind, so what was a little Canadian
weather next to all that?

She hadn't waited for Charlie to wake up. It was
more accurate, in fact, to say that she had snuck
around to make sure he wouldn't. She'd thanked
her lucky stars that she was a light packer, because
it was easy to throw her things together in the dark.
She'd done it in a hurry, as if that drowning she
feared so much was imminent.

She'd been hurrying down the old stone stairs
toward the hotel lobby before she could think
twice. And she'd been in a taxi headed for Naples
before daylight had really broken over the sea.

Hurry, something in her had urged. *Hurry.*

If she slowed down, she would stay.

Maya didn't let herself look back.

She'd flown to Rome, then got herself on the first flight she could find back to Toronto.

And all the while, her heart had kept hammering at her. That same panic had gnawed at her, not lessening in the least the farther away she got from the man who made her feel…too much. Much too much.

When she'd landed in gray, listless Toronto, it had been easy to convince herself that everything that had happened in Italy had been a kind of daydream. Something gauzy that couldn't hold up against the grim approach of a long Canadian winter.

"I'm glad you finally came to your senses," her sister said sternly when Maya turned up at her door. "I understand you had a shock, but it's as if you've lost your mind these past few weeks."

"Maybe I did lose my mind," Maya agreed.

But she didn't think she meant it in the way Melinda did. The truth was that she'd shut off her mind for a change, or Charlie had, and it was amazing how many things her body had found to teach her.

She knew better than to say something like that

to her distressingly unimaginative and unroman-
tic sister.

Instead, she set about the practicalities of sep-
arating her life from Ethan's, because every day
she remained linked to him felt like torture. And
she didn't really care if that seemed dramatic. She
needed him unconnected to her by any means possible.

The snow was coming down hard and she was
hideously jet-lagged, but she thought it was absolutely perfect timing to swing by the condo the
morning after she arrived. Very early that morning. She let herself in with her key, letting the front
door slam shut behind her. Then she walked into
the center of the space she had so carefully curated
to reflect the up-and-coming couple she and Ethan
had been meant to be..

Looking around, it felt like she was standing
in a hotel room. Or a stranger's house. A place
that had nothing to do with her and never would.
She took a deep breath in and realized that it even
smelled…off. Not like hers.

It didn't take long for the two of them to emerge,
looking sleepy and something like scared when
they came out of the bedroom to find her waiting
there in her own damned kitchen.

"Are you crazy?" Ethan demanded.

Maya smiled. "I own half of this condo, Ethan. I'm not crazy. I'm home."

She was pleased she'd taken a little extra time with her appearance this morning. She had been trying to erase the signs of her international flight more than she'd been attempting to impress her ex, but no matter why she'd done it, it felt better to be dressed well. She knew she looked sleek and sophisticated, polished to a cool shine, while Lorraine's hair was a tangled mess and Ethan blinked like an owl from behind his glasses.

"If you want to yell at us, just yell at us," Lorraine said.

Bravely, as if she was prepared to suffer whatever was necessary for her great and abiding love.

Maya rolled her eyes as she unwrapped her scarf from around her neck. "I don't want to yell at you. What would be the point? I have no desire whatsoever to play into this forbidden-love, martyr fetish you two think you have going on. Let's be practical, please. You want to stay in this condo? Make me an offer."

Lorraine looked as if she might cry but refrained. Ethan, on the other hand, glared.

This was the part where she usually backed down, she knew. Where she offered an apology to ease the tension and then started agreeing to things.

But she wasn't that Maya anymore. She stared right back at Ethan until he was the one to look away. Then they sat down at the breakfast bar and started negotiating.

And a few hours later, they'd hammered out a deal.

When Maya staggered back out into the snow already blanketing her hometown and showing no signs of stopping, she let the cold shock her system, even bundled up against it as she was.

This is good, she told herself sternly. *You need to freeze. You need to put out that fire however you can.*

And over the next few days that was exactly what she did.

She stayed in her sister's guest room while she arranged for her things to be moved out of the condo and put into storage. She searched for new apartments online and, when the storm let up, toured them in person. She talked for a long time on the phone with the managing partner at her law firm and found it a whole lot easier to smooth things over than she had expected it to be. Of course she and Ethan could work together, and seamlessly. Of course there would be no "unfortunate romantic blowback" on the firm. Of course everything could carry on as it always had, because that was what the firm wanted most. But then, Maya didn't want revenge. She didn't want anything from Ethan. She wanted to move on from him as if he had never happened.

And in the meantime, she had to figure out how to live in the black-and-white world she'd created for herself when inside she still felt wild and raw with color. Bleeding with it. Dreaming in Technicolor at night and waking up with tears on her cheeks, a weight where her heart should have been and that terrible, aching fire between her legs.

It didn't help that it was the darkest part of the year. She tried to lose herself in the Christmas lights that fought off the night, telling herself they were a promise that the sun would return. That she would, too, if she held on long enough.

Sometimes she even pretended she believed it.

But she'd returned to Toronto. She had chosen to resume her real life—the one that had nothing to do with staggering Italian vistas or a man who roamed about the cliffs of the Amalfi coast like a lion in blue jeans. That meant she couldn't hide from her responsibilities, and this time of year was all about duty and putting on a brave face no matter her internal battles.

She had two parties to attend and no interest in either one of them. There was the law firm's annual holiday party, where no one had originally expected her to make an appearance because she'd been supposed to be off on her honeymoon. But of course, they all knew she was back by now. They would whisper if she didn't show up with a calm smile on her face, exuding the sort of competence that was expected of her.

After all, she was supposed to be a high-powered attorney. That meant she was expected to be unflappable—and what better way to prove it than this?

As if that wasn't enough, there was also her parents' annual Christmas Eve party, where she would also need to parade about in front of so many of her parents' friends and business associates, all of whom had been sitting in that chapel waiting for a wedding that didn't happen.

She would have to somehow spin her failure into triumph, her personal mess into strength— because she was a Martin. That was what was expected.

But as Maya lay there in the guest room in Melinda's tastefully stark and minimalist house, accented with important investment art, she honestly didn't know if she had it in her.

And she realized it was the first time in all her life that she hadn't simply assumed that she could do whatever was expected of her, somehow. If she worked hard enough. If she extended herself. If she was too afraid of the consequences to fail.

It all left a sour taste in her mouth, if she was honest.

But if she had intended to shirk her duties, she would have stayed in Italy with the only man—the only *person*—she'd ever met who could make her forget herself entirely.

And delightfully.

She had come home to Toronto, so she dressed for her company party with exquisite care even though she would have preferred to stay in bed with the covers over her head like the teenager she'd never been. She chose a sparkling gown that skimmed over her curves but showed almost nothing. Because there was a power in restraint.

And she needed to assure everyone she knew that despite what had happened, she had all the power.

She practiced her chilly, faintly pitying social smile all the way over in her taxi. It was an expression she had learned at her frosty mother's knee and intended to employ with impunity tonight. After all, it was up to her to show how deeply unbothered she was by the wreckage of her personal life. It was up to her to act as if she was the one in control, no matter that she was the one who had been left at the altar.

It didn't surprise her in the least that the first people she saw when she walked into the firm's self-consciously glamorous party, up there on its glittering top floor with views all over Toronto, were Ethan and Lorraine.

Looking significantly more pulled together than the last time she'd seen them, half-asleep in the condo.

"Let me guess," Maya said as she handed over her coat at the door. "You decided to wait for me. So we could make a calm, amiable entrance together."

"You know how important it is to get the optics right," Ethan bit out at her.

Very much as if Maya was the one who had caused an optics problem in the first place.

She opened her mouth to remind him that the optics had not been awesome when he'd abandoned her on their wedding day with most of the people he was so worried about sitting out there in the chapel, but reminded herself that, really, she didn't care.

Truly. Deeply. She didn't care enough to fight with him. She didn't care enough to try to make him feel bad when she knew he didn't. She might never understand how she could have imagined herself in love enough to marry him one day and void of any feeling for him at all so soon after, but she didn't have to.

What she knew was that she was free of him, whatever that meant, good and bad and everything in between.

Maya contented herself with rolling her eyes at Ethan and started toward the party. Then paused when she felt Lorraine's hand on her arm.

"Maya. Please. You know… You know I don't care about optics."

Ethan bit off Lorraine's name. Maya looked down at her best friend's hand, then up to her face. And it was still so…familiar. She knew the back of Lorraine's hand better than she knew her own.

Was this what she wanted? That tortured expression in Lorraine's gaze? Finally, the kind of self-awareness she'd always been certain her friend could never—would never—possess? Or the grief that hung between them?

The way, Maya thought then, it always would. For who they'd been. And worse maybe, who they hadn't been to and for each other.

"We can't go back, Lorraine," she said softly. "You must know that."

"I know it," Lorraine replied, her voice thick. "I

do." But she shook her head, in a show of restraint that Maya would have said she didn't possess. "Of course I know it. I just… I'm sorry."

She squeezed Maya's arm a little when she said it, as if to underscore the apology. Then let go.

And Maya didn't know what came over her then. She was the one who reached out and caught Lorraine's hand before she could pull it back. Only for a second. Just enough to get her friend's attention.

"There's no way back, but that doesn't mean that someday, some way, maybe we might find a way forward," she heard herself say. And nothing in her rebelled at that notion, so she thought it was possible she meant it. "Maybe."

Lorraine's gaze met hers, bright with emotion and all their shared history. All those years. The particular language and vast world they'd created between the two of them, the geography of which only they would ever know.

Their whole, complicated life together, which Maya could either cast aside forever, here and now, or try.

At some point, try.

"Maybe," Lorraine agreed, her voice shaky.

As if it was a promise.

And Maya felt lighter than she had since she'd

left Italy as she walked into the big room, packed tight with colleagues and clients. There was entirely too much speculation in the gazes that landed on her, Lorraine and Ethan on Lorraine's other side. Everyone got the optics, just as Ethan had wanted.

She put the smile she'd practiced on her face, she held her head high and she began to work the room.

After all, she was good at it.

But there was something missing as she moved from one gleaming knot of people to the next. She could still do her job. She could smile here, insert a witty comment there, act confident and at ease. As if nothing had happened.

And yet she felt as if she was wearing someone else's skin. As if she was a puppet, going through the motions.

This is black-and-white and gray straight through, something whispered inside her when she laughed politely at a very wealthy client's joke that wasn't the least bit funny. *When what you want to do is shine.*

She snuck away after she'd done an exhausting round of platitudes, evasions and pointed commentary. She made her way down the abandoned, hushed hall, letting herself into one of the executive-level washrooms. It was single use, which meant she could lock the door and take a deep breath in peace before avoiding her own reflection in the mirror.

Maya didn't have any business to take care of, so she simply stood there. Wishing she felt more like herself again. Or not herself—but the person she'd been the last time she'd stood on this floor, a year ago at this same party, absolutely certain that she knew every last facet of her beautiful future.

She let out a hollow laugh at that.

Then, when she thought she had no choice but to head back into the fray and resume smiling until her cheeks hurt, she marched over and threw open the door.

And then stopped, because she was apparently having a stroke.

Or maybe she'd fallen, there inside the washroom, and hit her head so hard that she was seeing things.

Because the man who stood there didn't make sense.

He was dressed in another dark, bespoke suit that licked over that lean, hard physique of his and made him...*more*, somehow. More dangerous. More beautiful. More *him*. His dirty-blond hair was raked back from his face, his beard made him look like some kind of pirate and his blue eyes blazed with a dark, consuming fury she could feel like a punch to the gut.

Because she knew it was all for her.

"Charlie…" she whispered, unable to make sense of this. He stood there with his hands in his pockets, his body looking relaxed when she could tell that he was nothing close to relaxed. At all. Quite the opposite. "You can't… How… You can't be here."

"Too bad for you, babe," he drawled, too much Texas and far too much lethal retribution in his rough, low, gorgeous voice. "Because I am. And that means you're pretty much fucked."

CHAPTER TWELVE

THE LOOK OF shock on Maya's face was about the only thing that Charlie had liked over the course of this past week.

Because otherwise he was pretty much out of his mind, he was so pissed off.

Pissed off, in fact, didn't really do it justice.

He took a breath and kept himself on lock-down—but it was a close call with Maya standing there in a dress that sparkled, her hair a pretty cloud of curls like a halo he wanted his hands in and that mouth of hers slightly ajar in disbelief.

God, she was beautiful. Even when he wanted to take her apart—preferably while they were both naked, so he could enjoy it—there was no getting away from the kick of her. She was too potent. Too perfect.

He had watched her work this obnoxiously slick party like a sharp blade through butter and realized he hadn't fully appreciated that she was good at more than rocking his entire world. But he could tell she was from the way the people in the room looked at her while she did it. The way they looked at the weak, skinny dumbass who had to be her ex, then back to her. Maya was the powerhouse, no doubt.

And she was his.

Something the two of them needed to get clear on. Fast.

"You snuck out in the middle of the night," he growled at her, making no particular attempt to rein in the menace. "You didn't just run off down the street or take a really long walk to clear your head. You left the fucking country."

He already couldn't handle how beautiful she looked tonight and she only made it worse when she lifted up that delicate chin of hers, like she thought she was tough. "I had to go. You don't understand."

"You're right, Maya. I don't understand."

He moved, deeply gratified when she reacted as if he'd electrified her. She moved back, and he followed her into the very high-class bathroom. And then it was the easiest thing in the world to lock them both in all that marble and wood, far away from any prying eyes.

She might not know it yet, but his woman was in a world of trouble.

"Lucky for you," he drawled, not lifting his glare from her for even a second, "I flew all the way here so you could explain it to me."

"You can't be here." She still looked and sounded panicked, but the words were coming easier for her. He wasn't sure that was a good thing. "This is a party filled with lawyers. You can't crash it. We tend to take a very dim view of that kind of thing."

"Let's be real clear that if I wanted to con my way into some stuffy corporate party, I could. Easily. But I didn't have to." He let his grin get edgy. "I was invited."

She had backed all the way across the small room, the ridiculously high heels she was wearing muffled by the thick carpeting. He watched as she put her back against the wall, like that might save her.

"I don't understand."

But he could see she did.

"I made myself a new client," he told her, enjoying himself. "Or did you forget that I'm not just a dirtbag fling? This dirtbag comes with a hefty bank account. In the St. George name, which doesn't mean shit to me, but got your boss all kinds of excited."

"Charlie…"

"So this is what I don't get," he said, ignoring her attempts to steer the conversation in some other direction. If that was what she was doing when she said his name like that. "You wanted raw. You demanded real. So I gave it to you. And your response to that was to take off."

"I'm sorry," she said quietly.

And that was almost enough for him, because he wanted his hands on her more than he wanted to talk about it. But then he remembered what it had been like to wake up that morning to find her gone. To have to hunt her down, only to find she'd already left Naples. And soon after that, Italy.

"I can't say it's a surprise, because I feel like we already discussed what a runner you are," Charlie continued, his voice rough. "But the fact I should have known you were going to do it didn't make it any better."

"I'm not *a runner*," she snapped at him. "You can't arbitrarily decide I'm a thing because I did it one time, under very specific circumstances."

"Oh, okay." He even smiled at her as he said that and was gratified when she shivered in response. "You're not a runner. You just…run away. Whenever things get intense. I'm sure it's all a real big coincidence."

"Things had run their course." And even though her dark eyes were glittering and much too bright, she aimed that smile at him that he'd seen her use out there in the party. Remote. Regal. "I'm sorry if you had other expectations."

"Are you letting me down easy?" He laughed. "Is that what this is?"

That smile of hers deepened into straight-up pity. "I like you, Charlie. I do. But Italy isn't real life. It's not my real life, anyway."

"And this is?" He pushed himself off the door and stalked toward her. And he wasn't evolved enough not to enjoy the way her eyes widened as he came for her. She was so beautiful. And so full of shit. And he wanted to get his mouth on her and his cock inside her, more than he wanted to breathe. "Rich people standing around in a fancy room talking about all the money they're going to make?"

She scowled at him. "A holiday isn't real life. That's why they call it *a holiday*. Real life is different. There are certain expectations—"

"You talk a lot about expectations." He crowded her against the wall when he got there, putting a forearm up to brace himself over her head. That let him get his mouth nice and close to hers. "But whose expectations are they?"

"Mine," she threw at him, but her voice was so soft she was almost whispering.

This close, he could see her pulse go wild in the sleek, brown line of her throat. He could smell the scent of her, a hint of something delicate with notes of citrus.

He wanted to feast on her.

"You don't sound sure, babe."

She lifted her hands to his chest, as if to push him away. But she didn't.

"A wedding that didn't happen isn't a good enough reason to give up everything I've spent my life working for. It would be absurd to throw it all away based on a few days and some very bad behavior in Italy."

Charlie had been furious for days. It had settled in him like granite, heavy and harsh. It had taken a solid forty-eight hours to track her. Then another day or so to plan his course of action. To figure out she would be at this party and how best to get himself through the door. And he had done all of that with the same drumbeat of temper inside him, spurring him on.

Now—finally—she was right there in front of him, and that fury…shifted.

Into something a hell of a lot more like determination.

He was pretty scary when he was mad. But when he was determined? He was relentless.

Charlie almost felt sorry for her.

He pushed back so he could hold her gaze, and he liked the way she trembled. Her lips parted when he dragged his thumb over them, lazy and a little dirty. And he loved the way her body melted beneath his touch. He could see the heat in her dark, wide eyes.

He didn't say anything.

He kept himself braced against the wall and used his free hand to trace his way down her neck, applying just enough pressure to make her breath catch. Then he went lower, skirting her breasts so he could make it down to her hip.

She was already panting as if he was buried deep inside her, thrusting deep.

Soon, baby, he promised her.

He took his time reaching down, pulling up the hem of her long dress until he had it drawn up around her waist.

"Charlie..."

But she didn't tell him to stop.

He reached between her legs, cupping her pussy and applying pressure there, too. Over and over again, until he made his own rhythm through the pointless barrier of her panties. And better yet, she was lifting her hips to meet him.

Like she couldn't help herself.

"Now," he said, with a great satisfaction he made no attempt to hide. "Let's have a little discussion about truth."

"I told you the truth." But her voice was different now, rich with all that need and longing, and she bumped herself against his hand as she spoke.

"Here's what you need to know about me, Maya. I'm an all-in kind of a guy. If my stepfather hadn't died, I would have pledged myself to his bullshit forever, because that's how I roll. He raised me and I respected that. And I don't do anything by half. You asked me for real, I gave it to you, and you couldn't handle it."

"That's not true."

He made a sound like he was disappointed in her, but while he did it, he found his way beneath the soaked cotton of her panties.

And found her slippery and hot, and all this no matter what she said.

"You spent a lot of time telling me what a liar I was, and here you are. Lying to my face."

"It's not about what I can handle, Charlie," she panted at him. "It's about reality."

He dropped his mouth to her ear, circling that haughty little clit of hers while she bucked against his hand and proved herself a liar.

"This is reality, Maya. You're wet. I'm hard. And whether you know it or not, you're mine."

"You can't—"

"I told you I was possessive. Did you think I was kidding?"

She rocked her head back. There was moisture in the corners of her eyes as she met his gaze, her own wide and tortured and still filled with all that heat.

He traced her melting-hot folds as she fought to catch her breath. Again and again, until her hands turned into fists pressed hard against his pectoral muscles.

"I don't know how to do this." She didn't sound like herself, which was a good thing, because Charlie had left the version of himself he recognized behind a long time ago. "It's too raw. It's too much. I'm no good at it. I like things that are cut up into little pieces. Palatable. Small and so insignificant that if you lose one, you can go right on as if it didn't matter."

"Don't talk to me about other men when I'm the one making you wet, Maya."

"I'm not—"

"I'm not bite-size, babe. Too big. Too noisy. Too much, definitely. You're not afraid of any of that. You're afraid that you like it."

"I'm not afraid. I'm realistic."

"You're scared out of your mind." He leaned closer, scraping her throat with his teeth. And when she shuddered, he twisted his wrist and sent two fingers deep into her greedy little pussy. "You think I don't know why? You're not in control when you're with me, and you hate how much you love that."

"You don't… You're not…"

But she couldn't seem to finish the sentence, too busy was she lifting those lush hips of hers to meet each thrust of his fingers.

And he wasn't done talking.

"You're not going to control me. I'm not a handyman you can get fired if he pisses you off. With me, Maya, you're just a woman. A beautiful, horny woman who can't get enough of the way I take you apart."

He felt her tighten around his fingers, but she didn't hurtle over that edge. He didn't let her.

"Please, Charlie…"

"I make you beg, and you don't like that. I make you feel things, and you *really* don't like that." He kept up his pace, deeper and more deliberate with each stroke. "The reason you were so mad that I didn't tell you who I was isn't because you're upset at the idea that I might own that hotel. I think we both know that you thought that if I really was some no-account janitor, you got to be in control."

He laughed at that, there against her neck so it made her shudder. And then he stopped thrusting, keeping his palm heavy against her pussy but no longer giving her the friction she needed to come.

Leaving her there, strung out on that edge.

"Tough luck, babe. You don't get to control this."

"But you do?" she managed to pant at him.

He dropped his arm so he could cup her beautiful face, and he grinned at her. Lazy, full of himself and dirty as hell.

"Yeah, I do," he said. "Because that's how you like it."

She made a noise he'd never heard before. It sounded as if it was cracking open from deep inside her. Wild. Crazy. So insane and beautiful it nearly made him come, he liked it so much.

"I can't do this," she threw at him, loud. Like she'd forgotten there was a roomful of reality right down the hall.

"But here you are. Doing it."

"I can't give you what you want," she said. He heard the echo of his own words in that.

Still, he smiled at her, his fingers sunk deep in all her clinging heat. "You can. You will."

"How can I when I don't know what that is?"

And that, finally, was raw. An open wound, scraping them both.

But it was real. And that was what this was. That was the whole point.

"You're not going to know," he told her gruffly. "Don't you get it? You give everything. And I give everything. And it's scary sometimes. And hard. And fucking worth it, Maya. That's the point."

"Charlie…" She still sounded like her words were being torn out of her. "You can't say things like that. There are some things you can't take back."

"I don't want to take it back. I didn't fly all the way to Canada and subject myself to a room full of lawyers to take anything back. Catch up, Maya. This is already happening."

And he couldn't wait anymore.

He twisted his fingers, there in her sweet, hot pussy. And this time when he surged into her, he made sure to press down on her clit with each stroke.

And she went off like a rocket. She shook around him, shattering the way he wanted her to, her hips bucking wildly against his hand.

He still thought that watching her come was the best view he'd ever have, in this life or the next.

When Maya opened her eyes again, there was

water and there was light, and there was something else, too.

She made that noise again, wild and untamed.

As if she'd been set free.

Then she surged up on her toes, claiming his mouth in a ferocious kiss that he felt like fire poured down the length of his spine. She kissed him hard, deep. And then she launched herself against him, wrapping her legs around him.

When he held her there, his cock lined up perfectly with all that soft heat and her back against the wall, she reached down and fought him to open his fly.

"Hurry," she commanded him as he released himself and swept the head of his cock through all that sweet heat he'd made.

"Yes, ma'am," he drawled, like the humble and polite cowboy he'd never been and never would be.

And Charlie slammed himself home.

For a long while then, that was all there was. The perfection of the way she gripped him. The sweet slide of all that heat.

Hot. *His.*

And this time, when he pounded her over the edge, he went with her, because this was the promise they'd made. This was the kind of vow he'd view as blood. Sacred. And forever.

He held her there, still deep inside her, as the storm passed.

And when she opened her eyes, so deep and brown, he thought she could see all the way into his battered soul.

But what the hell. He welcomed it.

And not only because she made him feel brand-new.

"Everything," Maya said solemnly. "We both give everything."

"Everything," he agreed.

"Charlie…" She said his name in that way again, like a breath. And then this time, finally, she finished it. "I love you."

It made him hard all over again, thick and deep inside her.

He grinned down at her, because she was perfect. Because he was an all-in kind of a guy, and this was the best all in he could imagine. The rest would work itself out.

He had absolutely no fucking doubt.

"Babe." And he let his grin widen, because she felt like forever, she was entirely his and he planned to celebrate that the best way he knew how. "I know you do."

CHAPTER THIRTEEN

WHEN SHE DECIDED to truly disappoint her family, friends and employers, Maya threw herself into it with all the focus and intensity she'd brought to every other part of her life so far.

She led Charlie out of that washroom and straight into her world, as if she'd always been planning to put him right there into the center of it.

And once she stepped off the track she'd been on all this time—mindlessly, desperate to live up to other people's standards—Maya found everything she wanted was right there, waiting for her. Like international law offices in Rome that would love an attorney with her experience. There were options everywhere she looked.

It was possible she had only ever been as trapped as she'd wanted to be.

She used her parents' traditional Christmas Eve party to introduce him to her family, employing that very particular smile her mother had taught her—because it turned out, using it on her mother was a delight all its own.

"I was expecting more of a rebellion," she complained to Charlie after the party. "A big fight right next to the Christmas tree, you know. Something substantial."

"Parents love me," he said smugly, pulling her over his lap in the back of the car as the driver braved the frozen Christmas Eve streets.

"Mine love that you're a St. George," Maya corrected him, because of course they did. Her parents were nothing if not adaptable when it allowed them to be more mercenary.

"Whatever works," Charlie said against her mouth.

And then used those wicked hands of his to risk arrest, right there in the back seat, where she had to bite his shoulder to keep the sounds she made inside.

She never did find herself a new apartment in Toronto. She stayed in Charlie's hotel room instead, where he taught her more things about herself, one after the next. And they both taught each other about intimacy, so shattering and full and impossibly bright that it was clear to Maya there was no way she could ever resign herself to black-and-white or gray again.

"Marry me," he said, when he tied her up to

the bed in his hotel room and made her scream. As usual.

"You mean someday," she clarified later.

After she'd agreed, because she would have agreed to anything. And because she wanted to marry him, no matter how crazy that sounded. And after he'd made her come too many times to count, here in her deliciously ruined life that it turned out she liked. More than liked.

His mouth moved into that wicked curve that still made her heart pound. Maybe it always would.

"I don't mean someday. I mean now."

"Now?" she repeated, unable to pretend she wasn't shocked by the notion.

It was Christmas morning. Outside, the snow came down relentlessly.

And his eyes were so blue she kept forgetting herself and imagining they were back in Italy.

"I love you," he told her, with all the raspy solemnity of a sacred vow. "You can take five years to think about it if you want, but that's not going to change. So why wait?"

Maya knew all the reasons to wait. Because it was smart. Because it was practical. Because it was realistic, most of all, to take one's time before making such a huge decision—especially on the heels of the last marital decision she'd made.

But she'd already tried that route. She'd already lived that life.

And she loved Charlie a whole lot more, with every part of herself she hadn't known was there, in ways she had never loved Ethan. Or anything else.

"Why wait?" she asked, feeling giddy.

And better yet, safe.

This time, without the attendant panic.

Later that evening, at her parents' house, she announced their intentions. And found she didn't care, at all, when her entire family reacted with something less than the sheer bliss she felt.

Charlie held her hand, playing with the ring he'd put there, while her father lectured about caution, and somehow that gave Maya the patience and strength to smile her way straight through.

A real smile, this time. Because of all the gifts Charlie had given her, that was the one she thought she might love the most.

Whatever else they were, they were real. Together, they would always be real.

Her family might have given in to their dramatic side on Christmas, but they were Martins. And accordingly, a week later, they all stood there on New Year's Day while Maya and Charlie pledged themselves to each other forever, as if this had been the plan all along.

Her frosty parents even rustled up a smile.

"You know you'll come back here in a few months, wondering why I didn't stop you from making this mistake," Melinda couldn't resist muttering after the ceremony.

Maya eyed her sister. "If I do, you don't have to fix me."

Melinda looked startled. "I don't... That's not what I meant."

And Maya reached out and put an arm around her. "You don't have to be my doctor, Melinda," she said softly. "You can just be my sister."

She told herself it was progress when all Melinda did was blink at that.

"Everyone thinks we're crazy," Maya said with a laugh when Charlie bundled her into the car, headed for the airport and the plane that would take them back to Italy.

Where, she'd decided on yet another whim, they would stay. Because they could.

Because her life had been plotted out from day one. And now it was hers to do with as she wished.

And what she wished, more than anything, was to make it *theirs*.

Bright blue, shot through with all that color, and as raw and intimate and perfect as the two of them could manage.

Charlie looked over his shoulder, then shrugged in that way that made her stomach turn over in glee as he looked back at her.

"Who cares what they think? All you have to worry about is what I think."

"What do you think?"

"I think," he drawled, all that Texas and fire threaded through his voice, "that we're going to start with naked, work our way up to barefoot and pregnant, and figure out that happily-ever-after shit. In fact, I guarantee it."

And Maya didn't know how that would work. For the first time in her life, she didn't know what the plan was.

So she leaned into Charlie. *Her husband.* And she melted into the arm he put around her, and let it all happen.

One after the next.

Just as he promised.

* * * * *

MY ROYAL SURRENDER

RILEY PINE

MILLS & BOON

CHAPTER ONE

Z

I GAPE AT my outfit in the gilded full-length mirror—if a fishnet chemise, red leather G-string and matching choker with the word *slave* bedazzled across the front in black crystals could be described as an outfit.

"Oh no. No. No. No. Not a chance in hell." My vigorous head shake doesn't budge a single strand of thick hair from my lacquered topknot. "I can't step out of this room. Look at me! I'm practically naked."

It's not as if I'm a prude, either. On the rare occasion that I'm granted R & R, I'm more than happy to rock a skimpy bikini. But the French Riviera isn't waiting outside these walls. Feather and I are in downtown London, and I can't appear in public without proper knickers. I might be undercover…but I deserve proper underwear.

"But, love, that's the whole idea, innit?" Feather,

an avant-garde designer on the payroll of the British Intelligence Agency, smooths her asymmetric skirt while fluttering an impressive set of false eyelashes. "It's the perfect cover. One look at your jubblies and no one in the Lion's Den will imagine you're a kick-ass secret agent. They'll be too busy wanting to reach for a paddle. You look well fit."

"Oh, joy." My gaze connects with hers in the mirror and my whiskey-brown eyes narrow in mock ferocity. Feather's bright blue lipstick matches her eyes as she winks.

I don't return her saucy smile because lighthearted tone or not, Feather isn't joking. And while ridiculous, this situation isn't remotely funny. The Lion's Den is London's most notorious kink club, and in less than an hour I'll be walking through its depraved black doors, all my goods on full display.

This is what I've wanted. Plotted for. Dreamed of.

But in these dreams, I was always fully dressed.

"Come on." Feather clicks her tongue like a scolding schoolteacher. "Don't be a brat."

I exhale a frustrated breath, but damn it, she is right. I have to suck up my reservations for the good of the mission—and in this case that means going undercover to help British Intelligence as a BDSM aficionado. It's a far cry from last week, when I sported a chic Chanel suit and nude Louboutin heels while running the Hong Kong office for the Order, a top-secret international agency whose mission is simple: protect the world from itself. Order agents are carefully curated and come from all nations and walks of life to prevent wars, dispose despots and foil terrorist attacks. Sometimes we help out partners such as the CIA, Mossad or, in this case, my home country of jolly old England.

No one in mainstream society knows the Order exists, and it's better for everyone that way.

I'm a trained assassin, fluent in seven languages, an expert in poisons and knife play. I've worked my currently bare arse off to become a powerful, take-no-shit woman. Not someone who enjoys wearing a collar and parading about like an overprimped lapdog.

"I was instructed to pass along the final mission briefing after you were dressed." Feather hands over a sealed manila envelope. It's marked with a black marker slash—Z. That's how I'm known in the Order. All agents are assigned a random one-or two-letter name, our true identities protected even from those we work with. The name I was born with, Lora Summers, only daughter of a Cornwall couple whose boat sank off the coast of Calais, doesn't exist anymore. My records were purged right down to my birth certificate.

I'm a ghost. I've been one for years.

To work in the Order means to sacrifice the individual for the good of the group. Husband. Children. Simple Sunday mornings doing crosswords and eating leisurely breakfasts. Lives civilians take for granted, little acts of normalcy, have been denied me for the better part of two decades. But as I enter my early forties I can't help reconsidering my place in the world.

Maybe it's a midlife crisis, but the thought niggles like an itch that I can't scratch.

What if I want a new life?

"I'll fetch you a glass of cab sav," Feather mutters, the pucker between her plucked brows revealing a twinge of annoyance at my recalcitrance. "I know it's your favorite, and you need to loosen up before the Dom arrives."

My heart skips its next beat as the room's temperature seems to rise ten degrees.

The Dom. The Dominant. The man who is supposed to play the role of my master.

I try to snort and roll my eyes. *As if.*

Feather snickers and I know I've played the part she expects. Agent Z is a wordly badass.

Little does she know.

As Feather clicks out the hotel room door in her high-heeled boots, I rip open the envelope with shaking hands. The mission brief is printed in a pale green ink, sourced from the Nightshadow plant found only on the southern coast of an islet off Sumatra. The Nightshadow ink will fade in a few more minutes…leaving the paper utterly blank and these words undectable.

Mission: Lion's Den
Posing as "King" and "Princess," you and your assigned partner will infiltrate the Lion's Den and attempt to connect with club owner Dante Price. When not presiding as the ruler of Britain's kink underworld, Price allegedly smuggles arms to terrorist cells throughout Central Asia in return for heroin. We need concrete proof to get an arrest warrant. This means gaining his trust and being believable in your respective roles. Please note that sex acts (real, not simulated) and BDSM role-play are to be expected and embraced for authenticity. Both you and your fellow agent have been cleared for sexually transmitted diseases as per Order policy, and your hormonal birth-control shot is up-to-date.

It's not until I finish reading the mission that I taste the metallic flavor of blood. I've bitten the inside of my cheek so hard that I broke the flesh.

The sight of Dante Price's name will do that to a person.

Me more than most...

Dante Price is the baddest of bad guys. He makes a business out of chaos, profiting from human misery. Now he is mine for the taking. Not that this is a surprise.

I've waited to get him for years. It's finally time, and I'm ready. But that doesn't mean it will be easy. In fact, this will be the hardest mission I've ever done in more ways than one.

"Fuck me," I mutter, dropping the note to the floor.

"Sorry, love, it appears that will be my job," a deep voice growls from my left, and just like that the balcony door slides open, and in steps a blast from my past. The moment I've been waiting for with equal parts anticipation and dread.

He's over six feet tall and built like a swimmer, all broad shoulders and a trim waist; his flat abs are shown off to perfection by the tight tee over a pair of faded, low-slung black jeans. His close-cropped dark hair is flecked with strands of silver that match the small, sharp spikes gleaming along the arms of his leather jacket.

"Max?" My voice is nothing but a squeak. Not exactly the sultry, bored intonation I'd been re-hearsing for weeks in anticipation of this encounter.

"Agent X," he corrects coolly, his icy expression traveling my exposed body. "Nice to finally meet you in person... Agent Z."

"I..." A lifetime flashes past me in the span of seconds. This powerful silver fox with the wolfish expression was my first lover. After falling for each other at Frasier Academy, the Highland boarding school we both attended once upon a time, we stole away for a weekend to France. Maybe a cramped bed at a dodgy inn isn't the most romantic place for two teens to lose their virginities, but it was for me and Max—because it was *us*.

Before words like *duty* and *mission* replaced *hope* and *love*.

"Right. Well. You and I are going to have some serious catching up to do." He mutters the understatement of the year before glancing at his Rolex with a frown. "But that little reunion will have to wait. We're going to be late if we don't leave now."

It's only then that I register the tic in his jaw. The quiet, suppressed fury.

He is seriously pissed about this situation, and I can't blame him.

The room seems to spin, but I don't falter or faint.

He disappeared at eighteen, breaking my heart into a million tiny pieces. It wasn't until ten years later, well after I became Agent Z, that I discovered the full story of what happened to him. He had been recruited by the Order, as well.

I should have stayed away. But just over three years ago, I emailed him from the Hong Kong office, a short, perfunctory message on an arrest for a sex trafficker from Belgium.

He responded, asking a few clarifying questions, and we struck up a conversation of sorts.

And against every bit of my common sense, I eventually asked for a meeting. He had no idea I was Lora from Frasier Academy. He just knew me as Z. And I made damn sure he never saw my face. At my request, he wore a blindfold to every one of our meetings. I wore one, too. Mostly. It was for protection. So we couldn't betray each other if we ever fell into the wrong hands.

And so we began our torrid little affair.

In this way, I was able to have my lover back. He never recognized my voice or my body. I had more curves with age and made sure when I spoke to him it was only ever in a husky whisper.

I deceived him.

Now he knows the truth, and I don't have time to explain. Tonight we are assigned to a job where we are to revel in desire, where I'm to serve his every command. And from the way his nostrils flare as he opens the door, holding it for me, I realize that I'm about to be literally and figuratively fucked.

"Ready, Princess?" X asks.

But his expression is hard. I would bet he doesn't take deceit lightly. If the tables were turned, I'd be hell-bent on revenge, and I wonder with a tinge of both fear and desire if he feels the same.

"Of course, Your Highness," I drawl. "Lead the way."

X

My molars crush against each other as we slip into the Jaguar limousine; any more pressure and they'll shatter. The driver, a junior agent who can barely grow peach fuzz, closes the door behind us before reappearing again in the driver's seat.

"Pardon me for saying so, but I'm quite looking forward to this assignment, Agents X and Z. Your missions are legendary, both of you." His enthusiasm is mixed with his northern English accent. "I mean, X, that time you drove a Rolls-Royce onto the top of a train and then had to jump off? *With* an Edenvale prince in the car with you, no less!"

I open my mouth to cut him off, but the bloke barely takes a sip of air before rambling on again.

"And Agent Z—you wing walked from one plane to another, entered the aircraft from the storage hold and landed the beast after both the pilot and copilot had been *poisoned*. And you got them to the hospital in time to save them!"

I raise a brow at this, turning my attention to Lora. I mean—Agent Z.

The woman who has been fucking me—and with me—for years.

"That was you?"

She simply shrugs.

The rook—the Order's name for agents in training before they earn their crow's-feather tattoo—opens his mouth to speak again, but I press the button to close the soundproof partition.

"Thank you. That will be all for now," I say as the tinted glass slides shut, his eager young profile disappearing before he can protest.

The kid doesn't realize this gig isn't all about catching bad guys. It's about learning that the world isn't black-and-white, but merely shades of gray.

And the scantily dressed woman beside me is the grayest of gray characters.

Z stares out the window as we pull away from the curb, and I stare at her thigh-high black stiletto boots, the smooth-as-silk skin of her legs barely covered by the black netting of her—hell, I don't know what you call it, but whatever it is, it shows off every dip and swell of her curves. Beneath it, she's covered by a leather G-string and ruby-red

pasties that form an X over each nipple as if she's
marked them just for me. Coincidence—or another one of Lora's attempts to further toy with
me? It doesn't matter. She looks bloody fantastic,
and though I would never admit it to her, it will
require little effort for me to play my part tonight.
We're the same age, and if I saw her on the street I
wouldn't imagine she was a day over thirty. Whatever genetics are in her lithe body deserve a prize.

Fuck her for fucking me all those times and
knowing it was me.

"You never struck me as the type who played
games," I say with practiced nonchalance. If she
thinks I'm going to give her a big dramatic performance, she's got another think coming. She's
played me with ice-cold precision for years, so I'm
dialing the temperature to Antarctic levels.

She rolls her eyes but doesn't peel her gaze from
the window.

"And you said you loved me and disappeared
without a trace," she snaps. "Potato, po-tah-to,
Max. You were playing your little spy games years
before I was even recruited—years when I didn't
know if you were alive or dead. Don't try to tangle
with me or I'll tie you in knots."

"X," I say, my jaw tight. "I'm Agent X now. You
want to know what happened when they ripped me
from my life at Frasier? Max Vandenberg died a

thousand deaths until nothing of him remained. All that's fucking left is X."

She finally turns her head, her dark eyes meeting mine. "If you ever really loved me," she says coolly, "you'd have known it was me even with the blindfold. But you didn't. You never had a clue."

As if choreographed to her words, the car rolls to a stop.

The driver knocks on the partition. I tap out Morse code in response, permitting him to open the partition.

"King... Princess...we have reached our destination. Welcome to the Lion's Den."

I straighten my spiked jacket over my T-shirt and open the door to the dark alley that hides the club's entrance. I unclip the leash from my belt and turn to Z, tossing it onto the seat next to her.

"Should be as easy as jumping from one plane to another," I taunt. "Or as lying to a lover."

A muscle ticks in her jaw as she lets loose a soft growl.

"Careful, love," I tell her. "You're the sub, remember? You need to sell it."

She sneers at me as her knees fall open and she clips the leash to a ring on the crotch of her G-string.

I grab the free end and give her a slight tug, imagining the cool metal sliding against her folds.

My cock goes rigid, traitor that it is. But I take satisfaction in Z's slight squirm against the leather seat.

"When I say come, you come," I tell her, then lead her out of the car. It takes every ounce of effort not to allow my mind to wander to the dalliances we've shared over the years. The vise grip of her pussy on my cock. Goddamn it, she'd open so wide for me. She gave me everything except for the truth.

For the seconds we stand next to each other, she leans close and whispers in my ear. "If we make it out of here alive, I'm going to kill you."

I chuckle, though I know it's only partly a joke. Agent Z's reputation with the blade is legendary. As is her talent for escape. No one can capture her.

"I look forward to it, *Princess*."

And then I stride farther into the alley, the slack on the leash the determiner of how many paces she'll walk behind me.

Yes, we're playing our assigned roles, but it also allows me to case our surroundings and for her to have my back should I miss anything.

Not that I ever do.

I count the doors, none of them lit, and stop at the fifth one—an indistinct black door recessed in the nondescript redbrick rear wall of the building.

A camera above the door clicks and whirs as

we approach. Then the door falls open, revealing a dimly lit stairwell.

I wrap the leash around my hand and give it a soft pull.

Z sucks in a sharp breath and my nostrils flare. Fuck. I capture the scent of her erotic aroma.

"Tell me what's on the other side of that ring," I say, because it's either that or throw her up against the wall and take her bareback, thrust my cock in her to the root, make her milk every last drop of come out of me and see if that gets my head on straight.

She grits her teeth. "Make me."

CHAPTER TWO

Z

I HATE HOW my toes are cramped inside these ridiculous pointy boots. I hate the way the glue from my pasties itches my sensitive areolas. I hate the way London's autumn night chill pebbles my exposed skin with gooseflesh. But most of all, I hate how wet I am. I swear if I look I'll see my arousal shimmering on my thighs in a telltale gleam.

My body is compact and muscular, an instrument of death, honed to fatal precision, and yet with Max—*no, X*—looming over me, smelling vaguely of pine, oiled leather and mountain rain, my defenses crack. A part of me, a part that feels quite achy at present, wants to rub against his powerful form like a feral cat in heat, purring that he can use me any way that he sees fit. To acknowledge him as my master. My G-string is soaked and my mouth waters, remembering the velvet feel of his cock on my tongue.

But I got to where I am in the Order by being competitive, and I am compelled to answer the challenge in his eyes.

"As you wish," he growls and tugs me forward.

The wet leather of my G-string goes tight against my pussy, the cold metal of the leash ring skimming my clit. But I don't allow so much as a whimper to escape my lips. Keeping my face carefully bored, I clip down the steps behind him, concentrating on my balance and cursing the day that I ever begged my parents to send me to Frasier Academy. My life would have been easier if I never knew this man existed, because ever since I've been trapped in his orbit, it's as if he exerts his own gravitational pull.

No matter how many years I've known him, I can't get used to his presence. He's as addictive as heroin. The sexual chemistry between us could blow up Western Europe.

He glances behind and scowls. "Eyes down, Princess."

"Excuse me?" I bristle.

A muscle in his jaw ticks. "So help me, my sub will be well trained. Turn your gaze to the ground. You don't make eye contact with anyone unless I order you to, is that understood?"

"Fine," I spit. He's right. I have to be professional. Even if my job is requiring me to play a role that I hate.

He tugs my leash. "Yes, sir."

My breath hitches as my pussy responds to the pressure, and he snorts.

"Yes, sir," I mumble, lowering my gaze, my cheeks pink not from embarrassment but barely controlled fury. And still I want to lick every contour of the muscles beneath his Dom outfit.

"I might enjoy this gig after all," he says, almost to himself.

I glare at the floor, unsure whom I hate more. Him? Or me and my damn weakness.

And just like that we are at the bottom of the stairs. X pushes apart thick black velvet curtains, and we enter the Lion's Den.

Throbbing Euro trance music mingles with the sound of a woman's breathless moans. I dare a quick glance to my left to see a woman trussed up in what appears to be clothesline as a muscular man in head-to-toe latex pumps her slit with a fat crimson dildo while tugging her nipple clamps. A crowd gathers around them, clearly enjoying the spectacle from the way they stroke their exposed erections or finger their shaved pussies. At their feet, slaves kneel, heads down, men and women, all submissives waiting on the pleasure of their masters.

On the other wall, a young man is chained to a giant metal X while a dominatrix in a purple corset and crotchless panties paddles his exposed ass with an ebony cane.

Sprawled across a dining table in the center of the room, a nubile blonde stretches out, her naked body covered in small pastries. Dominants lounge in chairs around her, occasionally plucking a delight from her body as if she was nothing but a dessert plate.

Shocked, I return my gaze to the ground, grateful for a moment not to be the one in control. My thighs tremble as heat licks my core. It's like entering a sexual circus and erotic fun house.

It's not that I'm a prude. After all, for the last three years, I've been X's secret lover, allowing him to penetrate me in anonymous cars and hotel rooms all over the continent. But here I am out of my element. Cries of agony and ecstasy hit me on all sides. It's as if I'm a child, Alice of *Through the Looking-Glass*, and entering a wonderland of sexhibition.

"Hello, hello," I hear a woman purr in a throaty voice, addressing X. "Your little one is delicious."

"She is, isn't she?" X answers smugly, as if I'm a toy he's proud of.

And for the moment, I suppose that's exactly what I am.

"There's going to be a black-sheet party starting in the red room soon, very exclusive, invitation only."

I don't flinch. I don't give a sign that I recognize this woman. That she might view me as her friend.

Her name is Caro, and I'm about to stab her in the back—not literally, of course, unless she happens to get in my way. I have to be ruthless to succeed in this mission.

"Oh?" From the sound of X's voice, the frost and ice made flesh, he feels the same way.

It's not as if I'm unprepared for the mission. I did my research on fetish clubs. But even still…the butterflies darting around the pit of my stomach seem to have developed quite a case of stage fright.

"I'd love to play with your slave, if you're into sharing."

I jerk. *No!* That wasn't part of my plan.

Caro is taking advantage. I've been cultivating her friendship for years, a target who has been a henchwoman to the most wanted man in Europe. But she's a pain in the ass, and any traces of guilt I feel about my coming betrayal vanishes in an instant.

"I'm not," X snaps. "But I'll accept the invite."

Caro offers a sultry giggle. "This is your first time here, is it not? I make it my business to know all the clients."

"You own this place?" X asks nonchalantly; as if he could care less.

"Me?" Her giggle turns to an outright laugh. "Not at all. Daddy does."

Daddy. My lips almost twist in a sneer.

"I'm not a big fan of small talk," X announces abruptly. "Go ahead and lead the way."

"Okay, but if you aren't taking part in the fun, you need to stand on the side and remain quiet."

"Understood." X tugs my leash, and with a delicious shudder through my pussy, we're off again.

Daddy is Dante Price. The lord of this hell. And he is here, watching somewhere close by, and Caro is his head henchwoman.

A few twists and turns down a narrow hallway and the music fades into the background, even as the moans increase. My boots are washed in a rich red light. We must have arrived.

Without raising my chin, I dare to lift my gaze.

Busted. X is staring right at me. But that's not what causes me to gasp.

It's the fact that behind him, undulating over a twenty-foot mattress covered in black silk sheets, a full-on orgy is underway.

X

My jaw tightens as I tug Z's leash. I can feel her hesitation. Despite her outfit and willingness to play slave to my dom, she isn't prepared for this.

"I meant what I said," I whisper in her ear. "I don't share."

This time when I yank the cord, she follows more freely. She trusts my word, and she has no reason not to. I've never lied to her—aside from when I disappeared over two decades ago.

A chorus of moans erupts from all ends of the giant silk-covered mattress. A woman propped on her hands and knees gives oral pleasure to a man while receiving the same from a woman who lies beneath her. What seem like disembodied hands reach for Z. Before I can step between her and one of her admirers, someone succeeds in grabbing a handful of her net chemise.

She opens her mouth, likely to scream, so I don't waste a second. I cover her lips with my palm and wrap my other arm around her torso, wrenching her free.

"She's mine," I say coolly, dragging Z to a corner alcove, the last remaining free one in the room.

I know that Z can hold her own against anyone in this room, but I also know that she is out of her element here, whereas I've frequented clubs such as this across the globe. Never, though, with a partner and certainly not one who in my younger years took both my innocence and my heart.

Despite my feelings about Z's betrayal, if anyone else in this room lays a hand on her, I'll cut the appendage off before the assailant has time to blink.

I hold her body flush to mine, my cock rigid against her lush, firm ass.

"Twelve o'clock, nine o'clock, six o'clock," I whisper.

She nods, noting each alcove that hosts a dom and a sub in "private" one-on-one sex play.

From the intelligence I've collected, Price doesn't engage in the group acts, but he watches them. Those he finds most *entertaining* he invites into his private viewing room. All we need is to get a private audience with him and then we plant the seed. "Do you remember your role?"

She slams her ass into my cock, and I grunt from both the pleasure and the pain.

"I take that as a yes," I growl into her ear.

Anyone who wants to do business with Price needs an in. This is ours. Once we get an official invite, we become business associates of an arms trader who wants to check out Price's inventory.

I wrap my end of the leash around my wrist and spin Z to face me.

"Nothing we haven't done before, right?" I say bitterly. "And I've got something that'll make it like old times." I pull a silk blindfold from my pocket and tie it over her eyes.

"Fuck you, X," she hisses.

I grin. "That *is* the plan." Then I press a palm to her shoulder. "Now *kneel*, Princess, and show me how you worship your king."

She obeys, playing the part of the good little sub. But once on her knees, she does nothing more.

"Did I stutter, Princess?"

"No, Highness," she answers, whatever expression her eyes hold hidden behind the blindfold.

"Then tell me why you pay no reverence to your liege."

My cock throbs behind the zipper of my jeans.

"Because." She shrugs. "I'm a bad little princess. You're going to have to make me worship."

If we don't give Price a worthy show, then this evening was for nothing. So I grab the knot of hair on her head and yank it hard. Because of the blindfold, she doesn't see it coming, and she cries out as her head jerks. Then her ruby-painted lips part into a devious smile.

"Worship," I growl, giving the leash a slow tug, knowing the metal ring rubs along her folds every time I do.

She unbuttons my jeans and lowers the zipper, and there it is again, the smile that tells me this agent is far more trouble than I anticipated.

She rips my jeans to my ankles, nodding at the small weapons in each slot of the hidden holster that only she can see.

"What's the matter, X? Don't trust me?"

I raise a brow. "Not even a little bit," I say without hesitation.

She simply grins, then licks me from balls to tip—knowing despite her mask that I was commando inside my jeans.

She sucks me to the very base, and I grit my teeth to keep from roaring like a goddamn caged lion. Immediately, my body responds like I'm a teenager who needs one thing—to coat her throat. I begin to move my hips in time to her bobbing sucks, growling with pleasure as she exhales through her nose, controlling her gag reflex.

My fingers twitch, itching to bury themselves in her hair and imprint my taste on her tongue.

Damn it. I love every second of this assault.

If I am the dom, why the hell does it feel like she is the one in control?

"No," I grind out, realizing more than one thing feels off. "This is not the show Price wants."

I pull Z up and pivot her so she is against the wall. Then I lift her hands above her head to where handcuffs hang from a bar attached to the small alcove's ceiling.

I lock her there—arms raised and wrists shackled, her blindfold securely fastened.

"Pick a safe word," I tell her. "Quickly."

"Why?" she taunts. "You don't scare me."

"Not for here," I tell her. "For when we start working with Price. If we ever get separated—if you're ever alone with him and need out fast—we need a code word."

She bristles. "What if *you* need out fast? Why do you assume *I'll* be the one in trouble? Because I'm a woman? Honestly, X. I could kill you before you even knew I betrayed you."

"Maybe," I say. "If I still trusted you."

I pull another piece of silk from the pocket of my jacket and gag her, partly to play our role and partly so she cannot press the issue.

"The safe word is *La Seine*."

She thrashes as I strip to nothing, and I relish her reaction.

The first time we met as anonymous lovers was in the back of a limousine parked along the Seine River in Paris.

But it is also the place where at seventeen we spent the weekend holed up in a cheap inn where she gave me her virginity and I gave her mine.

Fucking hell, I was a fool. She all but told me who she was years ago, and I missed every goddamn sign. I wonder now at the betrayal she must have felt at finding her first love—a trained assassin and spy—unable to recognize the girl who should have been his.

I tear off her G-string and slam into her to the

hilt. The thrashing stops. Instead, our bodies pulse in time with the music beyond the walls. I lift her booted legs, and she hooks them around my waist. How I want to rip the gag from her mouth and kiss her until the decades between us melt away. But this night isn't about Max and Lora. It's not even about X and Z. It is a mission. A job. A means to an end.

This isn't tender lovemaking. It's a hard fuck.

And it doesn't change the fact that every thrust sends the memories swirling.

Her back slams into the wall, and she bucks against me.

It's our first year at Frasier. I sneak up to her table in the library where she sits alone and pull the book from under nose.

Slam.

"What are you reading?" I ask, wrinkling my nose at the old Agatha Christie mystery.

Slam.

"Nothing, now that you've stolen my book. Return it, if you don't mind."

Slam.

"Take it, then. If you can."

Slam.

She stands from the table as I hold the book high above her head. But in mere seconds she has

*my arm wrenched behind my back, and the book
falls to the floor.*

Slam. Z cries out around her gag and I'm breathing heavily.

*"I'm Max," I say grinning, my captor still
standing behind me.*

*"Lora," she says. "And you will never interrupt
me when I'm reading again."*

It took me years to win her over, but when I did,
she was mine and I hers. But we aren't lovesick
teens anymore. And despite what it does to me to
touch her like this, I remind myself of who we are
now—performers, saviors, killers. Am I a fool to
think we can be lovers, too?

I slide my hand between the place where we join
and roughly pinch her wet, swollen clit between
my thumb and forefinger. Z arches against the wall
and squeezes her legs around my torso. My cock
pulses inside her as we both rocket into oblivion.
My cock throbs as her body wrings me dry.

"I think I'm in love with you, Lora."

"I think you're crazy, Max. We just met."

She was right then, and hell if she isn't right
now. When did the crazy start? On the Seine two-
plus decades ago? Three years ago in that limousine? Down the street from the Royal Edenvale
Hospital the night I left the post I'd held on my

longest mission, with the royal family? Or was it everything in between?

I'd wanted to see her face, each and every time. Because despite her claiming I had no clue, on some level I must have known. But none of that matters now. Loving Lora or Z or whoever she is now puts lives at further risk. We will complete this mission and I will ask for reassignment as far from Agent Z as humanly possible.

It's the only option that gives us the greatest chance at survival.

CHAPTER THREE

Z

AS MY POWERFUL ORGASM ebbs and my shattered gasps return to a normal pattern of breathing, I uncurl my toes and sag limply, held upright by the handcuffs dangling from the ceiling. Blindfolded and gagged, I know how weak I must appear to every depraved leer in the red room, and look they surely do. I swear that I can feel their curious gazes crawling over my flesh like spiders.

A soft cloth presses between my legs, and I jerk at the unexpected contact.

"Shh. Easy now, Princess," X croons, his breath heating the sensitive shell of my ear. "Aftercare is an expected part of the scene. The dom always looks after his sub once they are finished." As he speaks, he expertly cleans his come from my folds, and despite my best effort, a furious tear breaks free, trickling down my cheek.

I feel X's confident movements falter.

"Lora." His voice is a low rasp. Not *Princess*. Not Z. Lora.

Another tear joins the first.

"What's the—"

His question is broken off by a slow clap.

"Magnificent performance."

I stiffen, recognizing that sultry purr. It's Caro, turning up again like the proverbial bad penny. At least she's not blowing my cover or Max would ensure I'd be fucked in a way that caused me considerably less pleasure.

"While you're not winning any kink contests, you two have a most intoxicating chemistry, which hasn't gone unnoticed. Daddy watched the whole scene, and I'm pleased to say that you've piqued his interest. He isn't prepared to invite you into his private playroom yet, but he asked me to invite you back tomorrow. This is a great honor."

"I'll check my calendar." X's response is frosty, arrogance infusing every syllable. He is perfect for this cocky dom role, acting like getting noticed by the dark god of the underworld is nothing out of the ordinary, as if our entire mission isn't relying on just such a meeting.

"Well…" Caro sniffs, obviously deflated. "If you come, Daddy has one more rule."

"I don't play by anyone's rules but my own," X snaps.

And the truth in his annoyed snark causes my sensitive inner muscles to clench even though he just wrung an earth-shattering orgasm from me minutes ago.

I force my dry throat to swallow, willing myself to get it together. I'm not a fifteen-year-old girl anymore, bringing my dog-eared copy of *A Room with a View* out to read beneath the ancient oak tree that grew alongside the rugby oval. While pretending to be engrossed in E. M. Forster's worlds in Italy and England, I always maintained an awareness of Max as he locked shoulders with his teammates, pushing, shoving and battering in a seething mass of rucking.

I'd find myself rereading the same page time and time again, too entranced by the look of utter focus on Max's face, the power emanating from his body and the near-palpable force of character.

I'd look away whenever he glanced my direction, pretending to study the clouds or a frolicking squirrel.

"He wants *her*." Caro reaches out and strokes my neck with what feels like claws, jerking me back to the present moment. "This little one is exactly his type."

Don't I know it.

My gorge rises. I've turned down Dante's advances for years, dangling the promise of my body like a carrot on a string. It seems his patience has run out at last. No doubt fueled by watching my little display with X.

I let it get personal.

Who is the idiot here? Me.

Shit.

"Touch her again, you'll answer to me." X's voice is deadly serious.

The Max I used to know was intense about sports, but off the field he liked nothing better than to joke around with his mates…or tease me ruthlessly.

Agent X, however, doesn't make jokes. Only promises. And his word is his bond.

"Is that a promise?" The woman sounds curious.

"We're leaving." X unlocks my handcuffs and tugs my leash.

"Wait!" I fumble to take off my blindfold, my fingers tingling as blood returns to my hands.

Then the blindfold drops and I see Caro nearly nose to nose. Her body is perfect and her dark skin is without a single blemish. Her bronze lips twist into a smug leer. "Like what you see, sugar?"

I don't wait for X's order before dropping my gaze to the floor. It's not that I dislike my looks, but I'm nothing special. Average height. Average weight. Brown hair. Brown eyes.

I could be a kindergarten teacher or a librarian.

I wonder if I'd have been happier in a simple life. And I think I know the answer.

Yes.

Somewhere behind me a woman begins to come in loud whimpers and suddenly I'm exhausted. This night is all so sudden and confronting and confusing.

My worlds have collided, and I feel thrust into a strange new universe.

X leads me from the club without another look or comment, and by the time we get into the waiting limo all I want to do is speed to my hotel, slip into my pajama pants and binge on online baking competitions until I fall asleep.

Instead, X doesn't release my leash.

"Why did you start crying in there?" His voice is tight, almost husky with some repressed emotion.

I look away, glaring out the window at the rainy London streets. The truth is that I don't know where my tears came from.

I thought I'd cried myself dry over Max. What we had. What we lost all those years ago. But apparently, when it comes to my first love, I have a reservoir of feelings.

I cry for a future denied me. One where I work a nine-to-five job. Live in the country with Max and have children.

Now, at my age, the promise of children is almost denied to me...unless I can find a way to get out.

But to buy a new future would sell out my past. Nothing comes without a cost. If I walk away from the Order, I walk away from my entire life.

"Lora, look at me when I talk to you," he growls.

"You don't get to command me outside the Lion's Den," I mutter as we pull up in front of our hotel. "Remember what's real and what's not. In the real world, you don't own me."

His eyes burn a deep midnight blue. "Is that a fact?"

"Ugh." I roll my eyes. "Whatever."

"That's the best you can do? I seem to remember a more extensive vocabulary."

"I've learned the value of brevity. *Go fuck yourself* has such a ring to it." I rap on the window to our driver. "Can I get my key, please?"

The young driver turns around. "Your key? There's only one, miss."

"You're kidding," I growl.

X chuckles. "What did you expect? If anyone follows us, we have to look like a believable couple. And in this case, it means sharing the penthouse suite in the Shangri-La Hotel. The Order moved our belongings in while we were at the club."

Ugh. Of course.

My daggers are all upstairs in my suitcase, so I have to settle for a death glare. "If we are living in forced proximity, I can't be responsible for my actions. I might smother you with a pillow in your sleep."

"I'm a light sleeper," he says. "But I'm sure we can find something to pass the time."

X

We ride up in the elevator in icy silence, glaring at the rich velvet wallpaper. Every time I open my mouth to say something, I think better of it and close it again.

She may have deceived me for a few years, but I kept her in the dark for decades. How do I begin to apologize for that?

There aren't words.

So I give her her space—as much as I can in the small box we're in.

She stalks ahead of me when we get to our floor, straight to our room and through the door, not bothering to hold it for me.

"Shit, Z," I mumble as I stick my foot in between the door and the frame before it slams in my face.

I slip inside and already hear the shower running in the bathroom. It takes everything in my power not to barge in there, to throw the curtain open and demand her attention as in the Lion's Den.

"Space," I mutter, reminding myself that what we just experienced was likely beyond her realm of comprehension or preparation. She needs time to let it settle.

So I stay in the suite's small living area, raiding the minibar and spreading out a feast of tiny bottles and delicacies across the glass coffee table. Before I can dig in, though, I'm hit in the face with a pillow, then a folded blanket.

Z stands in front of me in a plush white robe, the exposed skin on her chest and neck pink—likely from the scalding shower I'm sure she took. Her wet dark hair spreads long over both her shoulders.

In the twenty-plus years I've imagined her, I never anticipated seeing her like this would knock the wind clear out of my chest. She looks exactly the same.

It seems cruel to have her look so unchanged when everything else is different.

"You'll be taking the couch," she says coolly, her jaw tight, even as her whiskey-brown eyes hit me like a shot.

No woman has ever kicked me out of her bed

after sex, but then, we weren't exactly in anyone's bed tonight.

"Understood," I say. "Appreciate the amenities," I add, holding up my pile of linens.

She spins on her heel, heading toward the bedroom.

"Lora, wait," I call after her.

She stops but doesn't face me. "No one has called me that for years," she says softly. "Yet when you say it, it's like everything melts away and we're seventeen again. It makes me think you're Max when I know full well you're not."

I blow out a long breath. "You know if I could have told you, I would have. Don't you?"

She turns now, and tears streak her cheeks. "One night I fall asleep in your arms in my dorm room, and the next morning you're gone. No word. Not then, not ever again. Can you imagine how it felt? Did you hear my heart break? I swear I almost died from the pain."

I squeeze my eyes shut. "I was just a kid, Lora. And a moron. All those IQ tests they made us take? They were entrance exams. Apparently, my scores were such that the Order feared if anyone got their hands on me before they could put me through the program, I'd end up a weapon rather than a protector."

She scoffs. "It's all semantics. You're a weapon.

I'm a weapon. It's just a matter of who got to us first."

She's right. Yet something in what she said sets off a warning bell.

"Who got to you first, Lora?"

She doesn't flinch, her gaze remaining steady.

I stand and stalk toward her. Once in front of her, I cradle her face in my palm and ask the question again.

"*Who* got to you first?"

Her dark eyes burn with twenty-five years of fury, and in a blink she has me slammed against the wall, a blade at my throat, the cold metal taunting my skin.

"The. Order," she growls through gritted teeth. "Who the hell got to *you*?"

I disarm her in the fraction of a second, spinning her so now she's flush against the wall.

I press my cheek to hers, feeling her chest rise and fall with her quickening breaths, her perfect tits rubbing up against me.

"If we're on the same team, love, why the hell are you armed?"

She lets out a bitter laugh. "The same reason you wore that hidden holster to the Lion's Den. Don't make me break your nose, Max. I wouldn't want to mar that beautiful face of yours, but I'll do what I have to."

I retreat a step and hold up my hands in mock surrender.

"I'm not the enemy, Lora."

She turns around, her shoulders sagging a little. "Neither am I."

The problem is, in our line of work, you never can tell.

Several seconds pass before I finally let my shoulders relax.

"Nice work tonight, Agent Z," I say stiffly. And I mean it.

"Go to hell, Max."

There's the feisty Lora I remember. I can't help it. I grin from ear to ear.

She rolls her eyes and then stalks to the bedroom, the door slamming behind her so hard that it rattles the Impressionist paintings dotting the wall.

I take off the ridiculous spiked leather jacket and toss it on the marble floor. Since our bags are all in the bedroom, I decide to sleep in the jeans—and the ankle sheath that lies beneath…

Forget all personal connections. They will either betray you or be used against you. That goes for family, friends and even lovers. Consider anyone other than the agents you work with either an enemy or a liability.

That was the first thing they'd told me when the Order removed me from Frasier Academy. From the second I agreed to be an agent, I was forced to cut all ties outside the organization.

For twenty-five years I've been an orphan and a ghost, a man with no name, no past and no future. Only the next mission.

I prepare my makeshift bed and crawl in as exhaustion hits me like a runaway train. The couch is lumpy, but I've dealt with worse. Yet as I drift off, I swear I hear muffled cries coming from Z's room. I lift my head, and this time the cry is unmistakable.

Ice enters my veins.

If someone is hurting her, they are dead. But their dying will take time and I'll make sure every second is filled with inescapable pain.

I unsheathe a blade and creep soundlessly to her door. I slip inside, my senses on high alert, dagger raised to strike.

That's when I see her, alone in the bed wearing nothing but a Frasier Academy T-shirt, panties— and her own sheathed dagger at her ankle. I suck in a breath, for a second seeing the young girl I fell in love with. Has she kept the shirt as a memento of us—or is she playing with me, getting me to let my guard down because of a bloody memory? I hesitate, but only for a second as she thrashes right and left, a hectic flush on her cheeks as she sends the covers askew. This is no act.

I put my weapon away as my chest tightens. What horrors has she seen other than this night? If I had to venture a guess based on my own experience, I'd say it was more than any one person should be expected to handle.

I slip my dagger in its hiding spot and crawl cautiously into the bed. Dreaming or no, it is a dangerous thing I do with a woman I don't fully trust and who has no reason to trust me.

"It's okay, Lora," I whisper. "It's just me."

Her eyes open wide, and she pulls a handgun from beneath her pillow, aiming it unerringly right between my brows.

"It's me," I say again. "Max. I just thought you might need—"

She drops the gun next to the phone on her night table, then burrows into my arms.

"Only for tonight," she whispers, scooting closer. "Because I don't want to be alone, even if the alternative is you."

I huff out a laugh, pulling her to me. "Understood."

Her lips press to my ear, as gentle as a petal plucked from a rose. "And if you try anything like we did in that club, I'll castrate you before you can pull a weapon." Sharp teeth nip my lobe to punctuate her warning.

No matter how soft and supple she is, her body

is a deadly weapon. She knows a hundred ways to kill a man with her bare hands. And yet I'm not afraid. Shit. I can't get close enough.

"Of course," I say, grinning. "Whatever you need."

And because I haven't slept in days, I surrender to it now, Lora nestled in my arms. She hooks an ankle around mine, and we sleep, bodies tangled, chest to chest, and dagger to dagger. The lights of London seep between the curtains. Bad guys are out there. Plotting. Planning. But that's not my concern right now.

Enemy or liability means nothing, if only for the next few hours.

I breathe in the jasmine scent to her soft hair and for a moment revel in this most unfamiliar of feelings...

Peace.

CHAPTER FOUR

Z

I SLIDE OUT of bed before dawn. X might be a light sleeper, but I'm an expert at moving through life undetected. I'd have died a thousand times otherwise. In the bathroom I grimace at my reflection, the dark rings under my eyes hinting at a restless night. I've always looked younger than my years, but today it's as if the past has descended. My gaze looks ancient. I look like I've lived a thousand lives and I'm on edge from dreams that I can't fully recall. Only that they've left my stomach tied in a series of sickening slipknots.

Usually when I'm unsettled, sex helps calm me, but no way am I going to be mixing business and pleasure on this assignment.

This time your business is pleasure, an invisible devil on my shoulder whispers.

I bend over and splash icy cold water on my

face, washing away the traitorous impulse of my body to crawl into bed with X and wake him up by taking his cock in my mouth.

"No," I mutter, giving my reflection a stern wag of the finger.

I'll have to resort to plan B. When I can't indulge in a sexual release, running takes the edge off. It's in no way a pleasure, but it pummels my mind into order, allows me to sweat out stress.

I creep out of the bathroom, grateful we are in a suite, and change into yoga pants and a pale blue running top in the predawn dark.

I'm slinking to the door when the light turns on. I freeze, like a cat caught in the cream.

X, dressed in black athletic wear that makes love to his muscular frame, regards me coolly. My heart accelerates like I'm doing interval training.

"Going somewhere, pet?" he asks.

"You can see that I am," I snap, embarrassed to be caught scuttling away. Mortified that I needed the comfort of his arms last night. Frustrated that I'm craving his body heat more than my next breath.

"I'll join you." Not a question. God, he's such a cocky man. And damn if I don't love it.

"Ha." I roll my eyes, pretending to care less. "Trust me, you can't keep up. I run six-minute miles when I let loose in the parks."

"Impressive." He drops his chin, a hint of a smile tugging the corner of his wide lips. "That's fast."

"I know." I don't fuck around when I run. I beat the pavement like a horde of zombies are hot on my heels. It's the only way to get a much-needed endorphin rush, to clear my head of cobwebs.

"I'll try to keep up." He kicks back a foot and reaches to squeeze his ankle, pulling his leg in a deep quadriceps stretch.

His pants do nothing to disguise his rock-hard thighs, or the visible bulge.

"You can try." I force my appraising gaze away and stalk to the hotel door. "But trust me, you're going to lose."

"We'll see about that," he growls as I march into the hallway.

Our elevator ride is tense. He's standing three feet away and yet it's as if I can feel him against me, his touch branding my skin.

He doesn't look my direction. He says nothing.

I hate him right now. This was meant to be my time. A chance to outrun my demons. And yet now I'll be truly chased by an actual devil from my past.

I purse my lips into a grim smile. At least I'm going to kick his ass into next Sunday. There's something delicious about that fact.

We walk through the deserted but sumptuous lobby. Shangri-La is a five-star hotel and spares no expense, from the eight-tiered fountain to the marble columns to the cut-crystal chandeliers. It could be tacky but is more old-world Hollywood glamour. This is the type of hotel couples would pick out for their honeymoons or romantic getaways. Not to crash after spending nights in BDSM dungeons.

I refuse to make eye contact with staff, wondering if any of them recognize me from my nearly naked fishnet look last night.

We step out into London's early morning and the road is quiet, traffic not yet buzzing to life. Four classic black taxis idle at the hotel cab station, two bellboys in tailored uniforms shoot the breeze by their desk, and an elderly man is walking his beribboned Pomeranian, but otherwise we are the only ones out and about.

I set my GPS watch and reach to where my iPhone is strapped to a running armband.

"Which way are we going?"

"*My* plan is to hit the main parks… Kensington Gardens, Hyde Park, Green Park and St. James Park." It's a fun loop and one of my favorite runs in London.

X opens his mouth, but I start my Spotify running playlist and whatever he says is drowned out by Tom Petty's "Runnin' Down a Dream."

Without another word, I take off in a dead sprint. He doesn't catch up with me until Notting Hill station.

I'm surprised. He's quicker than I anticipated.

I've worked hard to be fast. When it comes to the Order's comprehensive physical exams, I've schooled most of the men in the Asian offices. I don't bulge with muscles, but I'm strong, my body nothing like a frail model. Instead, I'm compact and confident. I've been training for years.

I glance at X, who offers a smug smile.

"Hello," he mouths.

I can't wait to wipe that grin off his face. I've been going easy. Time to get my motor going. Pumping my arms, I up the pace. He lunges, trying to match me. He's powerful, built for sprinting, but I've trained for endurance. I've got a series of ultramarathons under my belt and have conditioned my body to accept and even crave the pain.

Might come in handy in the Lion's Den, the little devil on my shoulder purrs.

I don't turn around until I'm passing Royal Albert Hall, sweat slicking the skin in the valley between my breasts.

When I do, the path is empty.

I've lost him.

I should want to pump my fist, but instead I'm more aware than ever that I'm alone.

Like usual.

How I prefer.

But I can't quite tune out the cool wash of disappointment in my belly.

Did I really want X to chase me?

I start running before I answer my question.

If I'm going to survive this mission, it's critical that I don't overthink.

All I can do is breathe in and out. And survive.

X

Lora's fast as the devil. I'll give her that much. Secondary school may have been decades ago, but she's stronger than she's ever been.

Me? I'm not a runner. Maybe it's because I don't let myself get chased. Nor do I let anyone I need to apprehend get far enough away from me. I rely on ingenuity rather than speed or distance. It's why I'm scaling the rear of a double-decker bus right at this moment. If I've played my cards right—and I always do—I'll hop off in front of the Broadwalk Café ninety seconds before she'll run past.

Yes. I'm tracking her pace.

A tourist on the upper deck, a young boy with curly brown hair, watches what's going on behind the bus rather than what's in front or beside it. That's when he spots me hanging on to the rear emergency exit. He taps a woman on the shoulder, likely his mother, and points at me.

Her eyes go wide with horror. I wonder if she's worried for my safety—or if she thinks a strange man in running clothes illegally riding the bus is cause to worry for her own.

I plaster on my most disarming grin and wave with the hand that isn't responsible for keeping me from going splat onto the pavement.

Before she can sound the alarm, I see the coffee shop looming ahead—a beacon of caffeine and good old-fashioned cheating.

I jump from my perch as the bus slows but doesn't stop, my momentum carrying me across the street and over the hood of a Mini Cooper. Not that I couldn't have made it across the hood of a Land Rover or some other car of that height and caliber, but it was a Mini. I can't change that part of the equation.

What I can do is thank the gods that there is no line, so I'm able to rush inside. Then, with seconds to spare, I stand on the pavement with two coffees in hand and the biggest shit-eating grin, the likes of which I hope Lora has never seen.

She spots me while she's a block and a half

away, and as she approaches, I see her eyes are wide with incredulity.

"What in the world?" she asks as she runs past me and then doubles back to where I'm casually waiting with refreshments.

I hold a cup out for her, and she takes it begrudgingly.

"I'm not accustomed to losing," I tell her. "But I'm sure it's something *you* can get used to."

Her mouth drops open. "You're—you're an asshole."

I laugh, the heartiest laugh I've experienced in quite some time because no one—and I mean not a living soul who wants to continue living—has ever said something like that to me before.

"You call me on my shit," I say. "I like that."

She coughs on her sip of coffee, and a small trickle of it dribbles down her chin.

"No," she finally says when she's regained her ability to breathe and think. "No, X. You are not allowed to like one thing about me today. We're *business* associates. Nothing more."

I shrug. "You're fast. You appreciate a cup of black coffee, and you look amazing in formfitting running gear. That's three things I like about you today, and the day is still young. I'm guessing I'll like quite a few more by nightfall."

She groans and rolls her eyes. "You're not even

out of breath," she says. "You probably rode here on a double-decker bus or something."

I force myself not to react, to swallow the coffee that's in my mouth rather admit my guilt with an unguarded expression.

"Don't you know, Z? Our work is all about being creative. If you bent the rules to your will every now and then, you might actually have a little fun."

I wrap my palm around an item in my pocket. It looks like a tiny flashlight, the type of tool a person would clip to a key chain. It's got a small but ultrasturdy carabiner attached to it in case I want to clip into my belt loop or a backpack. That's not, however, what I'll be using it for today.

I point across the street toward a six-story apartment building.

Her gaze follows mine.

"Race you to the roof," I tell her, tossing the remainder of my coffee into a nearby bin. While it's a shame to let it go to waste, it's worth it to catch my opponent off guard.

And then in a flash I'm gone—down the walkway and into the street. But I hear the slap of sneakers against the pavement and know it has to be her behind me. I don't look back but instead keep my eye on the prize.

I catch the entry door with my foot as a resident leaves.

"Thanks," I say. "Sorry, love, went for a run and forgot my keys."

I don't wait for a response as I hear the door open again.

"You can't win, X!" she calls after me, but I know full well I can and that I will.

It's not until I'm halfway up the first flight of stairs that Lora catches up—and *trips* me.

I land hard on my knee and curse under my breath. Lora brushes past me and keeps running, looking back only when she notices I'm still down.

I've been shot and stabbed. I've been left to drown in an icy river and suspended upside down mere inches from a vat of hydrochloric acid. And I've survived every encounter with minimal fallout. Only once have I been held prisoner and tortured for any length of time. It was two years ago, not long after Lora and I began our anonymous trysts. The royal family believed it was a clandestine meeting, but instead I'd let my guard down, stepping into a vehicle I thought to be hers.

It wasn't.

I was blindfolded and bound to a chair in a dank room.

For twenty-four hours a man came in and asked me the same question.

"Who is Agent Z?"

While I did not recognize the voice, I knew the emotion in that tone. *Jealousy.* Whoever it was knew the answer to his own question, so what more was he looking for? It didn't matter. He wasn't going to get it.

For twenty-four hours they withheld food.

For twenty-four hours I did not speak, not even when they took a hammer to my knee.

Did I say I was held captive for a length of time? That was how long it took me to pick the lock with my cuff link. It only took me seven seconds to dispatch my captor once I did. I knew he wasn't the man behind my kidnapping, just a hired thug.

But whoever it was knew I was connected to Z. They knew I was meeting her that night. And if they were able to get to me, they'd eventually get to her.

But because I hadn't yet figured out why, I also hadn't told her. Because for all I know, Z *was* my captor.

"Go!" I wave her off and pull myself to my feet. Once the pain subsides, I continue my pursuit, and she sprints up the rest of the stairs. It doesn't matter. I'm grinning the whole rest of the way because even if she makes it to the roof first, she won't win.

Except, when I burst through the doors, she's not there. Instead, she stands waving to me from the roof of the four-story building across the street, the one to which I'd planned to zip-line with the carabiner in my pocket.

I shove my hand into said pocket and pull out nothing but air.

That sexy little thief, one step ahead of me the whole time.

"*Touché*, Lora," I say softly.

Then I massage my sore knee.

Who is Agent Z?

I have no fucking clue.

But I know Lora, and I know when she is hiding something.

The problem is… I don't have a clue what.

CHAPTER FIVE

Z

X IS DISTANT after my victory. The moment of fun seems to be just that…a passing moment, popped like a soap bubble.

I could dismiss his rigid posture and troubled gaze as evidence he's a sore loser, but my intuition whispers otherwise.

I'm not sure what's come over him, but I'm not sure that I care, either.

Correction.

I'm not sure that I should care.

In our line of work, emotions are dangerous. Feelings make for hesitation. All it takes is a few seconds to get yourself killed.

"Let's go," I say.

We return to the hotel without conversation, and once in the penthouse, X disappears into the bathroom. A moment later the shower comes on.

I'm kicking off my running shoes as there's a knock at the door. I open it to see a tuxedo-wearing Shangri-La staff member in front of a room-service cart.

"Special delivery," he says with a short bow.

"Oh, I didn't order anything." I scan his frame, looking for a hidden holster or other concealed weapon. You know, the usual for an assassin.

He doesn't blink. "I know." When he lifts up the lid of a silver tureen, beneath a bowl of lobster bisque, I spy the corner of a creamy envelope.

"What is this?" I mutter, realizing he isn't here to do me harm, but to pass me information.

"A message from a friend." Without hesitation, he pushes the cart toward the elevator.

I set the soup aside and tear open the envelope, wondering who it could be from. I hope it's not a reassignment. Not because I want to keep working with X but because I want to catch Dante Price.

Don't let him get under your skin. We're watching.

I freeze.

It's a warning, and I don't have to rack my brain to know who *him* refers to.

Max.

And the person who sent the note? I scan the room. I don't think it's bugged, but who knows in our line of work.

The shower turns off and I leap onto the sofa, grabbing a coffee table book and sliding the note into the pages before X emerges wearing a low-slung towel.

"Good read?" he asks just as I realize the book I've grabbed is called *Extraordinary Chickens*. It's photo after photo of obscure chicken breeds.

"Exceedingly," I say blithely, hoping that my flushed features aren't evident. I can't actually tell if my blush is from the mysterious note that I'm hiding or the fact that X's exposed glory trail is… well…glorious.

"We're going to have to up the ante tonight, you know," he says carefully.

I shut the book on the chickens and return it to the table before crossing my arms. I'll destroy the note as soon as he exits the room.

"What does that mean?" I arch a brow.

"It means that we are going to have to do scenes together. I'm going to have to own you, Lora, body and soul, if we are going to make it believable. And that means making a cerebral connection. I'm going to need full access, not just to your body, but to your mind and, yes, even your heart."

"Oh, really?" I wrinkle my nose even as a tremor undulates between my legs at the idea of giving myself utterly and irrevocably into X's care. "And let me guess, this goes one way."

Now it's his turn to furrow a brow. "Meaning?"

"You demand my utter complicity and yet offer me nothing. You…as always…intend to remain an enigma."

His nostrils flare and the muscles cord in his neck. "I'm to be your dom."

"So what? It's still me giving everything to you."

"That's exactly what it means," he snaps, dropping his towel.

I gasp.

He's bared himself to me, his arousal thick and firm, the dusky head nearly at his navel.

"Princess, you don't even get the catch, do you? You're the one who has control."

"Is that so?" He's got my attention. "Go on."

"You submit to me, but in return it's my responsibility to satisfy you utterly. Ensure not a single one of your cravings goes unanswered. Your pleasure is to be my obsession. It's about trust, safety and surrender."

"Surrender!" I leap from the couch, a sob lodging in my throat and I choke it down. "Once I gave you everything I had, and how did you treat me? You left, Max. You left without a word."

"Z," he says, warning in his voice.

"Cut the crap. I'm Lora. You're Max. If you want to pretend to be my king and me your pretty princess, or you as the mysterious X and me as

Agent Z, fine. But I know the truth. I know you eat cereal without milk for breakfast. That your favorite movie is *E.T.* That you are impossible to beat in chess and could have played professional rugby if you had wanted."

"Stop."

"Why should I?" I seethe.

"You joined the Order, too. You can't fault me for decisions you made yourself just because you did it years after I did."

"That's just it. I didn't make your decision. I would have told you, damn the rules. I wouldn't have left you with a broken heart. I found you *after* I became an agent. But before that? I spent an entire decade with this tiny broken place inside me that wouldn't heal because I didn't have the answers. All I had was what I remembered of us—of you."

"You aren't the only one with memories," he says in a strangled voice.

"But you won't let me in. You demand my trust, but I'm sorry. That is impossible for me to give you."

"Then we will fail before we have even started. Trust is the cornerstone of a dominant and submissive relationship, just as it is between two partners."

Damn him, I know he's right and I hate him for it. Even as my gaze is drawn to his erection. It hasn't flagged an inch, despite our arguing.

"Do you want to fail… Lora?"

My eyelids flutter, the emotion infusing his voice threatening to undo me.

"You know I don't," I grind out.

"And what about your own little game? How you duped me for years, using my body, never telling me who you really were. I'm not throwing this at you to explain away my own failings, but let's not pretend you are perfect, darling."

"I… I don't know what to say," I falter. Because he is right. But our dalliances were never a game to me. They were an intoxicating torment. I could never quit him, so help me, no matter how hard I tried. He is and always has been my drug. My addiction of choice.

"Just tell me that you'll help me," he says, this powerful, dangerous man who never relies on anyone.

I push a wayward lock of hair off my face, tucking it into my ponytail, and lick my lips. "Help you what?"

His eyes burn, turning me inside out. "Find my way back to you."

X

"Fine," she says, her voice softening. "Teach me how to connect. Teach me how to make Price believe we're the real deal so we can finally bring his ass in."

I offer her a ghost of a smile. She's in this for the Order, and she should be. But I'm disappointed. Not that I let it show.

I sit on the couch and rest my elbow on the arm.

"Stand, facing me, with your eyes fixed on mine."

"What are you— *Oh*," she says. "We're doing it. Is this, like, a scene?"

The corner of my mouth twitches, but I don't break. I am the dom. She will submit.

"As a hard-and-fast rule, one that you'll stick to this evening when we see Price, you will only speak when I ask you a question to which you must respond. Is that clear?"

"Yes—sir? I'm sorry. I am clueless. Should I call you sir, King, Your Highness? I mean, this should be a hard-and-fast rule, too, right?"

I sigh. "Highness will do."

She smiles. "Yes, *Highness*."

"Stay facing me. Do *not* break eye contact. And take off your shirt."

She opens her mouth to say something, but I watch as realization takes hold, as the rules start to sink in.

Z says nothing, but she holds my stare as she pulls her formfitting running shirt over her head.

"The sports bra," I snap. "*Off.* Let me see those perfect tits."

She clears her throat but does as I command.

Christ, she's beautiful, like a Renaissance painting portrait. Her creamy skin is like porcelain. Her pink nipples are firm and pert, and my cock responds with an almost imperceptible pulse. But Lora's mouth twitches. She saw me react to her, but she doesn't break.

"The pants," I say. "Lose them. And don't make me wait. I'm not a patient man, Princess."

She hooks her thumbs in the waistband of her Lycra running pants, but they don't slide off easily. She must be sweaty from the run. The thought makes me salivate. Even so…

"If you want my thick, hard cock inside you, you will not let me wait another second to see what you're hiding between your legs."

Fuck. I've touched and licked and penetrated what's between her legs. Last night at the club, though, everything happened in a blur. We weren't prepared. Tonight, however, we will be.

She finally gets her pants to her ankles and steps out of them. The whole while her eyes lock on mine, her gaze intent.

"Jesus, look at that pretty little pussy. What do you think, Princess? Is that not the prettiest pussy you've ever seen?"

"Yes, Highness. It's the prettiest."

There is trepidation in her tone, and for a second I begin to worry. But then I notice her shift her stance. Then she shifts again.

She's—squirming.

Fucking hell if my little sub isn't already turned on. This just might be a ton more fun than I was expecting.

"Touch that pussy, Princess."

She licks her bottom lip, then slips a hand between her legs. Her eyes never leave mine.

She sucks in a breath as her finger brushes her swollen clit.

"How does that feel, Princess?"

"Good, Highness," she says with a whimper.

"How good?"

"So fucking good." Her voice is tight, and I know she wants more.

"Then dip a finger inside, feel your dew."

She doesn't hesitate, a finger disappearing between her folds. Her eyes flutter shut as she lets out a moan.

"Eyes. On. Me. Princess."

She opens them with a start but says nothing. Good little sub.

"Turn to your right and press your torso against the wall, palms against the plaster, as well."

She pulls her hand from between her legs with visible reluctance. But she doesn't argue, doesn't take her eyes off mine. And it's in this moment that something clicks into place. Maybe she intended only to do this for the mission, but she is my obedient little princess now. She doesn't stare at me with a blank expression, nor does she looked confused or incredulous. She looks—trusting, like whatever I say or do next will be okay because she trusts me to keep her safe. This is all I want from her before we play our roles tonight.

I rise from the couch and stride to where she stands frozen against the wall, like a criminal in some prime-time cop show.

I shove a rough knee between her legs. "Make room for me, Princess, if you want your reward."

Her breaths come quick and uneven, and I can sense the fear, the anticipation.

She pivots her feet apart, leaving a generous opening between her legs.

"Do you…" I whisper in her ear, "want to earn your reward?"

"Yes, Highness."

"Then tell me to fuck you, Princess."

"Fuck me, Highness," she whispers.

"I'm sorry. What was that? I couldn't hear you."

I heard her loud and clear. I could have entered her right then and there, and my dick would have thanked me for it. But I want to hear the princess *beg*.

"Fuck me, Highness," she says at regular volume, but it's not good enough.

"I. Can't. *Hear*. You."

"Fuck me, Highness!" she cries out, palms slamming against the wall. "Fuck me, fuck me, fuck me!" she adds for good measure.

So I reach around her thighs and wrench her open just a bit more. Then I nudge her entrance with the tip of my slick, aching cock.

She cries out, so sensitive and responsive to my touch. It's how I know our little scene is working, that we have forged a connection, however brief it may be. She's out of her mind with need.

"Good, good, little princess," I croon before sheathing myself inside her to the very hilt.

I growl and bite her shoulder, and she arches against me.

"Are you ready to truly surrender to me?" I ask, her warm, silky heat threatening to drive me out of my goddamn mind. After all this time, after the countless anonymous trysts, I think I've found something I didn't even know I was looking for.

"Yes, Highness," she finally gasps. "I'm ready."

CHAPTER SIX

Z

"Good. Then hold that thought," X whispers in my ear before pressing in and then dismounting.

My eyes fly open as an unbearable sensation of emptiness fills me. "What the fuck is going on?"

He's already facing out the window, the light putting him in relief, highlighting the indents to his rock-hard ass and the defined musculature of his back. A thin scar runs down his right hamstring. I'm tempted to crawl on my hands and knees to it and lick it up to his sac, beg him to let me service him, humble myself to get that cock by any measure necessary, even if that means debasing myself.

I'm tempted, but that doesn't mean I've lost control.

Instead, I give in to another powerful emotion. Anger.

"Hold what thought?" I catch my nonexistent breath.

"You said you were ready. That's perfect. Fuck, I still feel your sweet cream coating my cock, Princess. But I want you hungry to serve me. Desperate with desire. Tonight, you are going to crave every last bit of pleasure that I give you."

"Jesus Christ!" I slam my knees together and unleash a frustrated scream. "You're the worst! The absolute fucking worst. Do you know that?"

He glances over his broad shoulder. His eyes, normally a midnight blue, are almost black with desire.

Restraint is costing him, too.

Good, because I intend to make him pay.

Easing open my legs, I skim my hands up my thighs. "You like this?"

He turns around, facing me fully, erection proud and ruddy. "You know I do."

I spread open my lips a little, let him glimpse my pink petals. "Control is so important to you. But you have to admit, losing it is also half the fun."

He says nothing, but he doesn't look away.

I dip one finger into my wetness, bring it out and lick the skin clean. "Mmm, yummy," I whisper.

Before my next breath, he's crossed the distance between us, his mouth slanting over mine, as he tears the taste of my pussy from my lips and tongue like it's his last meal on earth.

"You make me fucking crazy, you know that," he growls after drinking his fill.

I arch my brows. "You make me want to crazy fuck, so I guess we're even."

"You have a smart mouth," he snarls, two deep valleys appearing between his brows.

"There's one way to shut me up," I snap. "Put something in it."

I sink to my knees, and he pins my shoulders against the wall, presenting me with his engorged cock, precome beading the crown, his shaft slick from having been inside me. Madness overtakes me. I'm determined to make him shoot so hard that his balls feel bruised.

He gives an involuntary growl as I wrap my lips around him. He's not small, but I force myself to relax around his girth, greedy, taking him all the way to the root. I feel him deep, right at the back of my throat.

I glance up and realize why his eyes seem so dark. His pupils are so dilated they've almost eclipsed the blue irises. "Fuck, no one makes me harder than you, Lora. No one."

I know he's had other lovers, but in this moment I hate them. Just as I hate my own. I hate every second that I've lived without doing this, savagely sucking this man, claiming him, taunting him, bringing him to his knees.

Having him know me as his lover is night and day from indulging in anonymous trysts in luxury cars.

How many dreams have I had where I suckle his beautiful cock as he watches, knowing that it is me doing this to him. That I am the one who brings him such pleasure.

With my next suck, I take him so deep that his pubic curls rub against the tip of my nose.

"Lora. Lora. Lora." He chants my name. "So fucking good. So fucking good, Lora. The best." His eyes roll back in his head.

His thrusts grow uneven, and I can tell from tonguing over the frantic pulse in his thick vein that he's close to coming.

Perfect.

And with that, I pull back, shoving him off me before he can jet down my throat.

"What the fuck?" he cries in a strangled tone, gaze unfocused, hovering right at the edge.

"That's for fucking me. Or not fucking me, as the case may be," I purr, wiping my mouth clean.

"You're serious." He stares at me, incredulous.

"As a heart attack, *Highness*." I stand up and smooth my hair. "It seems that if I'm to be on edge tonight, you should be, too. Fair's fair, plus…you do want to be professional about all this, don't you?"

And with that I turn and stalk to the shower, grinning as I slam the door over his blue-balled groan of "Goddamn it, Lora."

Once I'm inside the bathroom, I reach beneath the vanity, finding the burner phone I've taped to the faucet. We've been playing a game, but I'm playing a more dangerous one, and it's time to make the first move.

X

Tonight the Lion's Den admits patrons before the sun sets. Many enjoy the added thrill of partaking in such deviant acts while the rest of the world heads home from a day at work or is just sitting down to dinner. The club pulses with a sexual energy unlike our previous visit. Or maybe it's my heightened awareness, the throbbing ache in my cock.

I could have relieved myself in the shower, though as much as I hate to admit it, Lora was right. My body should beg for it as much as hers. But while I pride myself on being a man of undisputed control, that woman could very well unravel me.

She walks behind me, her G-string leash wrapped around my wrist. Tonight I am dressed in a three-piece Italian suit, the cost of which could only be afforded by royalty—and spies. Lora wears the fitted bodice of an elegant gown. Her hair falls in glossy brown waves over her shoulder, and a diamond-encrusted tiara sits atop her head. If it wasn't for the black leather micro-miniskirt—necessary for easy access—and the boots that cuff just under her ass, she truly would look like a princess.

I flick my wrist and hear her gasp behind me. Tonight's leash ring is attached to a lipstick-size vibrator. Every time I tug, she gets a little thrill—enough to keep her begging for more but not enough that she falls out of compliance.

I turn over my shoulder.

"Did you enjoy that, Princess?"

She bows her head once, then meets my gaze. "Yes, Highness."

I grin, knowing that in her head she is cursing the day I was born. But the thought only makes me grin more.

A pixie-haired blonde wearing nothing but pasties and a G-string greets us with a warm smile.

"Highness, Princess, we have a room waiting for you."

I see Lora tense in my peripheral vision.

"We were hoping for something a little more private tonight," I tell her.

The woman's smile widens.

"Oh, he's given the two of you your *own* room tonight." Lora's shoulders relax.

"Right this way. He'll be watching."

And I'm guessing her feeling of reprieve lasted no longer than an exhale.

Pixie woman escorts us down a narrow hallway that dead-ends at a solid black door with a silver number one on it.

"His *best* room," she says, then inserts a key into the door. She pushes open the door to reveal red carpet, a plush bed with gray sheets and a quilted silver headboard that runs from the mattress to the ceiling.

Simple enough.

But I feel as if I'm in a fun house. Every wall is mirrored, as is the ceiling. And on the wall opposite the bed is a goddamn throne—oversize, upholstered in rich blue velvet, and atop a dais so the dom who sits in it can look down on his sub.

"A room fit for royalty, yes?" she asks, the tassels on her pasties swishing with every move she makes.

I nod. "Do thank your employer."

"Oh no, *Highness*. He humbly thanks you for the show—and for meeting with him and his associates in his suite after."

With that, she backs out the door, and I hear the tumbler click into place.

Lora's eyes widen, and she opens her mouth to

say something, but I cut her off before she blows our cover when we haven't even begun.

"Looks like we're not allowed to leave until I'm satisfied," I tell her, hoping the ease of my tone will lessen her worry. "Get on your knees," I add.

She obeys even as a strange energy emanates from her. "Yes, Highness."

"Do not look me in the eye when you are paying fealty, Princess. You will bow your head when you are on your knees." I don't know what is bothering her, but she can't raise Dante's suspicions while her lips are around my dick.

Once again she obeys, even though this wasn't in the script. When her head is bowed, her long waves obscuring any possible view of where my pants hit my shoes, I deftly slide my pant leg up an inch to remind her of the holster strapped to my ankle, the one that works as a virtual Swiss Army knife, a different weapon or tool in each concealed slot.

There's no situation we can't get out of, I try to tell her with this one small gesture. I could pick the lock and dispatch of anyone who gets in our way. We'd be out the door and in the car before the first scream was heard.

"Now stand," I tell her, "and remove your bodice."

She stands and meets my stare. "Your Highness, it ties in the back. I cannot remove it myself."

I yank on the leash, and she yelps. I can feel the vibration all the way up the cord.

"I didn't ask you a question, Princess. You know how I feel about you talking out of turn."

I spin her so her back is to me, but our eyes meet in the mirrored wall's reflection.

"What's your punishment?" I ask.

"A spanking for being a naughty princess."

There is amusement in her tone, and I realize she is enjoying this role play more than I anticipated.

I unzip her tiny skirt and yank it over her thigh-high boots.

I'm face-to-face with toned ass and the couple of inches of her lithe thighs that extend beyond her boot cuffs.

My cock strains against my pants.

Get the fuck inside her, you complete and utter wanker, it silently screams. *I have been waiting since she left us right when we were about to come.*

My cock hates me.

I give Lora's beautiful ass a firm slap.

She giggles.

"Do you like that, Princess?"

She wiggles her beautiful behind at me.

"Yes, Highness."

But I don't want to spank. I want to touch, to taste, to penetrate.

I touch the bodice, loosening the ribbon that ties it together before ripping it open.

"I said I wanted this off." The garment falls to the floor. Her pert breasts reflect back at me, the fun-house effect of the mirrored wall behind us making it look as if the two of us go on for infinity.

"Pinch one of those hard, rosy-red peaks of yours."

As she lifts a hand toward her breast, I give a tug on the leash, keeping it taut, thus letting the vibration continue.

She sucks in a series of tiny breaths. Her chest heaves, and her knees shake.

She's as out of her mind as I am. I know I'm supposed to be in control, but if I don't bury myself in that wet, swollen pussy soon, I might not leave this mission alive.

CHAPTER SEVEN

Z

I'M SECONDS FROM COMING when he drops the leash, turning lightly away even as his broad, beautiful chest rises and falls.

"Pick a number...one, two or three."

"What do they stand for?" I gasp, a bead of sweat trickling along the side of my neck.

"That's for me to know and you to find out," he taunts with an infuriating wink. "But know you'll win no matter what."

Before I can make the tantalizing choice, the door flies open with a loud bang and assailants dressed in tactical gear pour in, their faces hidden by black masks.

"What the hell!" I shout, inwardly grinning at how authentic my surprise sounds.

X responds in an instant, landing a back kick to the first man's neck. The burly attacker makes a garbled sound followed by a grunt as X does a neat leg sweep, taking out his legs and sending him flying. He knocks out the next two as I leap into action. But I'm naked, and the man in front of me has an assault rifle pointed between my eyes.

"Stand down or I shoot," he says in a thick Eastern European accent, and X instantly stills.

The black stocking mask blunts the leader's face, but not his thick lips, twisted into a menacing grin.

"I hope I wasn't interrupting anything important," he says with a husky, insinuating laugh. His leer bores into my exposed skin.

"Nothing we haven't done before," X replies in a casual tone, as if commenting on the weather. "Now, what can we do for you gentlemen?"

"You're coming with us."

"Ah," X says. "That's a problem. See, we have plans for this evening. We are going to be, ahem, quite tied up."

"Yes." The leader's eyes gleam. "You are indeed."

Five minutes later we are dressed and bound together in a van, back to back. "Happy?" I snarl over one shoulder, struggling as I test the knots. They are double tied and strong as anything I can do. "You and your big mouth."

"You love my big mouth, Princess," he whispers and even now, I have to admit the truth to his words.

I do love his big mouth. I love even more what it does to my body.

And if we survive the next few hours, I'm going to see that it is put to its full wicked use.

The van begins to rumble and X tilts his head to rest against mine. "How long will it take you to get us out?"

"Two minutes," I tell him.

"Bullshit."

"For that, I'm saying a minute fifteen."

He chuckles. "In your dreams."

"If I win, I want a favor."

"What's that?" he asks.

"*You* have to submit to *me*. Sexually. The next time we're naked and alone, *I'm* the master."

"Sure thing, Princess. Because there's no way in hell you are getting us out of this situation in seventy-five seconds."

"Count."

By the time he gets to twenty I've already worked the hairpin loose, and when it drops I catch it between my fingers. It has a fine blade on the underside, and I use it to saw through my wrist bindings. By forty-five seconds my hands are free and I'm attacking the knots at my ankles.

By sixty-seven seconds I've spun around and done the same for X.

"Sixty-nine seconds," he says when he's completely free. "Done!"

X

Before I knew who she was, I'd read of Z's many escapes from captivity in the logs of the Order. From being suspended on a rainforest zip line in Costa Rica to being locked in a crypt in Sicily, she always made it out alive. I'd heard of the infamous blade she wore in her hair but never saw it in action until tonight. If it can saw through the heavy cords that bound us, what can it do—or has it done—to human flesh?

Without wasting another second, I kick open the back door of the van.

"Shit," I hiss. We're on what seems to be a deserted road, which means we won't get bulldozed by other vehicles. But we're traveling faster than I anticipated.

"We need to jump," she says urgently.

"I know," I snap. "Maybe give me a second or two to figure out how to do it without both of us ending up bloody pulps on the side of the road."

"What?" she whisper-shouts. "You drove a car onto a train with Prince Benedict of Edenvale and his future wife, Evangeline Vernazza. And then you all jumped before the tunnel entrance took out the Rolls-Royce, and you're hesitating now?"

She has a point. But my hesitation isn't for fear of what will happen to *me*.

She pushes me aside and stands in the open doorway in her ball gown's bodice, micro-mini-skirt and those damned sexy boots. She'll die if she jumps.

That's when it hits me, my reason for hesitation. I'm putting her life before mine.

"Complete the mission," she says. "That's what we're here to do."

And then she leaps into the dark.

"Lora!" I yell, my voice strangled, and it's a sound I've never heard before.

And then, without another thought, I jump.

My shoulder hits the pavement hard, and I hear a pop as it dislocates, but I keep my head tucked, my knees to my chest as Newton's first law of motion plays out. An object in motion stays in motion unless acted upon by an unbalanced force.

Lucky for me, that force is gravelly asphalt.

When I finally roll to a stop, I do a quick check with my left hand, ignoring for the time being the searing pain shooting from my right shoulder all the way to my palm.

Nothing appears broken, but my knuckles are

bloodied, and I feel a slow, warm trickle down the side of my face.

I grin. In the grand scheme of things, I'm pretty impressed with the outcome of this escape.

But where the hell is Lora?

I pull myself to my feet, tucking my right arm against my torso.

"Lora!" I call, following the dark road the way we came. "Lora!" My voice grows louder and hoarser with each cry of her name.

There is no way in hell this is how the mission ends.

I'm running now, shouting her name, trying to prepare myself for the worst even as I refuse to believe that she could be gone.

It feels like hours even though I know it's only minutes, maybe even seconds, before my eyes adjust and I see a figure standing in the middle of the road, hands on hips, stiletto-booted foot tapping on the ground.

I'm out of breath when I slow to a stop. And there she is. Alive, with minor cuts and scrapes but other than that, no worse for the wear.

She wears a self-satisfied grin until she sees me up close.

"Max, oh my God. I thought you could— I mean all the stories— I assumed this was a piece of cake." She reaches a hand toward my head. "This needs sutures."

I wave her away. "That can wait. But you're going to have to fix my shoulder."

Her mouth falls open when she realizes the extent of my injuries.

"I—I don't know how," she says. "If I had a needle and thread I could stitch you up almost as quickly as I got us out of those cords. But I've never set a broken bone or dealt with dislocation." She winces. "How bad does it hurt?"

I lie down in the middle of the road.

"What the hell are you doing?" she asks.

"It hurts like fucking hell," I tell her. "But it's not the first time this has happened. So I'm going to talk you through putting it in place so we can get our asses out of here and figure out what's next."

She nods. "Okay. Tell me what to do."

"You can start by taking off those boots. You're going to need balance and leverage."

She doesn't question me, just unzips one boot and kicks it off. Then the other.

Jesus. My cock grows hard, not caring about the state I'm in. Because her smooth, lithe legs are all but bare to me now.

"You've got to be kidding me," she says.

I raise a brow. "What?" I ask with as much feigned innocence as I can muster.

"That *look*. You're lying there bleeding and broken, but your eyes say you want to fuck me until I've forgotten my name."

I grin. "I could do it, too." And it's a funny thing. In all my years in the service of the Order, which spans more than half my life, I've perfected the art of being wholly unreadable. But when it comes to this woman, I am a goddamn open book. And that's fucking dangerous.

She shakes her head. "I'd think you'd need both your hands to do that," she teases. "And that beautiful cock of yours."

"What about my tongue?"

She licks her lips and swallows. "Yes." Her voice cracks, and it's how I know that if I wanted to, I could fuck this woman into temporary amnesia. "Definitely your tongue."

I clear my throat, getting down to business. "Okay. Brace yourself against me by placing your toes on my torso."

She slides closer to me, pressing the ball of her foot against my side and keeping her heel on the ground.

"Good," I tell her. "Now grab my wrist and lift my arm slowly until it's about forty-five degrees from my body."

She doesn't hesitate but is slow and careful in her movement.

I hiss in a breath through my teeth. "That's it," I tell her, my voice rough. And for the first time since our kidnapping, I see some semblance of fear in her dark eyes. "It's okay, Lora. You can do this. All you have to do now is pull. Slow and steady. And no matter what I say, do not stop. You'll feel it when it pops into place. But until you do, promise you will keep pulling."

She nods and starts to pull.

I grit my teeth, growling softly. The pain intensifies, and the growl crescendoes to a roar. But she keeps pulling until finally there is that all too familiar pop and sweet fucking relief.

She lowers my hand to the ground and kneels beside me, running her fingers through my hair.

"Are you okay?" she asks.

"I am now, Princess."

She rolls her eyes.

"Hey," I add. "Tell me how the hell you jumped in those damned boots and survived."

She grins. "I guess you didn't do all your homework on me, did you?"

I raise a brow.

"When the Order found me, I was performing in a traveling troupe of aerial acrobats and trapeze artists."

I rise onto my left elbow. "You were in the circus?"

She groans. "It was much more professional

than that, thank you very much. But what you should be asking is what tricks I can do with my body that you haven't seen yet."

My throat goes dry. "We need to call in the incident and possibly make an appearance at the local base for a debriefing. After that, you are my master and commander on one condition." I slide my restored right arm up her thigh and under her tiny skirt where I know now—after seeing her stand above me—that she did not waste time putting on the G-string when we were kidnapped.

She gasps as my thumb brushes over her clit.

"And what condition is that?" she asks, her voice husky and breathless.

"You show me everything that body has been trained to do."

CHAPTER EIGHT

Z

AS MUCH AS it kills me, I step away from X's clever fingers. We follow the road to civilization until we finally recognize our surroundings. The wind blows cool from the Thames, bringing with it the briny scent of brackish water and a hint of refuse. I close my eyes and pay attention to the smells of the city, centering myself, finding my bearings. There is a faint hint of piss from the wall outside the Dancing Pony pub on the corner. The greasy aroma of a kabob shop. My own perfume and the faint hint of sweat from our exertion. The sheer scent of X.

Oh God, I could drop to my knees and bury my face between his legs like a nineteenth-century harlot plying my wares on the London streets.

"First things, first," I say before biting my lip so hard that I can't believe it doesn't draw blood. "We need some new clothes." It's chilly. Really chilly. Gooseflesh peppers my skin and my nipples are taut, for once not from this man's attentions. I can't stay outside dressed in, well, nothing.

"Clothes?" A muscle twitches in X's jaw. "I was rather hoping we could be dispensing with those."

I roll my eyes. *Men.*

"Do you mind thinking with the head above your neck for a minute, Max? I know you're injured, but surely you haven't forgotten why we're in our current situation. Or has it just escaped your notice that we were kidnapped from a sex club while on a secret mission to bust Dante Price? Which means our cover has been blown, and Dante was dispatching us." My shoulders stoop. "We failed, X. We failed the mission. Somehow we messed up." I kick at an empty soda can for extra effect and send it skittering across the road.

I glance at the man in front of me. I want to unburden myself, but I can't even trust X. Or Max. We have so many names. So many faces. It's a wonder that I don't drown in all the lies I tell.

But he is remarkably calm at the moment. I search his features for anything human, a sense that what just happened to him, to me, to us, left an impression.

But nothing.

Could he suspect anything? He's so incredibly calm. Impossibly composed.

Granted, I feel the same way.

I take a breath. Not too deep. I don't want him to see that my nerves are shaken.

"Sorry for that outburst," I mumble.

"Not a problem," he says, glancing up the street. A car turns. Headlights almost upon us.

We both jump back on instinct, taking shelter in the deep shadow of an alley dumpster. It's just a cab. Not more henchmen.

"You want clothes?" X asks, glancing over at me, a hint of humor entering his frosty gaze. "Follow me. Let's go."

I balk, crossing my arms. "Why do you get to choose the place?"

Think. Think. What's your next step here, Lora?

Ah, yes. My shoulders drop an inch in relief. There is a safe house across the Thames. After we give our statement at the local base, I can head there and regroup.

The only question is how can I get there alone?

Any trick up my sleeve, he likely has, too.

I'm going to have to up my game.

He assesses me coolly. "I'm not able to speak to what's going on in that pretty head of yours, but if you want to avoid attracting attention, I suggest you stick with me. At least for now. Unless—" his smile fades "—*you* had something to do with that stunt in the club. Tell me again how you're an acrobat who can jump from a van going forty klicks and land on her four-inch stilettos."

I glance at my boots, teeth clenched.

"You think I played a part in what just happened?" I say, my tone dripping with indignation. "Don't be ridiculous. Of course not."

I'm good at risky escapes, less good at convincing lies.

He gives me a skeptical once-over, and I feel the heat of his penetrating gaze all the way to my toes, which involuntarily curl.

Stupid, traitorous body. Wanting him even now.

I remind myself of the state he was in when he found me—his right arm held tight to his body, the wound on his head that only now has stopped bleeding, his voice hoarse as he called my name.

He was worried about me, wasn't he? I squeeze my eyes shut, scrolling through the mental Rolodex of briefs I read about Agent X—the stunts he himself pulled, the escapes he made. He fooled powerful men into wanting to be him and powerful women into loving him just to obtain information necessary to save the world. He was legendary before he was even thirty. And now?

Now I cannot sort fact from fiction. I know how well he's trained in the fine art of deception, because I've had the same training.

I could hook him up to a lie detector. Torture him. Inject him with truth serum and he wouldn't crack.

And I am freezing my ass off. In another minute, my teeth will be chattering.

"Fine," I snap. "But you are buying."

His chuckle is deep and rich, like dark chocolate, and leaves my mouth watering.

"Harrods." I cross my arms over my chest. "They're open for one more hour, and I am ready for some *real* clothes."

He arches a brow. "Harrods? You don't come cheap."

I blow him a kiss in return. "Darling, you have no idea. I want to hit the food hall, too. All this excitement has made me crave crepes with vanilla ice cream."

"Sounds delicious," he says, taking a step forward. Indeed, it looks as if he could eat me instead.

A cab rolls down the street toward us. I put two fingers in my mouth and blow hard, hailing it. "To Knightsbridge," I tell the driver as we slide into the back. "And step on it."

X

When we finally enter Harrods, it's thirty minutes until closing. Thankfully my phone and the small stash of cash and the one card I carry still sit safely in my pocket, having somehow survived the jump. This is Harrods after all, and despite who I may know on the inside, nothing here comes for free.

Z pouts, and the sheer honesty of the expression socks me in the gut…but I keep from visibly reacting. "I guess crepes are off the table," she says. "Clothes are more important, I suppose."

I wink at her. "Let me just make a quick call."

I step away while she wanders into the women's accessories and tries on a red cloche hat that, against her dark hair and creamy skin, looks absolutely gorgeous—until my eyes travel south to that ridiculous ball-gown bodice atop the shortest of short skirts, her legs still clad in those sexy boots. I laugh softly as the phone on the other end rings, reminding myself that the Italian suit I'm wearing is torn in several places from my landing, and the side of my face is likely covered in blood.

All in a day's work.

Someone picks up.

"X. Is that you?"

"Ewan, my boy," I say. "Still working the finest *crêperie* this side of the Thames?"

He chuckles. "You need me to stay open after hours, don't you?"

"We'll be there in thirty minutes," I say. "Just have one chocolate-banana crepe waiting, and we'll take it to go."

Ewan sighs. But I can tell my old friend is smiling. "Extra whipped cream for you?"

"Always," I tell him. "A million thanks. See you soon."

I walk toward a makeup counter as the woman behind stares at me in horror. When I get to a mirror, I see that my suspicions were right. The gash at my temple isn't bleeding now, but I do look a hell of a lot worse than I feel. Sutures will have to wait, but I do need some cleaning up.

"Can I—help you, sir?" the young woman—barely into her twenties, I'd guess—asks me. "A tissue? Or an ambulance, perhaps?"

I laugh. "That's good. You're quite funny…" I peer at her name tag. "Miss Gemma."

I grin, and despite my state, she blushes.

"Still got it," I mumble under my breath.

"What was that, sir?" Gemma asks.

"Oh, I was wondering if you had any of those makeup-remover wipes."

She nods earnestly, squatting behind the counter for a moment before reappearing again with a pouch of wipes.

"Thank you! Yes! These will do."

I grab the package from her and proceed to clean my battered face with the wipes. *All* the wipes. But when I'm done, I barely look like I jumped out of a moving van after being kidnapped at a sex club. In other words, it's just another day that ends in *y*.

I gather the pile of bloodied wipes and beseech poor horrified Gemma for a trash bin.

She lifts a small one from behind the counter, and I stuff the rags into it. Then I pull out a wad of bills, sliding them across the counter.

"For your troubles," I tell her. "And for keeping my visit here just between us."

Gemma nods, blushing again, and I know what she's thinking—that she's just met 007. This makes me laugh as I stride to where Z picks out a bag to match her hat.

Then I wonder. Is she my Pussy Galore? Was her reference to being an acrobat a hint to her being in on Price's arms trading?

A couple hours ago I thought she was dead and would have done anything to bring her back. Now I wonder. When we get to the final move in whatever game we're playing, will her weapon be trained on Price—or me?

* * *

"You're stunning," I tell her thirty minutes later when she's dressed in a formfitting black cashmere turtleneck, tight black pants and suede ankle boots. With the red hat and bag, she looks like she stepped out of Vogue in the '60s, the Audrey Hepburn edition.

She looks me up and down. Tonight I went rogue. Suits for me are everyday wear, so I decided to shake things up in dark-washed denim and a black crewneck sweater.

"And you look good enough to eat," she says, smiling at me with ruby-red lips, a shade she bought from Gemma while I was changing. "Which will have to suffice since we're too late for crepes."

I check my watch. "We will be if we don't hurry," I say. Then I grab her hand and pull her to the escalator and our next destination.

Her eyes widen when she sees Ewan waiting for us, a gorgeous chocolate-banana crepe waiting in an open to-go container.

"I waited for you so it would be fresh." He lifts a metal canister from the counter and covers the crepe with freshly whipped cream.

Z bounces on her toes, clapping, and suddenly she is not Z anymore. She's Lora twenty years ago, dragging me into a luxury department store just so she can window-shop from inside. But we don't leave empty-handed. I took her here for her first crepe.

"You remembered?" she says, her eyes shining as Ewan hands her the container and a fork.

I shake his hand, pressing into his palm more than enough for his troubles of staying open past his normal quitting time, then turn to Lora.

"Of course I remember. I remember everything about you."

Plus, I come here every time I'm in London and eat a chocolate-banana crepe so I don't forget this one thing that she loved.

We wave to Ewan and make our way onto London's streets, where we walk and Lora feeds me a few obligatory bites of her crepe before polishing it off herself.

"Do you really remember everything about me?" she asks when those beautiful red lips are free of both fork and crepe.

I nod. Though we walk side by side, we are noticeably distant as we start this jog down memory lane. Maybe, though, when we're done, she'll realize I'm someone she can trust rather than fear. And maybe, just maybe, I'll realize the same about her.

I glance at my watch. "They want us for a debriefing at midnight," I tell her. "We've got two hours to do whatever we want. You pick the destination, and on the way there, I'll tell you everything I remember about Max and Lora."

She worries her bottom lip between her teeth. "I'd like that."

I smile and shrug. "Then that only leaves one question. Where to?"

CHAPTER NINE

Z

"You sure this is okay?" I ask, licking the last of the whipped cream from the crepe off my fingers. I grin inwardly, noting that Max doesn't blink. His gaze is transfixed on my lips, and I make sure I get everything extra clean, just for his benefit.

"Of course," he answers, handing two tickets to the attendant. "I said you could choose."

We get into our capsule in the London Eye, the giant Ferris wheel on the southern bank of the Thames. We have it to ourselves despite the line. My guess is X slipped some extra pounds to the attendant to get it. We could sit if we want, but there is plenty of room to stand. And so we do.

Then the door shuts and we go up. The lights of London are soon laid out at our feet, and it's so quiet. As if the real world is far, far away.

I could tell him everything. Every last secret.

Every part of my plan. He couldn't run here. He'd be forced to hear me out.

But as much as I want to, my mouth won't speak the words.

"Let's review the facts," he says after a minute of strained silence.

"Let's," I murmur, focusing on Big Ben and the lights of Parliament House.

"Someone wants us dead."

"Do they?" I cast him a sidelong glance, trying to decide if he looks at all suspicious. "Because we are still alive. And in this line of work, if someone wants to kill an agent of the Order, they usually don't take chances."

He digests this a moment. "What do you think?"

"We were to be taken somewhere for questioning. Someone wants to talk to us."

"Usually those invitations consist of a polite phone call and a cup of tea."

I smirk, playing with a lock of my hair. "I'm guessing this someone isn't exactly one of the good guys."

"No." Two furrows indent the space between X's brows. "Indeed not."

"I'm guessing this bad guy also isn't Dante Price?"

X cocks his head and smooths a hand over his scruff. "Go on."

"Because the Lion's Den is his space. Why would he risk the reputation of the most popular kink club in the United Kingdom? His clientele insists on discretion. Safety. Not strangers barging in guns blazing."

"You're not wrong." He sighs. "I've been going back over all the people I've pissed off through the years."

I arch a brow. "And?"

His smile doesn't quite reach his eyes. "It's a long list."

"Mine too." My smile is also cool in return. "And guess who's at the top?"

"X marks the spot?" he queries.

I blow him a kiss.

"I don't trust you, Lora," he says at last. "I want to, but… I can't. The nature of our work has eroded the part of me that has faith. Don't get me wrong. I believe in love. I saw it when I worked at the court at Edenvale. But I've had to accept that for me… my life is safer going it alone."

"Safer for whom?" I whisper, taking a step closer, swinging my hips like a hypnotist's watch.

"Everyone who matters." His voice is rough gravel and grinds away at my self-control.

I take another step and close the gap. "Do I matter?" My lips graze his ear.

I can sense rather than see him tense. "More than you can possibly know."

"But you don't trust me."

"Not as far as I can throw you."

"And you think you can throw me far?" A challenge creeps into my tone. I don't know how to be honest. How to admit that all I want is him. And freedom to live a simple life. That my arms ache for a child. That I'm weary of dark alleys and darker deeds.

All I know how to do is deceive and seduce.

"I think I can throw you onto that bench and fuck you until you forget what day it is."

A delicious thrill shoots through me. At least we still have this. We'll always have this connection. "It's Saturday."

"That's enough talking, Princess." He seizes me by the waist in a sudden movement, hauling me up and sprawling me down on the bench. "And someday I might look at you and not want to bury my dick balls-deep in you, but today isn't that day."

"What romance," I purr sarcastically, even as his words drench my pussy. "Keep it up and you'll rival Shakespeare with his sonnets."

"If you don't stop talking I'm going to have to fill that smart mouth."

"With?"

He frees his cock with a quick jerk of his trousers. "This."

I make a show of licking my lips. "I was impressed when you bought me the crepe. I didn't realize I was getting dessert in the bargain."

That takes him by surprise, and his bark of laughter heats me even more than the sight of thick, gorgeous, uncut cock.

"Do you remember the first time I ever sucked you off?" I lean on my elbows and idly rub a thumb over the swell of my breast.

"How could I forget?" he rasps, crawling over me. "I didn't think I'd last a minute."

"You didn't," I tease.

"The second your tongue touched my shaft I knew there was a heaven. Fuck, I saw God."

"I hope you told her hello."

Before I can engage in any more banter he thrusts his cock between my lips and down I take him, down, down, down, because God, he's huge. Relaxing, I open my throat and make him welcome, breathing in his essence, the sandalwood of his shampoo and his own personal masculine musk. Pulling back I release his head with an audible pop before I unbutton my own pants. "Don't let me have all the fun," I say, wiggling my panties over my hips and then he's there, licking me hard and fast, his taste jolting through my body.

"I love the taste of your hot cunt," he groans as a mewling sound tears from my throat.

"What a coincidence, because I'd give your cock three Michelin stars."

"Shall we sixty-nine?" he rumbles, tension tightening his voice as a bead of precome shines in the deep slit at the head of his cock.

"Why not?" I wink, as my whole body judders in anticipation. "After all, it's my lucky number."

X

We dangle at the top of the wheel—just as my balls dangle above her plump, gorgeous lips. She truly is an acrobat, her lithe body more flexible than I could have imagined.

She licks my sac, and I shudder. I pay her back by plunging my tongue between her thick, swollen folds.

Lora gasps.

"I may not trust you," I say, savoring the sweet tang of her juices. "But I sure as hell enjoy tasting you."

My tongue swirls around her clit, and she retaliates by sucking me down from tip to base.

"Fuck," I growl, and she hums around my throbbing cock.

She wraps a strong palm around my shaft, and

her hand follows her lips, sliding me in and out of her naughty mouth.

I spread her open and bury my face in her, fucking her with my tongue and one finger while rocking my hips into her face. Then I put in two. Then three. I can hear the sound of her wetness and it turns me on even more.

"Max!" she gasps as my balls bounce off her chin. "Jesus fuck, Max! I can't— Oh my God."

I pump my fingers harder, impale her with my mouth, and she fucks me with hers.

My eyes roll in my head as we hurtle toward the point of no return.

With her ass pressed to the glass of the capsule, I feast on her until she cries out my name again and again, her body quaking as she rides the wave, undulates to the final pulses of my fingers, the laps of my tongue. And when she regains control, she devours my cock, taking me so deep I swear I feel her goddamn tonsils.

With one hand on my balls and her other gliding up and down my slick shaft as she takes me into her mouth once more, I reach the pinnacle, exploding inside her, growling like a wild animal, until I have nothing left to give.

I slide out of her mouth, and she brushes her forearm across her lips as she swallows all that I gave her. Then she licks her lips, her red lipstick smeared across her face and her cloche hat askew atop her wild chocolate waves.

I straighten and pull my pants over my fading erection, and she fixes hers, as well. Then I tug her onto my lap and kiss her swollen lips.

"Why?" I ask her. "Why fuck me anonymously for all that time when it's so much better knowing it's you?"

She shrugs. "*I* knew."

But I shake my head. "It's not the same, Lora, and you know it. Trust or no, it's infinitely hotter knowing it's your mouth around my cock, your pussy I get to taste."

She slides off my lap and onto the bench next to me.

"Stop it, Max. You're the one who said you're better off going at it alone. My little deception was the exact same thing—maintaining my own safety."

I scrub a hand across my jaw. "*Touché*, Agent Z. You've got me there."

The wheel moves with a jerk, and we're now minutes from the bottom, back where we started. What a metaphor for our relationship.

Highest heights. Lowest lows.

"It wasn't me," she says, continuing our previous argument.

"Nor was it me," I say. "But you'll never truly believe me. Nor I you."

She sighs, then reaches into her red bag and pulls out a compact. She opens it and gets to work going from looking freshly fucked to just fresh. And gorgeous. Always gorgeous.

"I guess you have me there, as well, Agent X."

When we reach the bottom, she steps out first, and I follow.

"One more stop before home base?" I ask.

She shrugs. "Sure. Why not?"

But there is a buoyancy missing from her step, and I feel the same weight pressing down on me.

Our cover is blown, and I can't know for sure if she's the one who blew it or not.

I hail a taxi and whisper the address to the driver. Tonight has been full of surprises. As an act of good faith, I want it to end with a good one before we have to get back to work.

We pull up short of the street vendor I know will be at this corner. And even before we get out of the car, Lora gasps.

"Oh, Max. You remember everything, don't you?"

Without answering, I step out of the taxi, then reach a hand in for her.

When she emerges, her eyes brighten when she sees the night florist. At least, that's what we always called him. During the day this section of the street boasts an outdoor market, but the flower vendor is never there. Only at night does he show up with his diverse collection, including Lora's favorite.

"Buy you a hydrangea?" I say, and her cheeks flush.

She practically runs to the cart, where there is a small line waiting to pay. She finds her favorite blue flower and grabs a stem that is wrapped in tissue paper and cellophane.

"I'll buy them all," I say. "If you want them."

She shakes her head, and her eyes glow with a sheen that might actually be tears.

"I haven't owned any sort of plant in over a decade," she says.

I nod because I understand. "For someone without a true home, plants are impractical. But you can own this for as long as our mission lasts."

She lets out a bitter laugh. "In our hotel room."

"Yes," I tell her. "In our hotel room. Don't trust me with your life, Lora. You don't have to do that. But trust that I haven't forgotten anything of our time together all those years ago. Not one damned thing."

"Okay," she says, her voice almost a whisper. "I'll trust that."

So I buy the vendor out of hydrangeas and give them to the only girl I've ever loved—who is now the one woman who has the power to either love me or kill me.

Or both.

She carries the flowers as we walk, my arm around her shoulders, until we reach a building with an unmarked door that doesn't have a knob, just a key panel on the door frame.

I punch in a number, and I hear a hiss of air and the snick of one dead bolt, then two, then three and four. Then the door pops open and we enter the home base of the London Order.

CHAPTER TEN

Z

OTHER THAN THE unmarked door, the Order's local base looks like any one of a thousand drab middle-class row houses in London town—brick, three levels, windows hidden by lace curtains. That's precisely what makes it so safe.

"Ah! Hello, loves." The elderly woman who greets us is wearing a housecoat and fuzzy pink rabbit slippers. Her hair is a soft white and pulled into a wispy bun. She could be anyone's grand-mother.

Though I know that inside her front left pocket is a garrote made of wire or fishing line. This mild-mannered granny is a highly lethal assassin, trained in the arts of strangulation techniques and master of disguises.

Agent G guards this safe house, and I don't have a clue about the appearance of her real face, the one hidden behind this elaborately deceptive mask. But once I had occasion to see her neatly dispatch two wannabe terrorists in quick succession, choking the life out of them before they could widen their eyes in surprise at their unexpected angel of death.

A television blares from the sitting room. I catch sight of a rocking chair, a paisley couch and a coffee table holding tea for one. For a moment my heart pangs—even though I know this is all an illusion, I can't deny it looks so…normal. I once had a normal life, too. A house. A mother. A father. I didn't kill. I wasn't hunted.

I walked my dog on country roads and listened to music in my bedroom.

The girl seems like a stranger to me now.

"Apologies for the noise. My hearing is going, you know, and I do so love *Doctor Who*."

"Indeed," I say in a deadpan tone, happy to carry on the charade. No doubt the television is blaring to cover up the sounds of an interrogation happening somewhere below us.

"If you wouldn't mind popping downstairs, I'm sure you will find something to occupy you. Now come in, come in, before you catch your deaths of cold."

She bustles us in and opens the plain-looking door beneath the simple staircase that leads upstairs. There is dark floral wallpaper peeling on the walls and a fine film of dust on the banister.

We step into the closet and press against the mothball-scented jackets.

"Where's the damn button," X mumbles to himself.

"It's behind me," I respond and press an inconspicuous button colored to match the paneling.

Without so much as a lurch, the floor begins to descend.

Because we're in a hidden lift, not a closet at all.

We come to a stop three floors below, and when I push open the door we aren't in sweet Granny's house anymore.

The hallway is a sterile white and the cement floor is illuminated by fluorescent lighting. There are four doors on either side, all a dull metal.

The one on the right, three down, swings open and out limps a slight man, around thirty, with pasty skin and thinning hair.

"Ah, Z, it's been a long time," he says, beaming at me while adjusting his cardigan.

I can't help but return the grin. "Beta, I didn't know you were in England."

He used to be my assistant in the East Asian office. Beta wasn't officially an agent of the Order, but he provided tech support—hacking, code breaking and the like. Very useful in a pinch.

"It seems fate has brought us together," he says, holding open the door for us to enter. "Please, please come in. Ah, and you must be the famous X."

"Famous?" X queries, sliding into a leather seat before being invited.

The room is full of state-of-the-art computers and surveillance equipment. Dozens of screens run dozens of complicated strings of code.

I don't know what any of it is for, but if Beta has been brought to London, things are happening. He is one of the best.

"The Order might be the most secretive organization in the world, but that doesn't mean it doesn't have its share of celebrities. I'm sitting with the A-list right now."

I don't waste any time. "We were attacked on an operation tonight. In the Lion's Den."

Beta swings to the closest keyboards and his fingers fly as he types in some commands.

A moment later, the flat screen above our heads blinks on and a grainy surveillance video begins to play. It may be black-and-white, but that doesn't mean it isn't incredibly obvious that the two people on the screen are X and myself. And…

And…

Oh my God. My pussy floods with arousal, drenching my folds. We are consuming each other.

I've never been one for pornography, but I can't deny the power of our connection up there on the screen for all to see.

No wonder the woman at the club tapped us for notice.

We are riveting.

Beta clears his throat. "Quite a good performance," he stammers.

"A-list," X reminds him coolly.

I give him a subtle sidelong glance. He might as well be carved from marble. No sign that seeing our passion in the sex club ignited so much as a glimmer of deeper feeling. He is master of self-control. And my fingers twitch as I resist the impulse to leap to my feet and scream, "Was it real, what you felt in there? Is any of this real?"

But I don't move a muscle. In the video, the door flies open and the henchmen pour in.

"I hacked this all off the security feed from the club an hour ago," Beta explains. "But I can't get a visual on any of the assailants. Their faces are all hidden, so it evades my facial recognition software."

"So where does this leave us?" X asks.

"It appears that Dante Price didn't order the hit. Chatter shows he was as surprised as anyone. In fact, after you were hauled out, he fled to an unknown location."

"If Dante didn't order the hit, who did?" I ask.

The door to the room opens as I speak and a tall blonde woman enters. "As far as we can tell, it was one of you," she says.

X

I don't react. I remain as impassive as ever, one of the many things I was trained to do. Acting shocked would be expected from someone who is innocent but also someone who is lying. And right now, I'm not letting on that I'm either until I know for sure who Z is. She is my Lora from decades ago, true. But she is also someone entirely new. And we are either allies or enemies. There is no in-between.

"So that would suggest a mole in the Order," I say calmly. "That would be a first, would it not, Your Highness?" I offer the woman a slight bow.

The blonde woman herself might be a stranger to Lora, but I know she recognizes Cordelia, queen of Edenvale—the kingdom I lived to protect for most of my career.

As expected, Lora's eyes widen, and then she bows, as well.

"Your Highness," she says. "I was under the impression that after you resurfaced you had retired for good."

I jerk my head, detecting a faint trace of jealousy in Lora's statement.

The queen nods, then strides toward me and wraps me in a warm embrace. I hug her tight. "You saved my life once," she says. "And my husband's and sons'. It's my turn to help you."

When we let go, Lora looks at us both with a tight smile, and the queen motions for us to sit at a small round table while Beta continues to study the various screens.

"You're correct, Agent Z. I have all but retired now that it's finally safe for me to be with my family. But I owe your partner a debt I'll never be able to repay. Stepping in to help was the least I could do."

On instinct, I rest my hand on Lora's chair. My thumb brushes the soft cashmere of her sweater, and she flinches ever so slightly. I have to bite back a grin.

Is she jealous of my connection to Queen Cordelia?

"Tell us what you know," I say.

"Price is bad," Cordelia says. "And we want him put behind bars eventually. But he wasn't the real mission. At least, not entirely."

I cross my arms and lean back in my chair. It seems this is going to get very interesting.

"Are you saying that we were decoys?" Lora

asks, forgetting all her lessons and letting her anger shine through. "That we did what we did—on *camera*—and that wasn't the real job?"

Cordelia presses her palms to the table, ever in control.

"Oh, Price is the job, Z. But what's worse than an outside enemy?" she asks.

Beta mumbles from his computer terminal, "The one who's right under your nose. Everybody *knows* that." He laughs at his pun then spins toward the three of us, eyes bright. "Did you hear that? *Nose* and *knows*? Brilliant, right? Absolutely brilliant."

He concentrates on his screens rather than us.

"So one of us is working with or for Price, then," Cordelia says. "And set up tonight's hit without letting him in on it so he would react accordingly—with complete and utter shock. Doesn't seem to make sense, though, does it? If we have a mole, you'd think he—or she—would have seen to it that the targeted agent or agents were taken out. It was a sloppy job to say the least. So what I'm going to do is interview you each separately, compare your stories, and we'll go from there. I'm going to need you two to stay the night. It's late already, and we can't be sure your hotel room is safe now that you've been made. We keep you under surveillance—"

"And Price gets away," Lora and I say in unison.

The queen hums. "Interesting" is all she says in reaction. Then she turns her gaze to me.

"Go and get that gash tended to," she says. "There's an infirmary—"

"I'll suture it myself," I inform her.

She smiles and shakes her head. "Of course you will, Max. I see not much has changed." She stands. "Come, Agent Z. I can't concentrate with all these screens. To the debriefing room, shall we?"

Z rises, as do I. "Of course, Your Highness." She barely glances my direction as Cordelia leads her out of the room. I pause, making like I'm checking my pockets for something I've lost, and then I stroll to Beta's side.

"Can you play that surveillance video one more time?" I ask him.

He obliges me without question. And I watch the two of us wrapped in such undeniable pleasure, however short-lived it was. Whatever the outcome of our story, I know this much—what's on that feed is anything but a performance.

This thought lingers at the back of my mind as I stand in front of a mirror tying off a third suture at my split-open temple. Two more and I'm done. Not half-bad for a night's work. Then I stare at the man in the reflection. He has salt-and-pepper hair and lines at the corners of his eyes. He seems to have a permanent five o'clock shadow and occasional dark circles under his eyes. I lift my shirt and map the many scars tattooing my flesh, each one a memory of a life I saved and others that were lost. I wonder when this man who looks so much like me ceased being a boy and turned into someone so jaded, weathered and untrusting. But I already know the answer. It was the day they tattooed the crow's feather on my arm, the day I pledged my life to the Order. I might have only been at the tail end of my teens, but it was then that the boy with his whole life ahead of him became both a preserver and taker of life, all for the greater good.

Wasn't it?

The question is getting harder and harder to answer.

I run a hand through my hair and then splash cold water on my face. When I step out of the exam room—the one I forbade the base doctor to enter—Lora is there.

She forces a bland smile.

"Your turn," she says. "Figured I'd come tell you—and see how you were."

I clear my throat, wanting to believe the concern in those deep brown eyes.

"Five sutures and I'm good as new," I say. "Don't worry, I know if—"

"If I wanted to kill you I would have already?" she interrupts.

I laugh. But the truth is, whichever one of us wants the other dead, it's not time yet. There's too much to learn no matter whose side we're on.

"Here," she says, pressing a thin metal card into my palm. "To get into your room."

I raise a brow. "Oh? Separate rooms, then."

She smiles softly. "Yep. But I'm right next door if you get scared when things go bump in the night."

I slide the key card into my pocket, then run the tips of my fingers along her hairline.

"Sweetheart," I say. "Don't you know? My favorite part of the night are the things that go bump."

CHAPTER ELEVEN

Z

"ONE OF US is guilty as sin," I whisper.

"Yes." His fingers roughly trail down the side my face, slide under my jaw and thumb my chin, forcing my gaze to stay fixed on his.

"And it isn't me," I add in a confident purr.

"It isn't me," he says.

"One of us is a liar?"

His smile is small. "Darling, we are both liars. Lying is what we do. It's in our marrow."

I lean into him, letting my breasts brush his chest. "It isn't all we do."

Muscles cord in his neck as he swallows thickly. "No, we have many skills."

I shimmy my hips a fraction closer, gloating at the harsh sound of his breath. I have to take my victories where I can. "So many."

He has the door open and me inside before I can take my next breath.

His knife is cool against my throat. He doesn't tremble. Neither do I. My blade is pressed to his throat, too, the tip teasing at the jugular. We dance on the edge, holding the other's death in the palms of our hands.

"I suppose this is what you call an impasse," he drawls lazily, as if our mortality isn't pressing in from all sides.

"I would call it admitting that you are the mole," I murmur. "Because I'm sure as hell not."

He rolls his eyes. "Because *of course* a mole would saunter through the Order's headquarters saying, 'It is I, the mole, here to steal intelligence for a price.'"

"Aha." I press the blade a fraction more—any more pressure and I'll draw first blood. "So you admit you are betraying the Order for money?"

"No." His nostrils flare in annoyance. "I simply said that is what a mole would be doing."

"Just tell me why you did it," I snap, annoyed to feel hot tears pricking the corners of my eyes. This isn't what I do. I'm not a crier. I'm ice. I'm stone. Now that the queen has been reinstated to the throne, I'm the most feared female secret agent in the world.

I'm not a woman who makes it a habit to blubber over a man.

Tension ebbs from his body as his gaze hoods. "Put down the knife, Lora. We need to talk straight for a change."

Shit. He takes me by surprise and I hesitate. He takes the advantage, twisting me around so my arm is pinned, the knife useless by my side.

Then a flash of sharp pain bursts from the side of my neck. The bastard stabbed me!

Wait, no… I grow light-headed. Max didn't stab me with a knife. He…he injected me.

"Sodium pentothal," he rasps in my ear. "The Order's own special version. I'm getting to the bottom of this."

The world moves slower, as if oxygen has transformed to invisible molasses.

"Truth serum," I giggle, shocked he pulled one over on me. I'm impressed. It's a first for me. "Are you fucking kidding me?"

"Sit on the bed." He pushes me down and I comply like a rag doll. "Lora. Pet, what the hell have you gone and gotten yourself mixed up in?"

My head lolls on my neck as I study his cruel, unreadable expression. I feel as if I've just woken up from a three-hour nap on a sun-drenched beach. As if I've had a bottle of wine and the world's best orgasm. The truth serum is taking over and making me totally uninhibited. I could try to fight the effects. But right now I enjoy losing my iron grip on control. And besides, if X is trying to manipulate me for information, his line of questioning will soon reveal all.

"You." I flop on the bed. "I've fallen into the X rabbit hole, and in X Land we are all mad."

He swears a string of oaths under his breath as he paces the room's perimeter.

"I am *trying* to protect you," he says.

"Mmm-hmm. Just like that time when we were climbing Ben Nevis and it started to storm?"

"Ben Nevis?" He pauses. "There's a trip down memory lane."

I close my eyes. "Isn't it though?"

Back at Frasier Academy, we went on a school trip to the tallest mountain in the British isles. When the weather turned foul, Max and I got separated from the group. We were caught overnight in whiteout conditions, huddled under an overhang of rock and clinging to each other for warmth.

"It was the first time we ever spent alone in each other's company. Remember how you told me stories that night?" I sigh, boneless and wobbly. "You told me how the Disney version of *The Little Mermaid* was bullshit and in Hans Christian Andersen's version the mermaid turns to sea foam at the end and loses her immortal soul."

"Not exactly the happiest tale. My game has improved since then."

"You told it so beautifully. It was the first time I ever really saw you. The *real* Max. Not just the rugby player who was stronger and smarter than all the other boys. You showed me depths that night and I've been drowning ever since."

"Drowning?"

"In you." My eyes grow heavy as sleep sets in. "Drowning in your depths."

X

My phone buzzes with an encrypted message. I do the obligatory ocular scan before it translates from what looks like the matrix to English. It's from Cordelia.

Lora's story checks out with yours. But something's still not right, just as you suspected. Her lack of injuries, her cool demeanor. I know of her history in acrobatics. That much is true. But she wasn't pulled into the Order because of it. She came here one night, pounding on the very door you entered through this evening, screaming for her life. We let her in, Max. We let her in because she said if we didn't, she would be killed. She was beaten bloody and thought to be a civilian. Her identification checked out. We let her recuperate, were prepared to wipe her memory and send her back onto the London streets. But she would whisper things in her sleep, things about a man named Peter. Frightening things, even for me to hear. We thought it was the man she was running from, but now we aren't so sure. He might be the man who sent a mole to us. I trust you've given her the sodium pentothal by now. Find out who Peter is, and if she is his mole, dispatch her at once. Surveillance is on in your room. We will be there if you need backup, but I don't suspect you will.

I clear my throat and look at Lora, so peaceful and beautiful in sleep. I sit next to her, take her hat off and run my fingers through her hair.

"Lora," I croon softly. "Lora, it's Max. Can we talk?"

She hums and smiles, her eyes fluttering open to meet mine.

"Hi, Max," she says, her voice so sweet I almost don't recognize it.

"Tell me about Peter," I say with practiced coolness.

She lifts a languid hand and rests it on my thigh, giving me a soft squeeze.

"Do we have to? Peter ruins everything," she pouts.

Good. She is still deep under the influence of the serum.

She grabs my hand and places it between her legs. "I'd much rather talk about what your capable hands and fingers can do to me. That's so much more fun."

My cock hardens in a fraction of a second, and my fingers twitch, inadvertently tapping where I know her beautiful clit hides beneath her pants.

"Peter first," I say, reluctantly pulling my hand free. "Then I'll give you whatever you want."

She rises up on an elbow and smiles coyly at me.

"You *know* Peter, silly. He was your biggest competitor at Frasier, and when he found out about you and me, he went ballistic. I can't believe you forgot."

My brows draw together. "Peter Cain?" I ask. God, I haven't thought about that guy since secondary school. Even then I never thought much of him. "I wasn't aware we were competing."

She crawls to her knees, then rests her hands on my shoulders. I can smell the perfume she must

have sprayed on when we were at Harrods. Chanel. Christ, she smells good.

"Of course *you* didn't know. You were always
one step ahead of him—in class marks, in athlet-
ics. You did break his nose in rugby, you know."

I chuckle. "That's rugby, Lora. It was nothing
more than that."

"He hates you. Hates you. *H-A-T-E-S* you, and
you never knew. You never even noticed, and that
only infuriated him more. You didn't know anything." She squeezes her eyes shut and grits her
teeth. "Make it stop, Max. I don't want to say anything else." She slides a hand down my torso, then
between my legs until she's cupping my balls.

I hiss in a breath. They're watching us, our
every move. They can see that she's fighting the
serum. And they can hear every word she says. But
this isn't how I wanted this to happen. Whatever
she's hiding, I won't let her incriminate herself if
it comes to that.

"Tell me, Lora. No one leaves this room until
the truth comes out."

She grips me tight, her palm rubbing up my
rigid cock. "Peter Cain wanted everything you
had, Max. Including me. I was broken when you
left, when I thought you must have died. And he
was there to pick up the pieces. He was also there
when I found out you were alive, and when that

knowledge wrecked me all over again. It's so stupid, but being close to him made me feel close to you. I knew it was terrible, but I was self-destructive."

Peter Cain.

Peter Cain.

The words niggle at a memory. What is it with that name? So he was a school rival? I vaguely remember the pain in the ass. The little lord who liked to pick on me for being a scholarship kid. Typical blue blood prick born with a silver spoon in his mouth. But I haven't thought of him in almost two decades. So he loved Lora and likely seduced her. I've been with more than my share of women over the years. I might have left. But I never loved any but her.

Wait.

The memory unfolds.

Peter. *Daniel.* Cain.

Our instructors always used our full names for roll call.

I rearrange the letters of *Peter D. Cain* in my head and can't believe it is this fucking easy.

Dante Price.

Peter Cain is Dante Price.

And that can only mean one thing…

Lora *is* the mole.

I open the music app on my phone and scroll

until I find what I'm looking for—Beethoven's Fifth Symphony. I set the volume at medium to start, and then I lean in to kiss the woman the Order likely wants me to kill. But before my lips touch hers, I whisper to her.

"There's a camera in the corner of the room behind my left shoulder and a gun holstered above the small of my back. I am at your mercy, Lora. Tell me the rest before it's too late. And then either kill me or turn yourself in."

Slowly I crank the volume a couple levels higher. Then I kiss her hard. She shoves her hands inside my suit jacket and reaches for the gun. Then she shoots out the camera and the electric panel at the door, and then points the gun straight at my forehead.

Tears streak her face.

"I loved you so much, Max. I still do. You broke me twice, and Peter put me back together. We were supposed to escape tonight like we did, but you were never meant to make it back to London. Peter may well want me dead, too, now that I didn't follow through with my end of the bargain. But I had to know. I couldn't kill you without knowing."

She's sobbing now.

"Knowing what?" I say, my voice low and controlled. She may have destroyed the door's computer locking system, but agents will burst through the door in minutes. Maybe seconds.

"If you *ever* loved me, too."

Gun or no gun, I shove my fingers into her hair and kiss her like it will be the last time I ever do.

"I have *always* loved you, Lora. Always. It has only ever been you."

The hand that holds the gun shakes as she loosens her grip and then hands it to me.

"I have to go, Max. But you'll know where to find me. Just promise you won't make it hurt too badly, and I'll do the same for you."

I grin and point the gun at the woman I love. I never miss, but I'm not in the right frame of mind now. Am I?

I retreat and wait for her to stand. Then I fire. The force of the hit knocks her back a step or two, but she doesn't fall. She glances at her arm, at the tear in her sweater where blood now seeps through.

"That *did* hurt," she says, eyes narrowed.

I grin. "I had to graze you at least. They'd never believe a complete miss. I'm too damned good."

She shakes her head at me ruefully. A drop of blood hits the floor.

"My turn," she says, holding out her palm.

I give her the gun. "You'll never get out of here," I say. Though I know she will. She must know the ins and outs of this house if it is the one where she trained, where she planted herself as a mole in the Order and from which she will now be a fugitive.

She strides to me, beautiful, sexy and lethal. She brushes her lips over mine and then, as the music crescendoes, whispers in my ear. "I chose you, Max. Remember that after all this time, I chose *you*."

Then she clocks me in the temple with the butt of the gun, and everything goes black.

CHAPTER TWELVE

Z

THANK GOD. I think he fell for it. What an idiot. A devastatingly handsome, frustratingly enigmatic, utterly maddening idiot. What can I say? I hopelessly love this man.

I kneel down and press my lips to X's forehead near the small angry wound I put there by his previous injury. "I'm so, so sorry, my heart."

I'm not apologizing for the horrible headache he'll have when he wakes up. That is a necessary evil. I'm apologizing for lying. For letting him believe that I was the mole. That I would betray him and my fellow agents for money or spiteful vendettas.

I smile ruefully as I rise to my feet, reaching into my pocket to remove the small vial of pure adrenaline and throw it back to overcome the groggy sensation of the truth serum. I mean, technically I *am* the mole.

But I had to go deep undercover for this mission if I wanted a prayer of taking out Peter once and for all.

Peter Cain, aka Dante Price, might want to fool the world into believing that he is the king of the underworld, spawned from hell, that he entered London fully formed with sin in his veins and a penchant for fine leather.

Max and I both knew him when he swaggered through the halls of Frasier Academy wearing sweater-vests and tweed pants, a lost little lord, the overlooked third son of a duke.

I did arrange the sex club storming earlier this evening, but that was only because Dante was planning on assassinating X at the club tonight. The tip from my sources that I contacted at the Shangri-La Hotel on that burner phone in the bathroom confirmed it. But there is no way in hell that was going to happen on my watch. Not that anyone can know.

Shouts ring out in the hall, so I back away from the door. If I go out there now, I'm as good as dead. Only one choice here. After shooting out the lock's keypad, they'll have to break the door down. I barricade it for good measure, I hope buying myself much-needed seconds before leaping up and grabbing the air vent. It releases and I land on the floor quiet as a cat, tossing the vent cover onto the bed above X. I allow my gaze to rest one last time on the man I have loved all my life. The only man I've ever truly given my heart to. And then I remove Cordelia's utility belt from my purse, the one I nabbed upstairs during our session with Beta. I unhook the small grappling gun and shoot it through the air shaft. Good thing I don't suffer from claustrophobia. I'm disappearing through the ceiling as the door bursts open with a sonic boom.

Yep. Exactly as I expected.

After all, this is the Order we are talking about. They aren't going to mess around and let me run away without putting up a hell of a fight.

The problem—at least for them—is that they don't truly know who they are dealing with.

I army crawl through the vent, turning right, then left and left again. A few months ago, I had Beta show me the safe house's air-conditioning/heating schematics under the guise of creating a risk-management plan for evading airborne biological warfare. I was lucky enough to get the full tour on his computer—and am grateful for my ability to remember everything I saw.

I'm Agent Z. Quiet. Dependable. Deadly. I will deceive my own to save them, even if it means taking down the enemy on my own.

Peter Cain likes to call me his spider, and believes that I'm spinning webs of deceit throughout the organization that aims to take him down. But he never fully trusts me even as he is desperate to believe that I want him…and that since Max first left Frasier, that I have only ever wanted him. Peter's even fooled himself into believing my deep love for Max was nothing more than an adolescent infatuation.

But he forgets that I'm so much more than an expertly trained spy. At my core, my deepest truth is that I'm simply plain old Lora—a woman who loves with her whole heart and refuses to give up on the only person who's ever mattered to me now that we've found our way back to each other.

I am a keeper of secrets—both for the Order and for myself. Peter claims his evolution into Dante Price was natural—that becoming one of the world's most powerful criminal minds was his destiny. But I do not suffer fools like him. Everything Peter Cain has done—every twist and turn he's taken from what could have been a formidable path in life—has been for one purpose and one purpose only: love.

Well, at least the bastard and I have one thing in common.

Once I realized Dante Price was conspiring to hunt down and execute the Order's most lethal agent, X, I reconnected with him and revealed my secret identity. I flattered and manipulated Peter until he was confident that he was the one who had always held my heart, and to prove my words I pledged to give him X's head on a platter and betray the Order.

And he believed every honeyed lie.

For now X is safe. I got him out of the Lion's Den by radioing in a crackerjack team of rogue commandos loyal only to me. All I had to do was text them my symbol—Z—and they knew to get us out.

Peter probably still has no fucking clue what happened.

The plan was for me to escape with X in an anonymous part of the city and get him to the safe house.

Riding up in the Eye wasn't part of the plan but my own selfish decision, reckless as it was.

My pussy gives an involuntary throb.

I needed one last taste. One last worship of Max's gorgeous cock.

My throat clogs with unshed tears. All I want is a simple life. To leave the Order and live free to love as my heart chooses. I'm tired of action. Of mayhem.

I want to be in the real world. Not the shadows.

I reach to my hip, blow a lock of hair out of my face and remove a knife from the belt. This is one of Beta's personal inventions and a favorite of mine. I click the small button on the side and the blade turns red. Pressing it into the side of the vent, it slides through the metal wall as if it was butter. Luckily, I'm small, so the hole doesn't have to be large. I wiggle through and tumble through the air in a neat somersault, landing right in the Order's secret subterranean garage. I race past the rows of expensive sports cars, beelining to my pick at the end, up against the exposed brick wall.

God, I love a Ducati bike.

I might want a simple life, but that doesn't mean I don't have expensive tastes.

I jump onto the motorcycle, turn the key and gasp as the engine reverberates through my body. My heart pounds in my ears.

A dismayed shout rises in the distance, but whoever it is, they're too late.

I hit the gas and I'm up the ramp. The scanner near the steel doors identifies my retinas and slides open, letting me disappear into the night.

I duck my head and accelerate. As much as my heart breaks to leave X behind, I've got things to do and scores to settle before I have a slim shot at a happy-ever-after.

X

I wake in the infirmary atop a metal table, Cordelia standing over me with her arms crossed and eyes narrowed.

"How long was I out?" I ask.

"A couple of hours."

"Don't look so worried," I say dryly.

Her expression remains impassive.

"You don't miss," she says, her tone biting.

I reach a hand to my temple, feeling the knot under my skin.

"Would you mind keeping the volume down?" I say. "This is my second head injury tonight."

The line of her regal jaw pulses, and I know she will not be easy to appease.

"You don't miss, Max. And neither does she. So tell me what the hell is going on."

"She's the mole," I say. "Is that what you want to hear?"

The Edenvale queen rolls her eyes. "Then why did she make it off the property alive?"

I swing my legs off the table and sit up, my head throbbing. "Did I mention the double head injury? Maybe I neglected to mention in our debriefing that I jumped from a moving van and dislocated my shoulder."

She clucks her tongue like a worried mother hen. "Oh, you told me, Max. You also told me you were not in love with this woman, and I believed you. That was my first mistake. You *know* love has no place in what we do."

I let out a bitter laugh devoid of even the faintest trace of humor. "Says the agent who now lives happily with her king of a husband, three sons and growing brood of grandchildren. If anyone understands what it is like to betray authority for the one they love, I'd expect it to be you."

She opens her mouth to either protest or put me in my place, but I don't give her a chance. "I *know* you lost decades with your family to keep them safe, but I lost decades, too. With Lora. So please, get off your sanctimonious horse and remember your reunion with King Nikolai. Remember how your son and his Nightgardin queen united her kingdom with Edenvale, saving them from a war that would end with more casualties than either of us would care to count."

She throws her hands in the air. "I'm the one who perpetuated that feud. If I had maintained my allegiance to Nightgardin's Black Watch and disposed of King Nikolai—"

"Then you'd have killed the only man you ever loved. But you couldn't, could you?"

She groans, her haughty, laser-sharp gaze fixed on mine. "Tell me one reason why I shouldn't lock you up without so much as a trial until this mess is over—or longer."

I grin. "Because she has my gun."

"I fail to see how this is a positive."

I shake my head. "Cordelia. Your Highness.

Agent Z escaped with *my* gun. And I have no doubt she will be meeting up with Dante Price—who I now know is Peter D. Cain."

It takes a second to register, but then recognition sets in, and she actually gives a girlish giggle.

"I always told you that you were insane for putting a GPS chip in your weapons. No self-respecting thief would hang on to them long enough for you to…"

She trails off.

"Long enough for me to track them, retrieve them and dispatch the thief. But—"

This time she cuts me off.

"I can't believe I'm going to say this, but I'm letting you go, Max. Track her to Price and bring her in. *Alive*."

My smile widens. "And Price? Permission to dispatch of the criminal mastermind?"

She shakes her head. "Alive, as well. He is not a one-man operation. We need as much information as we can get from him. Do you think you can follow orders this time?"

I hop off the table, caring nothing for the physical pain I've endured tonight.

"Of course, Your Highness." Sure. I'll bring Price in alive *enough*. But I'll have some fun with my old school chum first.

I take the liberty of kissing my former partner once on each cheek.

"You know," I say, "if you didn't think I went soft for the woman I love, you'd think I planned it like this all along—that I knew she was the mole and wanted her to lead me to Price."

After all, I always knew the mole wasn't me.

"Go," she says, waving me out with a curt gesture, even as her eyes are bright with unspoken emotion. "Before I change my mind."

She and I have a long history. This moment means the world.

And with that I'm out the infirmary door and soon on the streets of London.

I pull my phone from my pocket and launch my tracking app. A soft green light blinks on the city map as I remember Lora's whispered words to me, that I'll know where to find her.

Truth be told, I didn't need the tracker. It was just my backup in case I couldn't trust her. And, well, I can't. But there she is, exactly where she said she'd be.

"Hello, love," I say. "Looks like I'm headed to Paris."

Despite how many hours behind her I am, the blinking green dot doesn't move. And then I reach her at the Pont des Arts over the Seine. Our favorite place in the world.

"If I wasn't here," she says when she sees me approach, "would you have changed your mind? Killed me next time you saw me?"

I shake my head. "You betrayed the Order," I say. "But you didn't betray me. That means I can still save you."

She huffs out a breath. "In case you hadn't noticed," she says, "I don't need saving."

I close the distance between us and pull her to me.

"Fine," I tell her in a soft voice. "But maybe I do."

I grab her hand and lead her to the other side of the bridge.

She comes with me willingly.

When we get to the street, the Rolls limousine is waiting.

Lora gasps. "This is where I had you meet me for our first anonymous get-together."

I nod. "There are silk blindfolds inside. For old times' sake. Seemed a nice touch, don't you think?"

"What about Peter Cain?" she asks. "You're giving up on him? You know I'll never willingly lead you to him."

I laugh, then wrap an arm around her. I tuck her

hair behind her ear and lean in to whisper, "Who said anything about willingly?" As I feel the shiver run through her, I press the thin adhesive to the skin behind her lobe.

Toss the gun in the river, I think to myself. *I'll never lose you now.*

We climb inside, and I fasten her blindfold over her eyes.

"Don't wear yours," she says hesitantly. "For the years that I knew and you didn't, keep *me* in the dark while you know the whole truth."

She doesn't need to ask twice. I place a palm on each of her knees and push them open.

"I have my own brand of truth serum," I tell her, then slide a hand up her thigh until my fingertips press along the line of her folds beneath her pants.

She licks her lips as I admire how swollen she is. I can see her body opening before my eyes, softening, begging for my affection.

"Do your worst, Agent X," she says.

I knock on the vehicle's privacy divider, and the limo starts to move, navigating the Parisian traffic.

I chuckle. "Oh no, no, no, love. I always do my very best."

CHAPTER THIRTEEN

Z

I'M PLAYING A dangerous game, but no matter, it's one that I mean to win.

This man beside me is a liability, but as I sped my motorcycle through the tunnel beneath the English Channel, I decided that like it or not, I'd have to factor Max into any future equation. Because even as I put kilometers between us, I couldn't deny the truth anymore.

It turns out that while I'm a masterful liar, I can't fool myself.

He is my weakness, so I have to try to survive my passion.

And it's a heady freedom to throw caution to the wind, when most of my steps are so calculated, every risk assessed, and assessed again.

X is the category-five hurricane in my insular

world, blowing apart my defenses and leaving me exposed.

And right now, he seems intent on exposing me.

He eases me onto my back and works my pants and thong from my hips. I curl my fingers into the limo's black leather seat as he spreads the softest part of me open with his thick, callused fingers. Anticipation grips me as I wait for a stroke or a lick.

But nothing comes.

"What are you doing?" I whisper, my question ragged.

"Looking."

"At what?" Good lord, I'm beginning to squirm.

"At the most perfect pussy that's ever been or will ever be."

"I bet you tell that to all the women." I moisten my lips. He's had his fair share of lovers over the years. I know this, and even though it's irrational I hate each one. I hate everyone he's ever touched that wasn't me.

"No. I don't," he says flatly. "Do you know how much you haunted me over the years? I felt like I searched for what I had with you over and over and over. But I never got close. Hell, I never got in the same ballpark."

"If you want me to apologize, you're going to be disappointed."

"Here's what we're going to do. You like to play games. And I can see from the way this sweet wet honey slicks your clit that you like me near you. But if you want to be rewarded with my affections, I need something in return."

"Ooh. Do tell. I love a good quid pro quo. Is it another sixty-nine? It is my lucky number."

"As tempting as that sounds, I'm afraid this will be more straightforward. I want information. You give me an answer and I'll give you…"

I moan as he taps my clit, jutting my ass forward.

"Pleasure."

"Fuck you," I grind out, annoyance burning a hole in my belly. "I'm not playing that game. Tell that queen you love so much she can fuck off, too."

He growls his own annoyance. "I told you as plain as I can. I've only ever had the misfortune to love one woman. And right now, she's a little tied up."

He's got my wrists bound over my head in an instant.

I make a show of wiggling. It's a good strong knot. Not enough to keep me contained, but enough I'd have to work to free myself.

"I don't want information for the Order, my love. I want information for me and me alone."

"What do you mean?"

"You have a lot of gaps in your history. Fill in a few."

I buck my hips up, taunting him with my bare sex, knowing the sight of my soaked folds will drive him wild. "I would rather you filled me."

"Question one," he breathes in my ear, and behind my blindfold my eyes roll back into my head. "Who were your parents?"

I freeze. A question that I don't expect.

There is no way he can know the truth.

Except this is Max.

"Go on," he whispers, a slight taunt amid the gravel. "You know I suspect."

"Tom and Portia. They died in a boat accident."

He settles his weight over me, and it's goddamn delicious. Again his hand creeps between my legs, skimming my inner thighs.

"And they were also Agents Alpha and Omega, weren't they? Leaders in the Order, credited along with Queen Cordelia for bringing the group into the modern day and making it relevant again."

"How did you know?" I rasp. "No one knows. I hacked into the system and destroyed their files after their deaths, just like they instructed. There is no record. I am sure of it. They had wanted to guarantee I was protected and could never be tied to them."

"I remember."

"What the fuck are you talking about?"

"I was there."

"That's impossible. I was alone in their cottage. You were gone. You'd disappeared months before."

I don't talk about my parents. I don't think about my parents. Their deaths ended my childhood, and while I know they never wanted this life for me, it was the only way that I could have closure. That I could move forward.

He stills and rests his forehead lightly against my own.

"I know because I was there when they died."

The world stops.

"What? That's impossible. You never met them."

"I was undercover. My first assignment with the Order. I was part of a pirate ring with links throughout eastern Africa. My captain had taken a hostage, a wealthy businessman whose family threatened to create a war to return. Your parents were to pick up the hostage and head out via boat, but we were betrayed. There was a shootout. Your father died instantly, but your mother… hell, Lora. I didn't know she was your mother. The hostage survived, barely, and I blew up my ship, taking him through the water to your parents' vessel. Your mother was alive, Lora. And I held her as she left. And that's when she told me about her beautiful daughter. The light of her world. Her sweet princess. And when she said your name, I knew. It was you.

"I went to find you. To comfort you. But you'd left Frasier Academy. And so I went to your parents' home. You were there. Deleting files. Burning records in the hearth."

"You watched my pain and said nothing?"

"There was a cost to me." He pressed a kiss to my neck. "It killed me. A part of me died that day. But I realized as I watched you that I wanted you to have a chance to be free. That I had to turn my back on you because I'd sworn an oath to the Order. And I didn't want that world for you any more than your mother did. You were so smart, Lora. Scratch that, you are so smart. Much smarter than me. You could have been in politics or the UN. A professor. Anything that would have kept you safe from this life."

"I'm not safe and I'm sure as hell not sweet." I wrap my thighs around his hips and bite his lip so hard I draw blood. "I hate you for telling me this."

"I know."

"I love you for wanting to protect me."

"I know."

I seethe in frustration, my buttocks tense. "You are an arrogant bastard."

"I know." This time he chuckles, though, a deep,

musical rumble that draws me into an unwilling smile.

"Why did you ask me a question you knew the answer to?"

"I wanted to see if you'd lie."

"I'm a good liar."

"We'll see." He takes a ragged breath. "I have a few more questions. But first, I think you earned a reward."

X

I push her knees open.

She squirms on the leather seat. I know she's humoring me by keeping her wrists bound, but the fact that she is playing along means she wants to, well, play.

I slide my hands up her silky thighs until my thumbs rest in the crease where legs meet pelvis. Up and down I stroke along the natural lines, so close to where she begs to be touched but not touching her yet.

She whimpers, and I relish the sound. "Why the fuck are you teasing me?"

I smile. "It's not teasing, love. It's appreciation of every angle and curve, every line and crease of your unbelievable body." I skim up and under her sweater, hissing in a breath when I find her braless, too. "Like this," I say, tracing the half-moon of the underside of her breast. "This beautiful shape that is all you, only you, and *mine*." I pinch her hardened peak. "Tell me you're mine, Lora."

She sucks in a breath. "Yours," she says, breathless. "Only yours."

I lift her sweater over her head and watch her skin pebble. I take her nipple into my mouth, swirl my tongue around it, then pull back and blow softly.

Her spine arches.

"Max, you bastard. Fuck me before I break free of your pathetic knots and knock you out again."

I laugh. "You're terrible at bluffing when you're out of your mind with need." I rub a finger over the bump at my temple. "You'd never leave me before I satisfied you. And don't forget that I *let* you get away before." I slide a hand between her legs, running one finger between her warm, slick folds. She pushes her pelvis against my touch as she hums a soft moan. "I should have killed you, and I didn't."

"And now?" she asks, her voice thick with desire.

"Now you're to lead me to Price or Cain or whoever the hell he is."

I enter her with one finger, then two, and she cries out, throwing her head back against the seat.

"And if I don't cooperate?"

I add a third finger to let her know I'm serious, and she bucks against my palm.

"Just—cooperate, Lora."

The Order before everything else, I chant in my head. It's the mantra drilled into us during early training—beaten into us when we fuck up. All for the good of the world, the safety of humankind. We sacrifice so others don't have to.

So if it comes down to it and Lora compromises the mission, I will have to do what I've been trained to do.

She rides my hand, fucks it as I pump my fingers inside her. I tease her wet, swollen clit with my thumb and she lets loose a feral growl. It's then that I slide out from inside her and reluctantly pull away.

She twists and turns and moans. "What the fuck are you doing, Max?"

"It's time for another question," I say.

Her jaw tightens and her teeth clench. "Fuck you."

I grin. "Oh, sweetheart, I plan to. But not just yet. Not until you cooperate."

She groans. "I hate you."

I laugh. "I see you tread that thin line as often as I do. Now, if you want me to tend to that aching pussy of yours, all you have to do is tell me where you're supposed to meet up with Price, and we'll get back to the business at hand."

"He'll kill you the second he sees you," she says. "Don't you get it? All he's ever done—all he's worked for has been because of you."

I lean in and bite the lobe of her ear. She gasps.

"Don't you mean," I whisper, "because of *you*? Because no matter how many times you tell him— no matter how many times you *bed* him—deep down he knows you never loved him. You're a good actor, Lora. But you can't fake what we have."

I glance up to see her wriggling free of her ties, so I buy myself more time by yanking them tighter. I kiss the skin she's rubbed raw on her wrists in her attempted escape.

"Where is he, Lora? You wouldn't have come to Paris, to *our* place, without him nearby. If you miss your rendezvous, he'll be suspicious, no? So let's not keep our old friend waiting."

She groans, but I can hear the sliver of defeat in her voice. And a sliver is all I need.

"There is a café around the corner called Très Bon. Behind it, down a small staircase, is a door that will lead you to what you're looking for." She sighs. "Jesus, Max. Don't get killed."

I chuckle. "I don't plan on it, but just in case, I think I'd like to enjoy my last meal."

I spread her knees wide and bury my face between her thighs, lapping her wet, aching sex from bottom to top, my tongue lingering on her throbbing clit.

In a fraction of a second, her hands are free, her fingers tangling in my hair as she kicks off her shoes and wriggles out of her pants completely. She throws her legs over my shoulders and my brain melts.

"That's my girl," I say, shoving my hands beneath her and gripping her gorgeous ass for purchase.

I don't plan on dying anytime soon. But if I do, it'll be with the taste of Agent Z lingering on my lips. Not a fucking bad way to go.

CHAPTER FOURTEEN

Z

AFTER I SHATTER into a million pieces, I try to recover my focus. Not easy when I'm well aware Max seems to want a full meal.

But the time for pleasure must be paused, at least for now. My mission isn't over.

First, Max asked questions. But not the right ones.

He doesn't understand why Peter Cain hates him so much. Does Max believe a criminal mastermind rose to power simply to get revenge on him for a rugby injury? Max seemed to take it in stride.

I have to admit; I'm impressed.

Second, he thinks I've bedded Peter.

God, the very thought makes my skin crawl, but I can't convince him otherwise. Not now. He'd assume I'm lying.

But I need to get him to see the truth before the final showdown.

It's the only way we will make it out alive.

"We have to talk," I say.

"I see." He helps me put my clothes to rights. "You've gotten yours and now you want to say your piece."

"Don't you see? I want peace."

He arches a brow.

"I want out, X. I want to leave the Order. You know my parents were in deep. My whole life has been lived with an invisible ax over me. I've done my time. I've done damn good work. But I don't want to die. Not yet. Not when I've never had a chance to live on my own terms." I take a deep breath. "Or to love on my own terms."

His other brow rises to meet the first.

"Haven't you ever wondered why Dante Price, aka Peter Cain, hates you so much?"

"He was jealous of me? He wanted you?" Max shrugs, arrogant to his core. "Who cares? The why of it never really worried me. He's an entitled ass."

"The why should have made you wonder." I tie the silk blindfold around my neck as a scarf. "The why is the reason."

"Are you going to speak in riddles all day?"

I gape at him. For such a smart man, he can be woefully thick. His blind spot on this issue is the size of the black hole at the dark center of our galaxy. He is so perceptive except for when it comes to himself. "You have no idea, do you?"

"Damn it, Lora. No idea of what? I'm still trying to comprehend you walking away from the Order. For the last time, spit it out."

His command is punctuated by a loud crash that sends us both flying to the floor of the limo, a tangle of limbs.

"Rear-ended," I gasp, my rib cage aching. I evaluate my body. Nothing is broken, thank goodness.

"That was no accident." X pulls a gun from a hidden holster.

"No." My mouth presses into a grim slash. There are never coincidences in our line of work.

There's a staccato pop of gunfire ahead and a cry. That must be the driver. None of the bullets puncture the bulletproof glass.

"You tipped off Price." Max gives me a cool dead-eyed stare.

I bristle. "Of course not."

He is every ounce an agent of the Order. This is the man who stands at the wall, protects the world even if it means he must be ruthless in turn. "Give me one good reason to trust you."

"Max. Love." There is no way to say it except to say it. "Peter Cain is your brother."

He jerks, his surprise almost imperceptible. "What?"

"Peter Cain… Dante Price…he's your brother. At least, your half brother."

"But…that's impossible."

"Is it?" I lean in speaking quickly. We don't have much time. "His father was the earl of Northumberland. You come from Northumberland. You don't know who your real father is."

"Mother didn't like to speak of him."

"He was her employer. She was the maid to the earl's wife. They had an affair while his wife was pregnant with her third child. You were the product of that affair."

"This is impossible."

I caress his clenched jaw. "You are opposites, but with similar features. You are dark. He is light. But that is where the resemblance stops. Because your heart is good. And his…his is twisted."

"Why didn't he ever tell me the truth?"

"And expose his father's affair? He's far too proud for that."

"But you knew?"

"He did have feelings for me. *Does* have feelings. And he likes to drink too much sherry." I shrug. "When he drinks, he talks. After we reconnected recently, he told me about how he found in his dead father's papers some tuition bills for Frasier Academy, but they had your name on them. Not his. He did some fact-finding and uncovered the whole secret. That's the crazy part of it all. Your father barely tried to hide it. It was almost as if he wanted to get caught, like he wanted to acknowledge the son he was proud of. He secretly supported you and paid for you to attend boarding school, but he did little to cover his tracks. You just never looked."

"And all this time I thought it was a scholarship."

The window behind him shatters, glass shards filling the air.

We're out of time. He's found us. Dante Price knows I betrayed him.

But the face that appears isn't Peter Cain. Nor a paid goon. It's a friend, wiry and squinting behind thick spectacles.

"Beta?" I gasp. The last person I expect to see here is my bookish friend from the Order. "What on earth are you doing? Did you shoot our driver?"

"L-L-Lora. Fancy meeting you here."

But then he peels off his face, one quick gesture and the features change. Whatever was Beta is cast to the concrete. And there he is. The opposite of X in every way, and yet utterly familiar.

"Hello, Lora." Peter Cain smooths his thin blond hair with a smug leer. "And Max. I'm afraid the real Beta is all tied up. Has been so for a few days in fact. But where are my manners? Long time, no see, old chum."

X

I scramble for my gun, having lost it in the crash, but Cain is quicker. He grabs me by the shoulder and injects something into my neck. I know it's not truth serum. It's not information he seeks from me. Everything slows, my movements sluggish. But I fight to remain conscious. I stay awake long enough to see him backhand Lora, tie her up and gag her.

Strange, but I see the resemblance. As the darkness closes in, I curse myself that I never noticed before.

Lora doesn't scream or fight, and I both love and hate her for that. She does it for me. Because despite wanting out of this life that has consumed us both for so long, she would never leave an agent behind.

She would never leave *me* behind.

My last thought as darkness pulls me under is that brother or no, I will kill Peter Cain.

My eyes open, but I can see nothing. Either it's pitch-dark wherever I am, or whatever Cain injected me with has affected my sight.

My limbs are stiff, aching, but I'm standing upright. I realize my hands are bound above my head. I try to wriggle free, but rough metal chafes at my skin.

"Chains," I say aloud. "Nice touch."

A light flickers in the corner of whatever room I'm in, and I wince as it illuminates fully, my eyes too sensitive for the sudden change.

"Where's Lora?" I ask through gritted teeth.

My captor claps slowly. "Bravo, Max. Really. I do love how you let her think you were dead for two decades—how you fucked your way across the world all in the name of saving those less fortunate—and now you're playing the protective lover. It's such bullshit."

I blink hard, forcing my eyes to adjust, and see Peter Cain emerge from the pool of light.

He wears a well-tailored suit, much like what I wore on a daily basis while in the employ of the royal family of Edenvale. But where my hair is thick and salt-and-pepper dark, his is fair and wispy. But he's no longer the slight, strutting lording he was in school. He has filled out, his body clearly the benefit of intense training, and I do not doubt he would be a formidable opponent in hand-to-hand combat.

I'll still win.

Cain clasps his hands behind his back. "What if I let you go right now? You can tell the Order where I am, and they can send their minions to retrieve me. You save face, prove your loyalty, and sweet Lora and I move on to our next location as the chase continues. All you have to do is exactly what she asked of you—help her leave the Order."

This is a game. There is no way he'd let me set Lora free.

"What the hell are you talking about?"

Cain clucks his tongue. "Come on, Max. This was never about her. She was a great tool to use against you, but you know the truth now. I heard everything she told you in that limo—everything she was *supposed* to tell you like she was spilling her heart out. But come on…*brother*. She's betrayed you more than once already. What makes you think this is any different now?"

I yank at my iron chains, knowing if I pull too hard I'll dislocate my shoulder again, but the pain does nothing to deter me.

"Enough games, Cain. What the hell do you want?"

He shrugs. "If you won't let me leave with her, then take her from me. Kill her."

"Fuck you." I spit the words at him.

He blows out a breath. "I was afraid you'd need some convincing."

He taps on the wall on the opposite end of the room we're in, and a scene lights up on the other side of a window.

I thrash and growl as I stare beyond the glass, straight at Lora. She's chained to a wall much like

I am, but her ankles are shackled, as well. Where I am fully clothed, Cain has her dressed in nothing but the mesh chemise she wore our first night at the Lion's Den. She is blindfolded with the silk scarf she wore in the limo. But blood trickles from the corner of her mouth and from her nose.

"Lora!" I roar. "Lora!"

Cain hums. "She can't see you," he says. "Or hear you. In fact, I already told her you escaped, killed a guard and left her for dead. She thinks I'm trying to get her to spill secrets on the Order." He laughs. "She doesn't even know that the Order's mole has been nothing but my biggest pawn."

My brows crease, and Cain laughs.

"You thought I loved her and wanted you dead, yes?" He shakes his head. "On the contrary, bastard brother of mine." His smile morphs to a sneer. "It has only ever been about destroying you, and tonight I will."

He mumbles something into the face of his watch, which sits on the underside of his wrist.

Almost immediately someone dressed head-to-toe in black, his or her face masked, as well, enters the room carrying a small dagger. He drags the blade across Lora's thigh, a superficial enough wound, but one that bleeds bright crimson red.

She doesn't flinch, but I do.

Something feral tears from my chest as I thrash

so hard at my chains that my wrists bleed and my injured shoulder pops clean from its socket.

I don't fucking care. Not when I am helpless to save her. Not when he wishes to torture me by torturing her.

"I've got all the time in the world," he tells me. "Of course, my associate won't kill her. Only injure and maim her enough for you to change your mind. Once you do, it will only take a bullet to put her out of her misery. I will remove her blindfold, though, so she can see who her *savior* is."

I squint at what I swear is a smile playing on Lora's lips. Then I see her hands moving ever so slightly in her chains.

Cain is an idiot.

"Actually, Cain, your time is running out. The only person dying here tonight is *you*."

CHAPTER FIFTEEN

Z

I CAN GET FREE whenever I want. But when I make my escape, it will be at a time of my choosing.

Cain has tried to make me believe that Max escaped, that he sold me out and left me behind to face a traitorous death alone.

But I know my Max wouldn't leave without me. Just as I know Cain would never kill me.

The thug in front of me rips off my blindfold and sneers. I pretend to cower, make my eyes go round and hitch my breath.

The idiot believes it.

His gloat makes me sick. This asshole is a man who likes to hurt women.

I'll make him pay, but for now I'm going to rest and save up my strength.

I flutter my eyes, let my head loll and pretend to swoon in abject terror.

"That's right, bitch," he spits. I can hear the smug tone of self-satisfaction. It will be glorious to wipe it off.

Meanwhile, I let my mind wander.

How strange to have Peter and Max together. A surreal reunion.

I met both of them when we were all teenagers, just turning fifteen.

I'd just started noticing boys.

Max was the sporty one. The achiever. He was always the best at everything, even though he made it seem easy.

It was only if you watched him carefully, studying his nuances, that you could see how much he pushed himself. How he might have an easy smile and nonchalant shrug, but he'd tear his body to pieces to win.

I did some light hacking on him. Not hard. Frasier Academy records were like taking candy from a baby for someone with my abilities. I learned he was a scholarship student. Then I learned about who paid his bills.

I tried to care for Peter when he was there for me after Max disappeared. I truly did. He was fascinating, but also cold. It was like admiring an iceberg in the North Atlantic. And his depths were as treacherous as my own.

"Blend in," my father had said when they'd dropped me off in Scotland.

"Never let anyone see how special you really are," my mother had whispered in my ear. "The world is a dangerous place. Someday you will meet someone you love, but never let down your guard all the way."

And in that moment I realized that even though she madly loved my father, she never let him know all of her.

And I resolved to be the same. Beautiful but distant. Confident but lethal. And, of course, charming.

If I half succeeded in following in her footsteps, I'd be a force to be reckoned with.

And I'd like to think I have.

But I've had enough.

Someday I want to stand in the sun, on a beach, far away, where no one knows my name or history. And I want to look over one shoulder and see a man who knows me to my core and still wants me. Who isn't scared by my past. By the fact that I can kill a man with my bare hands. I want him to see my strength but also my gentleness. I want to truly be known.

And if I get out of here alive, I want that man to be Max.

I let my thoughts steal to him. Even though

Peter didn't have proof until years later, my guess is he suspected Max was his bastard brother long before. Bad things happened to Max at Frasier. A pipe burst in his room, ruining his laptop, one for which he'd had to scrimp and save.

Then one night there was an electrical fire when he was lifting weights after rugby practice. He almost didn't make it out alive.

When I lost Max, Peter was my only connection to the boy I loved, so I didn't push Cain away. I kept my enemy close. I never gave him any true affection, but I always let the promise of seduction remain on the table. It kept him in my orbit. I don't know exactly what it was about me that fascinated him. Probably the idea that Max wanted me.

As a private person, I tried to hide our growing connection. How after we were caught in the storm we began to spend time in the library together. How I began to learn that he was so much more than a star athlete. That he was kind and brave and dreamed of adventure. He had grown up poor—his mom had worked herself to the bone to provide for him while being diagnosed with cancer right before he went to Frasier.

Then one night we kissed in the nonfiction section. His tongue slid over mine with a confidence well beyond his years, as if he had done this a hundred and one times and knew my body better than my own.

One kiss led to another and another and then kisses in other places. I remember the first time I opened his pants and saw the full, proud length of him. The size had scared me. How was it going to fit in my mouth let alone between my legs? But then I looked up and saw Max watching me, lips parted, open awe in his blue gaze, and I realized it was just the core of him, and how could I ever be scared of his essence?

Even now after all these years, the memories of my early fumbles with Max drench my pussy. But it's more than a physical craving. When Max is with me, I feel as if I have a home, an anchor in the storms of my life.

And I know he is somewhere close by, no matter what Peter says.

I've pretended to care for Peter for so long just to keep tabs on his plotting against Max. I've had to bear witness to cruelty and jealousy. How he felt like his father loved his secret son more than his legitimate ones. And how Max fooled everyone into thinking he was so amazing. Peter's hatred blinded him from the fact that Max was competent and respected for good reasons.

Peter enjoyed manipulation. He wanted to inspire fear and took pleasure in causing pain. He saw the world as chaos and thrived on instability.

I played a dangerous game pretending to be his friend, but it's time to beat him.

The guard mutters to himself that he has to take a leak. And the minute he steps into the bathroom, I free myself from my chains. I have a lover to save.

X

It takes everything in me not to react when I watch Lora escape. There is no way Cain truly knows her if he is fool enough to think those chains could bind her. She played him better than she ever played me. Which means she never cared for him. I take comfort in that.

Who am I kidding? I'm gloating. Cain just doesn't know it.

"How would you have me kill the woman I love?" I ask, toying with him enough to keep him occupied. Beyond the two-way mirror, I watch Lora dispatch her attacker with an upturned palm to the face as he returns to the room zipping his damned fly. Blood pours from his nose as he goes down like a sack of potatoes. But Lora is quick to catch him before his body hits the floor, easing him onto his side, likely so he doesn't choke on his own blood.

She is more merciful than I would have been. Even though Lora was just her playing her part, watching that asshole drag a blade across her skin was enough to wipe the definition of mercy clear from my memory.

Cain strolls closer to me, his arms still clasped behind his back.

"A bullet between the eyes would be too easy," he says. "Not personal enough. I was thinking more along the lines of strangulation. I want you to watch the life leave her eyes. I want you to feel the blood stop beating through her veins."

Come on, I think. *Just a little closer and I can take you out myself, Cain.*

Instead, I grit my teeth. "Why?" I growl. "Because of your goddamn *daddy* issues?"

Cain lands a jab across my jaw. My lip splits where it hits my teeth, and I laugh, spitting blood at him as I do.

"Guess I hit a nerve, huh?" I taunt. "I didn't even know the man. Yet you've made punishing me your life's work. Might be time to reevaluate your priorities, Cain. Because they're a little fucked."

"Silence!" he roars, backhanding me on the other side of my face.

I try to shrug and am reminded with searing pain that I dislocated my shoulder again.

"Fuck!" I grind out. Then I force my best placating grin. "What do you say we get me out of these chains, maybe open a bottle of scotch and talk this out like we are both civilized men…instead of man and the sociopath we both know you are?"

He steps in closer, likely to hit me again, his false sense of security now heightened by my injuries. So I strike.

First, it's a side kick to the ribs, then one lower to the knee I remember he injured in a horseback riding accident at Frasier.

He roars in pain as he goes down.

"Hey. What are the odds? We've both got a bum knee. Think it's in the genes? Or am I just repaying you for the gift you gave to me a while back?"

He sneers, and I have my answer.

He rolls to his good knee, scrambling to get up, but his hand braced on his side tells me I likely cracked a rib or two. It'll take him a minute to get to his feet.

On his side now, he pushes up on an elbow toward the back wall. Toward the window to Lora's torture chamber. But she's not there.

Cain lets loose a monstrous howl.

"Where. Is. *She?*" he yells into his watch.

And that's all it takes. Two armed men burst into the room beyond the window, pointing their guns in every direction.

Though I'm not religious, I say a quick prayer, hoping to hell the glass is bulletproof.

"Now, Lora!" I shout, knowing she must be near.

A door hidden in the wall to my left opens, and she slinks in, catlike in her grace.

"Hello, boys. How's the family reunion going?"

Cain is on his feet now, but he's unsteady. Other than my busted shoulder and lip, there's another thing that makes me uneasy.

Cain's maniacal smile.

Then I see it. From the cuff of his suit a dagger has appeared. He grips it tight in his palm while his other holds tight against his ribs.

Lora's jaw tightens. "Don't do anything stupid, Peter. There are two of us and one of you, and your idiot goons are searching an empty room trying to find me. Can they hear us through the glass? Would they even know to look this way, or are you so mistrusting that they don't even have a clue about the mirror?"

I raise my brows. "Darling," I say. "Did you know I was here all along?"

She smiles her broad, beautiful smile. "I had a hunch."

"Enough of this two-to-one bullshit," Cain says. "You can't free him before I can kill him."

He strides toward me, but his breathing is labored and uneven. He presses the tip of his blade above my heart.

"If she loves you like you think she does, then it will ruin her to watch you die just as much as it would have ruined you to kill her. If your last memory is watching me break the woman you love, then I still win. Isn't that the first rule of your precious Order? The Order before everyone else? Personal ties are liabilities. And you two went and fell in love anyway."

He pushes the tip of the blade through the first layer of skin, and I say nothing. Despite the searing pain, I don't even flinch. No way in hell I'm giving him any sort of satisfaction.

"I've loved him since we were teenagers!" she cries. Cain pauses, fist still tight round the dagger's hilt, and I hear the desperation in Lora's voice. "But you've never loved anyone other than yourself. And that, Peter, is *your* liability."

As she says the words her fingers play with her hair. And it's all the time she needs, the distraction just enough to pull the jeweled hair clip free—the one that isn't a jewel at all but a lethal blade.

Like Robin Hood's arrow, the weapon hits its target—Cain's hand—before he can register that she's moved. The dagger falls as blood pools in his palm and down the back of his hand, running down both sides of his wrist.

He stumbles in shock, hits the window wall and slides to the floor with a hideous wail.

I sigh. "Have you come to rescue me?" I tease.

She runs to me, cupping my cheeks in her palms. "You've looked better," she says.

I laugh, then wince as the weight of my body tugs at my bound wrists. "Think you can get me out of this and maybe perform your magic on my shoulder again?"

She looks at Cain, strides to where he's collapsed and pulls the hairpin blade from his palm.

He writhes and swears at her through gritted teeth.

"Should I kill him first?" she asks.

"Not if you want your ticket out," I say. "If we bring him in and you turn yourself over to the Order's authority, you'll likely be able to bargain your way to freedom."

She strides toward me and in a blink unlocks my chains. My injured arm falls limp at my side, and I hiss.

She braces her foot against my thigh, takes my wrist in her hand and pops my shoulder back in like she's done it a thousand times before.

Then she kisses my bruised temple where she knocked me out with my own gun. She kisses my bruised cheek, my busted lip—every injury I've incurred in the past twenty-four hours I've been with her. And I wouldn't change a second of it.

"Come with me, Max. Leave the Order and live the rest of your life with me."

CHAPTER SIXTEEN

Z

MAX FREEZES IN MY ARMS, his muscles rigid with the implication of my statement. "Leave." His voice is steel and strikes at the defenses around my heart, leaving invisible bruises. "Lora… I can't leave. The Order is my life."

What about me? I want to scream. Shake him. Slap him silly and stomp my feet like I'm two years old and throwing the world's biggest temper tantrum.

The heat leaves my body in a rush, and a cool sludge fills my stomach like December pond water.

Max and I are practiced liars, but I know when he speaks the truth…and right now is one of those times.

Peter spits out a mouthful of blood and laughs from the ground, a husky wet sound tinged with a wheeze of pain. "Oh, this is rich, my old friends.

Rich indeed. Lora, you stupid git, you thought he loved *you* more than the precious secret society to which he has devoted his entire life? And here I thought you were the brains of the operation." He snickers again, spittle flecking the corners of his mouth.

"Shut up, Peter," I say, rising and stalking toward his cowering shape. No more is he the confident lord of the underworld, the cocky prince of darkness. I could crush him like a cockroach under my heel. "Quit speaking in my presence or I swear by all that is holy I will end you right here, right now, and there won't be enough left over to make a midnight snack for a bloody vulture." My patience is wearing thin.

Peter presses his lips so tight that a ring of white appears around his mouth. "Watch your tongue, bitch," he snarls.

"Make me," I taunt him right back, flinging the words in his face. The toe of my boot longs to press down on his neck. I've killed in my line of work. All agents have, but never without justification.

But tonight I'm ready to commit murder. The world takes on a red hue.

"Lora." Max places his hand on my shoulder. "Think, Lora. Don't let him get to you."

Oh, Max. His hands feel so good on my body… so right.

I am tempted to close my eyes. I feel the latent strength in him. It grounds me and makes me want to go boneless. For him I'd consider giving up and giving in, remaining in the Order. It would be so easy. And I'd have Max. At least some of the time.

No… I would have *X*, and I can't settle for that anymore. I want the boy I fell in love with and the man I know he can be.

I can't live without love anymore, snatching stolen moments, never in control of my choices but instead sacrificing everything for a cause. I will not do it. That path would be the end of me. The plan was to save Max, even if that meant betraying the Order. I've done that. I don't want to go down the same path my parents did. I have dedicated years of my life to the Order and regret nothing, but now I need to live…and love…on my terms.

Peter's eyes gleam, bright with hate and triumph. He sees my defeat and savors the victory.

"You're never going to win him away," he croons. "He might not have ever known our father, but they are so much the same. Single-minded and stubborn. You will never have what you want."

The doors fly open and agents pour in. They are dressed in black tactical gear and brandish military-grade assault weapons. Surprise, surprise. The Order is here to save the day. No doubt they were tracking X the whole time.

But as they lead Cain away, I don't hear the words of congratulations from those in the room. I hear Peter's mocking laugh boring into my skull.

"Come on," X says, taking my hand. "We have to talk."

"What more is there to say?" I whisper wearily, feeling a heavy weight descend on me like I'm a hundred years old. And yet I don't want him to pull away. I want his hands everywhere, spanning my waist, squeezing my ass, caressing my hips, teasing my breasts. This man makes magic with his hands, and I want to fall under his spell.

He pulls me close and presses his lips to my ear. "I'm not planning on talking. What I want to say to you is more than words."

Then he turns, holding my hand and leading me from Cain's lair with arrogant certainty.

I should hate him for it, but it only makes me love him more. Passion crashes through me, sending my heart adrift in a confusing confluence.

I follow, letting him think he is in charge. But then I pull him into a dark alcove before we reach the door. I've been his virgin lover. His secret mistress. His sex slave. His ally. His enemy.

But tonight he will be mine or nothing at all.

"What is it?" he asks, concern lacing his tone.

"You never asked—what tricks my body can do that you aren't aware of."

Even in the dark I see his eyes widen and his lips curl into that roguish grin I've loved since I was a teen.

I slide my foot up his leg until it reaches his hip. On instinct, he wraps his hand around my ankle, his eyes dark with need as they meet mine.

I simply nod, and he straightens my leg until my heel rests on his shoulder,

"Lora," he says, his voice hoarse. But to hell with words. Right now I need to *show* him that we were made for each other, that in a world where so much doesn't make sense, we do. "Your injuries."

I shake my head. "I don't feel any pain right now. Do you?"

He shakes his head.

I unbutton his pants and tug the zipper down. His cock throbs inside his boxer briefs, and I set it free, my hand strong around his thick length.

"Lora," he whispers now, and I quiet him with a soft *shh.* He nods in understanding, neither of us wanting to reveal ourselves to the agents just outside. So he slides his hand from my ankle down to where the chemise has ridden up to reveal me bare underneath.

He sucks in a breath through clenched teeth when his fingers reach aching, swollen clit.

I whimper, so sensitive to his touch, but I need to be the one in control here, so I grab his hand

and thrust it above his head, slamming it against the wall. Then, his cock still in my hand, I rub his wet tip against my center.

"Fuck me." They are the only words I speak before he pivots to press my back against the wall instead of his, then lowers himself enough to enter me.

He growls as he grabs my ass with both hands, lifting me so my other foot comes off the ground, and then slams into me.

"Harder, damn it!" I order. "You can't break me, Max. Do you understand? You. Can't. Break. Me."

I chant the words silently in my head, trying to make them true.

He plunges inside me again, my ankle on his shoulder taking him to depths I didn't know were possible.

I bite his lip, drawing blood as my fingers tangle in his hair.

"We fit," I say against him. "Do you understand?"

"We fit," he grinds out, and then his thrusts come faster, his cock filling me near to bursting as I let go as I never have before, coming with a silent scream as Max explodes inside me.

He can have me like this for all the nights to come. Or he can choose the Order.

But he cannot have both.

X

My head swims as I lead Lora outside.

What the hell was that? It's not anything we haven't done before and yet it was unlike any other time I've been inside her.

I need to think—need to regain control of the situation, to separate fantasy from reality.

I scan the scene before us. Aside from several tactical vehicles waiting in the alley outside, there are two ambulances—one to take Cain away, as his wounds will need mending before he can officially be taken into custody, and one that stays behind to tend to anyone with less serious injuries—mainly me and Lora. Beta was found in the London warehouse where he was captured and held over a week ago. Luckily it seems like the old boy will pull through unscathed.

The puncture wound over my heart is superficial, and the emergency technician makes sure my shoulder is back in place properly. The wound on Lora's thigh is worse. The tech cleans it and tells us he can close it with surgical glue.

"You both should see a doctor," Cordelia insists. She, of course, led the extraction team, relying on the tracking device on my gun and another I swallowed in the form of a capsule, its effects set to wear off in the next hour or so as my body metabolizes it. The one on Lora was strictly for me. All that mattered was that I found her first, that I got answers before the Order dealt with her.

"Ah, Your Highness," I say. "Since when have I ever done what should be done?"

She rolls her eyes and hooks her arm through mine.

"Let's walk for a moment, shall we?" the queen says, then turns to Z, who is being tended to in the ambulance. "I trust you'll stay in one place until we return."

"Yes, Your Highness," she says flatly.

We stroll beyond Cain's compound. Lora wasn't lying when she claimed it was beneath a popular street café. We emerge onto the main street. In her civilian clothes, Cordelia blends in more than I do in my state, but no one seems to pay us much attention.

"She wasn't working for Cain," I start, but the queen cuts me off.

"Agent Z betrayed the Order. No matter what her intentions were, that cannot be overlooked."

I stop at a well-lit corner, my gaze fixed on hers. "She saved my life, Your Highness. And in doing so, she did protect the organization. Cain would have stopped at nothing until he ended me, and I have a feeling you've known that for quite some time."

She sighs. "That you and Cain were brothers? Of course we knew. We weren't certain about Price being Cain, though. We needed Agent Z for that confirmation."

My jaw tightens. "So you were using her from the beginning."

Cordelia lets out a mirthless laugh. "That's what we *do*, Max. We use whoever has the information to get the information. Then, depending on whether or not our sources are expendable or valuable…" She trails off.

"Lora is *not* expendable," I say through gritted teeth.

She looks regretful. "No. Not expendable. But also no longer valuable. Her loyalties lie with her heart, X. Or should I say *Max*? Because that is who you are to her. The question is, who is *she* to you?"

I find Lora waiting in front of the closed café, sitting at one of the empty outdoor tables in hospital scrubs.

"How is it that no matter what you're wearing, you're the sexiest woman I've ever seen?" I ask.

She laughs. "So?" she says half-heartedly. "Am I to be executed or set free?" She forces a smile.

"There are a few minor hoops you'll have to jump through—information you'll need to turn over—but Cordelia will expunge your record once you do. It will be as if Agent Z never existed."

"And you?" she asks. "It's still the Order before everyone else?"

I hold out my hand. She hesitates for a second, but then she takes it.

I lead her not to a limousine but to a parked Rolls-Royce, much like the one I used to drive for the royal family of Edenvale.

"I'm not fucking you blindfolded in a car tonight, Max," she says as I open the passenger-side door for her.

"I wouldn't dream of it," I say with a grin. "Okay, that's not entirely true. I dream of doing all sorts of things to you in any number of vehicles, hotel rooms, penthouses, et cetera. And of you doing some very naughty things to me, as well. But alas, we'll save those fantasies for another time. Tonight is—different. Will you let me show you?"

I don't need to convince her, not after what just happened inside that building. Everything is different. We can't go back. What remains to be seen, however, is where we go from here.

She sighs. "Okay. But do me a favor. Never call me Agent Z again."

We drive for an hour in complete and utter silence, the weight of what she's asked of me filling the air between us.

Finally, we turn down a narrow gravel road that ends at a small country house well outside the Paris city limits.

All we can see is what the headlights of the car illuminate—the whitewashed brick and wrap-around porch, the swing hanging from the olive tree in mild disrepair, but it's fixable.

"I don't understand," she says.

I clear my throat. It's been so long since I've uttered the words.

"This is…my home. At least, it was many years ago. It's not much, but it's where my mother raised me until she sent me to Frasier."

Lora blinks and swipes a finger under her eye. "This is—your childhood home? Does your mother still live here?"

I shake my head. "She left this place many years ago, sold it." I clear my throat, swallow over the lump that has surprisingly risen there. "I was informed a few months ago that she'd passed away. It was a small ceremony—her burial. I went. After not contacting her for over twenty years, I laid her to rest. She was, as far as I knew, the last of my living kin, which meant no one I loved was left who I could endanger because of who I was and what I did."

"Oh, Max." She cups my cheek in her hand.

I lean into her palm, pressing my lips to it and kissing her softly.

"But if you leave now…" I say.

"I'm out," she says without hesitation. "This was it for me—ensure your safety from Cain and then take my life back."

I nod. "I know. It just means that I was wrong."

Her brows furrow. "About what?"

"About there being no one out there left whom I love."

Her breath hitches.

"I love you, too, Max. Do you get that? But I love *Max*, not Agent X."

I nod. "I get it. But all the things X has done in the name of the greater good—some were terrible things, Lora. So even if I am still Max to you, you need to know that he comes with all of X's strengths but also all of his faults."

I don't tell her of what Cordelia and I spoke of on our walk, or of what was left to me in my mother's will—the only thing she owned, which I now know must have been a gift from my father. I need to know that regardless of my future this woman I have loved for what feels like my entire life loves X and Max equally, because we are one and the same.

"May I take you inside?"

Lora's eyes widen. "But how? I mean, who lives here?"

"No one right now," I tell her. "So I thought we'd stay here for the night."

She nods, so I lead her out of the car and straight into my past.

CHAPTER SEVENTEEN

Lora

"WHAT ARE YOU DOING?" I yelp as Max sweeps me off my feet.

"I mean to do tonight right," he whispers in my ear, deftly opening the front door and carrying me over the threshold without missing a beat.

Hope floods me, and the pleasure is so acute that it's almost pain. "So does this mean you will leave the Order? That it can be me and you, a simple life at last?" The words don't taste real on my tongue. I can't believe this fantasy might come true. The idea practically takes my breath away, then Max slants his mouth over mine and I'm a goner. Our tongues tangle, parry and thrust. It's like fencing, a fight to the death, hungry and intense, where we will both win or lose, and neither is certain of the outcome. It takes me a few seconds to realize he hasn't answered my question.

Instead, he grips me tighter with one hand, then leans forward and swipes crockery off the table. There is a sound of porcelain crashing on stone. The air is dusty and smells like dried chamomile and lavender. From my quick scan over his shoulder, I see a sitting room where the furniture is hidden by sheets. They look like ghostly sentinels.

He eases me onto the large farmhouse table.

"Do you know how much you torture me, just by existing?" he growls, smoothing my hair from my face and casting a searching gaze over my features. "Lora, I can't be near you and not lose my mind."

I press my finger to his mouth. "You never answered my question."

He bites me near the knuckle and slowly, seductively licks the sting away. "I know."

I wait to see where he goes with it, but he seems resolute in his silence. Instead, he presses his lips to my temple, right near my hairline. Then each eyelid. He kisses the tip of my nose, the edge of my jaw, the hollow of my neck.

"Do you know what I hate?" he rasps.

"Evasion?" I quip.

He snorts. "Clothing. And you, love, are wearing entirely too much of it."

I glance at my less than sexy attire—the hospital scrubs the ambulance driver gave me so I wouldn't have to wear the sex-club outfit Cain forced me into. Max peels me open gently as if I'm a rare and exotic flower. Each of my garments drops from my body like a petal.

And then I'm down to my hospital-issued panties. With a sharp tug he rips them off before pressing the thin fabric to his nose and inhaling deeply. "Goddamn delectable," he says, his eyes dark and intense.

"So you have me on the table. Now what are you going to do with me?"

"Feast." He drops to a crouch and spreads my legs. His tongue dances around my clit in a slow, seductive motion, lapping at the hood before tracing my slick inner lips. Then he fucks me with his tongue, plunging it into my aching heat while pressing the pad of his thumb against the tight rosebud of my ass, shocking me with an unfamiliar sensation that bucks me off the table.

He relents with a smirk. "Dirty girl, I can see you like that." He nuzzles my thigh. "What else do you like?"

I should tell him to stop, to level with me and let me know if he is going to be mine for forever… or just tonight.

But then he makes his last question rhetorical by slipping a finger into my slit and pressing against the sensitive nerves inside my inner wall, pumping them in a slow, relentless rhythm as he gives my clit a hard suck, pulling from me the first of what I can safely bet will be many orgasms. I'm not finished throbbing when he has his dick out and buries himself in me to the hilt, though he's still fully dressed. He pumps my wetness before tugging me down and pressing my breasts together, using the moistness from my pussy to coat his cock and lube it for what turns out to be an epic titty fuck.

I lap at his ruddy head as it emerges from my cleavage, grinning when he hisses a breath.

"You've liked to be in control, haven't you, my love," I whisper. "Always one step ahead of everyone."

"My life depends on it," he snarls, slamming me harder. "And yours, too, of late."

I sit up and shove him hard, sending him off balance, and he lands on the floor with a dull thud. Then I climb off the table and stand above him, my legs spread, my sex in his face.

"What if I ordered you to eat my pussy?"

He doesn't hesitate before answering. "Your wish would be my command, Lora. Anything you want." His lips curl into a crooked grin. "But I know how you love a good rogering."

"Rogering." I laugh in surprise. "Who uses that word anymore?"

"Me. Right now," he quips. "Now, are you going to use me like I know you want to?"

"Oh…you have absolutely no idea."

I fall to my knees, straddling his thighs, and take him inside me in one sharp thrust.

"Jesus. Fuck," he growls, his eyes wide.

"I should wash your mouth out," I purr, removing his silk tie from around his neck. Then I push it between his lips as a gag, which I tie behind his head in a deft knot.

All the while I rock and roll my hips, a slow undulation that I intensify by milking him with my inner walls.

Max's eyes roll in his head as I work him harder, faster. I use him for my basest needs—I want him to know how it feels to only have part of me, since that's all I can have of him. And yet I can't keep emotion from what I do. Because I love this man. I am ready to give everything to him, and yet I'm still held back because I don't know if he'll meet me halfway or if he'll run away forever.

X

I let Lora take what she wants from me, just like I did all those times we met anonymously. I left her, and I own that. But it doesn't mean I wasn't ass over elbow in love with her the day I vanished and broke her heart.

For half my life, I've tried to put her out of my head. Because the Order came first. When they offered me a career that meant my mother could afford the treatment that would add decades to her life, that she would be free of any financial burden for as long as I served the agency, I couldn't say no. Not after all she sacrificed to give me a life she never could have had. So I jumped at the opportunity, even if it meant giving up a certain part of my life. Anything or any-*one* else taking priority over the Order would be a liability to me and a danger to whomever might hold that rank.

So I spent my early adult years doing anything I could to push Lora as far from my mind as possible. I was hardly celibate. Instead I dived headfirst into meaningless encounters for the dual purpose of either satisfying my basest needs or acquiring much-needed information.

But the moment she was back in my life, it was as if she never left.

Because she never had.

As the final orgasm rocks through us both, she collapses over me, her face buried in my neck.

"Max," she murmurs against me. "Oh God, Max."

For a while we lie like that, me stroking her sweat-dampened hair, until she finally rolls off me.

"Where can I get cleaned up?" she asks matter-of-factly.

I reach behind my neck and untie my silk gag. "Bathroom is down the hall and to the right," I say. "But Lora—"

She doesn't wait for me to finish as she gathers her strewn clothes and takes them with her. The last thing I see is her beautiful, perfect ass before she disappears around the corner.

I'm left alone with my thoughts and my half-hard cock hanging out of my pants. I chuckle at what a sight I must be, my multiple cuts and bruises, and my exposed cock.

What a fucking life this has been. What would it be to stop, to put it all behind me for something stable and normal?

I clean myself up and follow Lora back to where the bathroom and two bedrooms hide on the west end of the cottage, only to find her curled up in my childhood bed, wrapped in a quilt my mother made, sound asleep.

I rap softly on the door frame, and she stirs but doesn't open her eyes.

"Lora?" I say softly.

"It's okay, Max," she says, her voice heavy with sleep.

I kick off my shoes and climb into the small bed behind her, snaking my arm beneath her and pulling her tight.

"It was never okay," I whisper, but this time she doesn't stir.

Her rhythmic, deep breaths tell me she's asleep, so I let the rise and fall of her chest lull me, as well. It's just before sleep takes me that everything finally falls into place.

My internal alarm assures I wake along with the rising sun. I leave Lora deep in slumber and take the car to the Paris safe house Cordelia and the team stayed at last night, not giving a shit that I will likely have to wake her to do what must be done.

But when I get to the door and punch in the security code, the door swings open to reveal Her Highness wearing a gown befitting a queen—which I remember that she is—and with a mug of tea in her hands.

"I expected you much earlier than this," she quips, the corners of her mouth curled into a knowing grin.

"I told you last night to sell the cottage," I say, and something in my chest squeezes so tight I think my ribs might break.

"You did," she says. "I was planning on meeting with the buyer this morning." She looks me up and down and narrows her gaze. "But I suppose you're here to change all that, are you not?"

I grin. "You found a way to make it work, Cordelia. You have your husband again. Your sons."

"Only after they spent over two decades thinking I was dead. That was my price for betraying Nightgardin, my home country, for the love of a king. What price will you pay, Max? I live in a palace flanked by guards, and still there is risk. Do you pretend to think a country cottage is as safe? The Order may have Cain, but there are likely others who know your identity now. Lora's, too."

This only makes my smile grow wider. "Do you think anyone making an attempt on my or Lora's lives would walk away with their own?"

She rolls her eyes. "Always so cocksure."

I wink. "Always."

Hours later, I push through the cottage door and slam it shut with my foot, somehow having managed to unlock it even though my hands are full. I'm greeted with a palm slammed against my solar plexus as my back hits the door. A small blade rests against my throat.

"Good morning to you, too, love. Care for a coffee or a chocolate-banana crepe?" Both of which are in my hands.

"Damn you, Max," she says, backing away. Her

chest heaves, and her voice shakes. "I woke and you were gone. I swear I was eighteen all over again, and I thought—I thought…" Tears streak her cheeks, and I realize I've fucked up royally. "I know I asked too much of you last night," she continues. "But I thought I'd at least get a goodbye this time."

"I'm not gone," I say softly. "What I mean is, I'm not *leaving*."

She shakes her head. "I don't understand."

I set the boxed crepes and coffee on the side table next to the door and approach her slowly, hands raised, not wanting to spook a woman holding a weapon.

"This isn't just my childhood home," I say. "It's mine. I own it now, thanks to my mother. And up until last night, I was going to sell it because I didn't think I could do it, Lora. I didn't think I could do what you were asking."

I reach for the knife still gripped in her white-knuckled fist, and she relinquishes it.

"Why?" she asks.

I shrug and decide that nothing is better than the truth, however ordinary it is.

"I don't know how."

She lets out something between a laugh and a sob. "I don't, either, you idiot. But I love you enough to learn."

I let the knife clatter to the floor and take her

into my arms, finally surrendering to what I've deprived myself of for too many years. I dip my head, bringing my lips to hers. "I love you enough to learn, too. How do you feel about my home being *our* home?"

She clasps her arms around my neck and pulls me tight. Then she whispers her words against my lips. "We're going to need a bigger bed."

CHAPTER EIGHTEEN

Lora

MAX FEEDS ME the crepes bite by bite, kissing the chocolate from my lips in slow, leisurely licks. He doesn't say much, and I'm uncharacteristically silent, as well. My heart is so full that I feel as if words might break me into a thousand pieces. When I'm done with my breakfast, he takes my hand and leads me outside into a cottage garden filled with lavender and rosemary. Ancient apple trees ring a white picket fence, and orange butterflies flit amid rosebushes.

"I feel like a princess in a fairy tale," I whisper.

He turns to me. "You sure this is enough for you? There will be no assassinations here. No terrorist plots. No bad guys chasing you through city alleys. I hear the most exciting news in these parts is the old farmer, Jean-Luc, up the lane, who often drinks too much sherry and lets his cows escape."

"I will have to be on my guard." I grin, tilting my chin up to face the dappled sunlight filtering through the trees. "Cows can be very dangerous."

"You could trip on a watering can."

"Or fall off a hay pile."

We look at each other and burst out laughing.

"Will you be bored?" I ask.

"With you in a five-kilometer radius? Never." He leans in to press a kiss to my temple. "I wasn't sure I'd be able to leave, and now I can see that wasn't the reason for my hesitation at all."

"Oh? What was the real reason?"

"I was afraid of hurting you. It's my biggest fear. My only fear, to tell you the truth. Every time I've ever pulled away from you has been for one reason—to keep you safe."

"But I can look after myself."

"Exactly. Which means I was being cowardly as shit. And that didn't sit quite right."

"Max the coward?" I tease.

"I'd rather cut off my left nut than let you down."

"Please don't." I step forward and cup him between the legs, squeezing playfully and giggling as he hardens in my hand in an instant.

"You're like a teenage boy," I say.

"Around you, I feel like one. All fumbles and awkwardness. And I'm about to make it worse." He drops to one knee and I press my hand to my mouth as he produces a small black velvet box. "Lora, my love, I've spent the better part of two decades committing myself to the Order. But I'm turning away from that path to pursue an even bigger commitment. I want you, all of you, the good and the bad. The simple woman who wants to start a garden and the badass who can kill a man from twenty meters with a thrown blade. I've made so many mistakes in my life, but loving you was never one of them. And I'm hoping that you'll give me the honor of my life in agreeing to become my bride."

I sink to my knees, my legs shaking as my eyes brim, bright with unshed tears. "You were my first love, Max. And you'll be my last love, too."

"Is that a yes?" he asks, taking my hand and slipping on the most gorgeous diamond ring I've ever seen.

"I can hire a skywriter if that helps," I quip wryly. "Because my answer is yes, yes, a million times yes."

"And there's more," he says pulling me to him, slanting his mouth over mine for a perfect, pure, gentle kiss.

"What else can there be?" I whisper. "You've just given me everything I could ever want."

"Not quite." He moves his lips to the side of my neck, fastening his mouth on a sensitive place that makes me squirm with pleasure. "I want to give you a baby."

My eyes fly open. "Are you serious?"

"Your birth control shot from the Order will be winding down soon," he says. "And at our age we have a limited window. We have to strike while the iron is hot."

I tackle him to the ground and cover his face with kisses. "This iron's hot, all right."

"A child of our own," he says with something approaching wonder. "What a wonderful, terrifying thought."

"Every single day we are together from this point forward, I am going to live an amazing life. You are the sun in my day and the song in my heart. Our first kiss, our first time together, our first *I love you*. I remember them all. Every memory is cherished."

He slides a hand under my shirt and palms my breast and my body arches in response. "And we will make so many more."

EPILOGUE

Max

"MARI? MARI?" I call through the Hall of Mirrors in the Edenvale palace. "Good lord, where has that girl run off to?"

A sneaky giggle drifts from over my head.

I glance up and freeze, heart leaping into my mouth at the sight of my four-year-old daughter sitting astride a stuffed stag's head near the top of the twenty-foot-high wall.

She wiggles her fingers in a cheeky wave.

"Hi, Daddy!"

I've faced down assassins in the mountains of Pakistan. Swum with great white sharks off the Cape of Good Hope. Tested poisons in the Amazon that could kill a man in five seconds.

And I've never been so terrified on a daily basis as I am raising a daughter.

I pass a hand over my head, now almost completely silver, thanks in no small part to the little hellion above me. Lora likes the look.

"There you are, darling." She calls out the greeting as she turns the corner in a knockout red dress. "Did you find her?"

"Uh…up there?" I point.

"Mariam Portia." Lora's hands fly to her hips. "What on God's green earth are you doing up there?"

"Sneaking," Mariam says smugly.

We named our daughter for both of our mothers. It still gets me when I hear Lora say it—when I realize where we began and how far we've come.

"We have to get to the great hall in Edenvale," I say, checking my watch. "It's almost time." And it's not every day Edenvale has a coronation for a new king. King Nikolai has finally chosen to abdicate and live out his retirement in a love nest high in the mountains with his queen.

It's a new day in the country where I spent so much of my career, and time for Prince Nikolai and Princess Kate to ascend the thrones and hopefully have a long and happy reign.

Lora and I enjoy our quiet life in the French countryside together—well, *quiet* isn't the right word for it.

A knife goes whizzing through the air and embeds itself in some molding across the corridor.

"Bull's-eye!" my daughter crows. She is an expert knife thrower, like her mother before her, and together these two women rule my heart.

"Come on, you little devil," I say and Mari drops through the air in a tucked somersault, landing as gracefully as a cat.

"That's your daughter," Lora says in mock annoyance, but I know she is brimming with pride over her feisty only child.

"We are lucky, aren't we," I say, drawing Lora in and pressing my cheek to the top of her jasmine-scented hair.

"The luckiest," she demurs.

"Ew, you two aren't going to play kissy face again, are you?" Mari isn't shy about saying what she thinks.

"Of course we are," I say, dipping my wife. "That's what you do when you find a princess and live happily ever after."

And from the enthusiastic way that Lora kisses me, I think she agrees.

* * * * *

COMING SOON!

We really hope you enjoyed reading this book. If you're looking for more romance, be sure to head to the shops when new books are available on

Thursday 27th December

To see which titles are coming soon, please visit
millsandboon.co.uk

MILLS & BOON

LET'S TALK
Romance

For exclusive extracts, competitions
and special offers, find us online:

f facebook.com/millsandboon

🐦 @MillsandBoon

📷 @MillsandBoonUK

Get in touch on 01413 063232

For all the latest titles coming soon, visit
millsandboon.co.uk/nextmonth